Queens and Spies

The Watchers Series: Book 5

Eilidh Miller

Cover Photography by TJ Drysdale

Cover Design by Matthew Weatherston

Griffith Cameron Publishing

ISBN - 978-1-955212-06-9

Chapter 1

<u>London, 1940</u>

"I swear I don't know what you're talking about!"

"Ye see, now ye are lying to us, and that will nae help ye," Euan said from where he leaned against the wall, watching their target. "It will only make things worse when we have to resort to. . .other. . .measures to get the truth out of ye."

The target's eyes went wide with fear, his complexion paling even further as he stared at Euan, quite clearly imagining what those things might be.

"Those men you have been talking to? Nazi spies," Grace added, drawing his attention back to her as she crossed her arms over her chest. "They're planning to invade England, and they want you to help them."

Her fingers tapped impatiently on her arm as she awaited his response to this new piece of information, the flash of her red nail polish catching the light from the desk lamp standing in sharp contrast to the drab gray of the darkening room. Aside from the fire, the tiny lamp provided the only illumination present in the dingy flat in East London. Dusk was coming, a time when one would normally turn on the lights. But not here. Not now.

The young man shook his head vigorously. "No. No, that isn't the plan! You're lying!"

"Did ye nae just say ye did nae know what I was talking about? I knew ye were being dishonest," Euan quipped as the young man tried to stand up, only to have Euan grab his shoulder and forcefully shove him back into the chair.

"Oh, but it *is* the plan and has been all along," Grace continued as though the previous exchange hadn't happened. "It's why they're asking you to build bombs."

He stopped struggling against Euan's grip and looked at her curiously. "How did you know that?"

"I know a lot of things, *John*," she said, watching with no small amount of satisfaction at his surprise when she knew his name. "Now, where did they tell *you* they would use them?"

"They said they'd take them back to Germany to disrupt their supply lines."

"Wrong. The plan is to use them in the Tube stations where people are taking refuge during the air raids."

His face became a mask of horror at the revelation and showed he wasn't faking his lack of knowledge of the real plan or that the men he'd been talking to were actually working against England. "No . . ."

"You *do* realize what the deaths of so many would do to the morale of the entire country, don't you?"

He answered with a slow nod of understanding.

"I thought you might, so I'm giving you a chance."

"A chance?"

"For you to agree to stop what you're about to do. I know you don't want innocent people to die, and that's why I'm telling you all of this."

"Who *are* you?"

"It doesn't matter who I am. All *you* need to know is that we've been sent to help you avoid the biggest mistake of your life, one that would cause all those deaths. If you think, even for a moment, they won't kill you once they have what they want, you're fooling yourself."

"Someone is coming now to meet with me and collect the

plans," he said, the rush of words tumbling out of his mouth even as his voice quaked.

"Where are the plans?"

John pointed a shaking finger at a tray sitting on the desk. "Under there."

Grace turned and moved the tray aside, picking up the schematics he'd talked about and studying them. "Are there any other copies?" she asked without lifting her eyes from the pages.

"No, but if I don't help them, then —"

"Don't worry about them; they're no longer your concern. I said I was here to help you, didn't I?"

"Yes, but —"

He ceased speaking as Grace walked across the room and threw the papers into the fire, where they at once flamed up and turned to ash, the pages blackening at the edges and curling in on themselves, leaving one part of their mission complete. Grace returned to where Euan stood with John. "Now, let's get you out of here, shall we?"

"Where?"

"The United States. They're waiting for you at the embassy. Gather a few things. Quickly."

John moved in an instant to follow her instructions, grabbing a case from beneath his bed and hurriedly packing things into it. Clothes, some small, framed photos, specialty pencils and other tools used by engineers, whatever meant the most to him. The decisions as to what really mattered to a person always came into stark relief when they had little time to choose, and she always found it intriguing to see what they selected.

Once he was done, Grace headed for the door, and he followed her with Euan behind them to make sure he didn't run. As she opened the door, the person John was supposed to meet stood on the other side of it. He surveyed her with interest, and she stepped back to let him inside.

"Who is this, hmm?" he asked, his accent telling them immediately that he was English, not German. A homegrown traitor.

"Just some friends, Ed. They came round to pick up a book I borrowed from them since they were in the neighborhood."

"Is that so?" Ed looked Grace over once more, this time appraisingly, clearly liking what he saw and thinking about things other than his meeting for a moment. "Perhaps they can help us."

"I think not," Grace replied.

"You don't even know what I would ask you to help with, so how can you be sure?"

"Doesn't matter. Not interested."

"Since when are you friends with Americans?" Ed asked John.

"I am nae American," Euan snapped, seeming offended by the very suggestion.

"She's here going to school. That's how I know her."

"You're a terrible liar, John," Ed said before he examined the other two. "I know my own kind when I see them."

Grace's smile was wry. "Clearly not. I'm not a spy."

"That's what we all say," Ed replied. "Besides, how would you know that's what I meant?"

"Except that, unlike you, I mean it, and because you're not being very subtle."

Ed produced a knife and held it up between himself and Grace, whose expression became one of annoyance rather than fright. "I think I have some friends who might get you to say otherwise," he said in a menacing tone that had zero effect on anyone except John.

Euan rolled his eyes. "Ach, here we go."

"You have friends?" Grace replied, her words dripping with sarcasm as Euan smothered a smile behind his hand.

"I should just kill you," Ed replied, angry at not only his threat not being taken seriously, but also being insulted by a woman.

"You could certainly try," Grace said with a small shrug.

"I would do more than try," he said, moving quickly and shoving the blade into Grace's chest then retracting it.

"Jesus, what are you doing, Ed?" John shouted. "Have you gone absolutely mad?"

Grace made what sounded like a pained cry and doubled over, but it became clear the cry was fake when it faded into laughter as Grace stood up. Ed still stood there, the bloody knife in his hand, and his face went slack as he watched the wound, clearly seen through her blouse, disappear.

"What the hell?"

"Oops," Grace said with a wicked smile, taking advantage of his shock to grab the arm of his knife hand and pull it out straight. Twisting his arm, she brought her elbow down onto the back of his, the move forcing his elbow the wrong way and breaking his arm. Ed screamed in pain, but Grace silenced it as she yanked him forward and slammed her elbow into his nose before turning and driving a fist into the side of his face.

Euan made no attempt to intervene on her behalf because he didn't need to. They'd worked together long enough that he'd long since stopped panicking at the first sign of trouble near her when they were in a mission. As the man crumpled to the ground, Euan nodded and grinned proudly. "Nicely done, love."

"Thanks," Grace said, her smile triumphant.

"What in the hell is going on?!" John cried out, a hint of terror in his voice as he stared at Grace. "*Who are you*?!"

"Your salvation," Grace replied. "Let's go."

Euan gave John a slight push forward as Grace turned and walked out of the flat, stepping over Ed's unmoving body on the floor. They were running out of time for today, and she was more than tired of being here. Once the sun went down over London, the bombs started dropping, and that got old *fast*. They needed to get John to the embassy before the nightly air raids began and it became too dangerous for anyone to be outdoors.

Stepping out into the street, the trio picked their way through the hellish landscape that was London during The Blitz. Debris littered the streets, and the burned-out husks of what had once been buildings loomed in the darkening sky. It wasn't a short walk to the embassy so there wasn't time to go on foot, but they were lucky to find a cab to hail when they emerged onto the high street. John was silent, clutching his suitcase against his chest. There were no more questions to ask, and he probably didn't want to know the answers to them anyway.

As they arrived at the embassy, Grace turned to him. "This is your stop. Go up and ring the bell, tell them your name, and they'll let you in. They're waiting for you to show up. I suggest you answer all their questions and answer them honestly because if you don't, they'll have no problem handing you over to Scotland Yard and you won't like what *they'll* do to you."

"What they'll do?" he croaked. "What will they do?"

"They'll fast track you for a hanging, John, and your friend Ed is going to find that out quite quickly. In fact, I'm fairly certain they're picking him up now. I'd be sure to give his name and explain before he has the chance to point the finger at *you*."

John nodded and got out, shutting the door and practically running for the stairs. Grace and Euan watched as he rang the bell, the door opened, and he went inside. Grace released a small, relieved sigh. They were done.

"Curzon Street at Park Lane, please," Grace said to the driver.

The driver wasted no time, surely ready to drop them off so that he could get out of the streets to the safety of his own home. There was no conversation between her and Euan for safety's sake, though he reached out and took her hand in his, lifting it to his lips and kissing it before resting their joined hands on his leg. When they arrived at the corner they'd requested, Grace handed the man all the money she had left, about £20, as Euan got out of the cab. She'd no longer need it now that the mission was over, and she always felt it was better served going to the final person who assisted them in-mission.

The man's eyes widened, and he looked at her in shock. "I will try to source some change for you, miss."

"No need. Keep it for your trouble. Better hurry and get home," Grace said with a reassuring smile as she took Euan's extended hand and stepped out of the cab.

"Thank you, miss!" he called after her before he drove away.

Euan kept hold of her hand, and they hurried down the still, silent street. They might not be able to die on a mission, but that didn't mean they wanted to be outside when the Luftwaffe started dropping bombs, as they'd been doing every night for weeks. Thankfully, none had hit their flat, but there'd certainly been ones close by, far closer than either of them would've liked. No place in the city was safe from the onslaught. The sound of the bombs dropping, the rattling explosions, made them both tense, but they'd managed it together. It was a sound they were intimately familiar with and could live the rest of their lives without hearing ever again.

When they reached their door, Euan pulled the key from his coat pocket, unlocked the door, and hustled them through it before shutting and locking it. It was pitch black inside because of the wood placed over the windows in case they shattered, and Grace switched on the lights. Once the foyer was illuminated, Euan reached out and pulled her into his arms.

"Are ye all right?" he asked, and she didn't miss the note of concern in his tone.

"Fine."

"He did nae hurt ye?"

"No," she said, looking up with a small smile. "But you know perfectly well he couldn't."

"Does nae mean I like to see it."

"I know," she said, reaching up to stroke his cheek, "but I'm fine, I promise."

"Must admit I liked seeing ye knock him out, though," Euan said through soft laughter.

"And I'll admit that I liked seeing the look on his face when he realized he'd just made a massive mistake."

"Oh, aye, that was priceless, but it always is. However, ye know how much it gets to me when ye do things like that."

"You're so strange," Grace said, laughing.

"Because I like to see my wife lay waste to the man who tried to kill her?"

"Because it turns you on."

"Well," Euan said, his lips twisting into a wry smile. "Cannae deny it does."

"See?"

"Does that make me strange, though? I dinnae know that it does, and I have a feeling a lot of men might feel the same. It is a nice reminder for me that ye are nae as ye seem, all sweetness and light."

"How could you *possibly* forget that?"

"Because it is so rare to see. Remember what I said to ye when I first met ye? Ye are nae as placid as ye seem. When ye do that, it shows me that fire in ye I so love."

"And you kind of like the idea that I can llrt you a little?"

"A little," he said with a small teasing smile as he turned them and pressed her back against the wall, putting his lips against her ear. "The question is if I will let ye," he whispered.

Grace couldn't help the small laugh that left her at his words. "You're never shy about asking when that's what you want."

"Nor will I be unless ye are nae willing and ye always are."

"I've no reason to say no, have I?"

Euan smiled before he pulled back and kissed her. "Ye are a wicked lass, and God help me, I love ye for it."

Grace grinned, but it faded in an instant when the air raid sirens began their high-pitched wail. Looking at the door, she didn't bother hiding the panic she felt at the sound of them. Euan hustled her away from the foyer wall and deeper into the flat where it was safer, away from doors and windows. The first bomb hitting sounded uncomfortably close, and Grace buried her face in his chest as he wrapped his arms around her. It was going to be hard to concentrate enough to reach out to The Council for extraction, and just as she tried to do so, the planes roared overhead, and several nearby explosions sounded.

"Grace! Call for the —" Euan got out before an explosion silenced him.

The bomb landed so close to their flat that it felt as though the shock wave levitated them for an instant before it propelled them to the floor. The glass in the windows shattered, the force of the blast pushing them apart and sending Grace sliding across the floor as they both screamed. Euan scrambled across the short distance and grabbed her by the ankle, dragging her to him and wrapping her up, covering her as best he could with his own body out of pure instinct.

"Christ! That was right behind us!"

Grace fought to focus, to tune out the sirens, planes, continuing explosions, and sounds of panicked screaming outside. She felt like crying, but she managed to gain enough focus to open the connection to The Council. *Watcher Cameron for The Council! Mission complete! Get us out! Quickly!*

In the next moment, there was nothing but silence, and it told her in an instant that they were safely out of there before things could get worse, if they even had. Euan unfolded himself from his protective position around her and sat up on the floor, and a shaking Grace followed him, more than relieved to find them in a debriefing room. Glancing over at Euan, she found him similarly relieved, and they embraced in a moment of silent gratitude for the ability to escape. Bombs were terrifying no matter what their advantages might be, and neither of them knew how it would work if they got hit by a bomb. They'd decided long ago that they didn't want to find out and did nothing that would test it.

When the panic subsided a bit, Euan kissed her forehead, smiling as he picked up her hand to hold it in his, and frowned. "Yer red nails are gone. Ach, that is a shame; I rather liked them."

"I'll get a manicure when we get home, if that's what you want," Grace said.

"Ooo. Aye, do."

Grace laughed at him as the door opened and Councilwoman Rochford entered with another of the members. Seeing them on the floor, she raised an eyebrow. "Should we come back later?"

"No," Grace said. "A bomb dropped near us before we got out."

Rochford grimaced. "That sounds terrible, and I am glad you are safely back with another mission completed in your stellar fashion. Are you ready for debrief?"

"Aye, very," Euan said. "I am ready to go home."

CHAPTER 2

"Vanessa, whose playlist is this?" Drew asked as he sat in front of a table and scrolled through the files on a laptop used expressly for music. It stored a rather impressive collection of tracks, something Vanessa hadn't considered when she'd sent him over to look for something for them to listen to.

"Which one?" she queried as she joined him and peeked over his shoulder. "Oh, that's Euan's, but Mal uses it, too."

Drew chuckled. "Ye live with metalheads."

"Yep. Though they tend to only listen to the really heavy stuff when I'm not here."

"What does Grace think, or do they limit it around her as well?"

"She turns it up."

"What?" Drew said in shock, turning around in the chair to look at her. "Seriously?"

Vanessa smiled, amused by his expression. "Not the answer you were expecting? But, yeah, seriously. She's not what she seems, and her musical tastes span a bunch of genres. She definitely doesn't mind this, but it all depends on her mood, really."

"I would nae have thought that of her. At all."

"You should know by now, thanks to your work, that appearances can be deceiving."

"That's true, but people can still surprise me."

"Here," Vanessa said, reaching around him and selecting an album to start playing. "She's been really into this new album by an Icelandic band recently. They're one of her favorites and

Euan surprised her by taking her to a small show they were playing in Whitby last month."

Drew closed his eyes to listen and then nodded. "I like this. I'll have to pick it up for myself. Very chill, which would be nice after work."

"Not *too* chill, though. Wouldn't want you being so relaxed when you see me that you just go right to bed."

"Now, why would I do that, hmm?" he asked, his lips spreading into a small smile as he opened his eyes and pulled her down into his lap to kiss her. "Ye are far too interesting for that. Besides, I never want to go right to bed when I get off anyway. It takes me a while to settle down."

"I know," she said, returning the smile and tapping the tip of his nose with her fingertip. "I'm always happy to sit up with you."

"Aye, ye are, and I appreciate it. Even if that's by video call or just a regular phone call. I wish it could be in person more often than nae, but I understand why it cannae be."

Vanessa sighed. "Only way it could be is if you moved closer, but then you'd have a longer drive to work."

"Aye, but it's nae an issue yet," he replied as he rubbed her back. "We're making it work as it is, and that's fine for now."

"Yeah, well, Euan and Grace are pretty good about giving me time off between their travel schedules. There's usually at least a few days between trips, but more often it's a week and I can spend that with you."

"I'm glad they do. It's good of them to nae tie ye here all the time."

"They wouldn't. They're way too conscientious to keep me from having a life. Besides, they like you a lot, so I know they go out of their way to make sure we're able to see each other."

"I like them, too, and am just as glad I've gotten to know them better as I am that Euan introduced us. They're both fascinating people."

"They really are," she said, knowing it was truer than he could even imagine and wishing she could explain it to him.

It would make things quite a bit easier. . .or perhaps not. Her phone pinged, and she pulled it from her pocket, opening the message from Caia telling her that Grace and Euan were in debrief. "Oh, they'll be home soon."

When they'd restarted their missions a few months ago, they'd set up a system: The Council alerted Caia that her Watcher was in debrief, as they always did, allowing her to prepare for their bodily return, and there was a phone provided for Caia by Euan and Grace, who used it to relay the same message to Vanessa so she could prepare for their return on her end. Caia's phone was from the current period, used only for that purpose and left in the mission room. This method of communication also gave Vanessa a way to let Caia know through a coded message if they had company so that she didn't show herself to anyone else and so Euan and Grace could pretend to come back into the house instead of downstairs. This deception relied on a bit of juggling, usually consisting of Vanessa getting Drew to go with her into the kitchen so that he wouldn't be able to see that no cars came up the drive to drop the pair off.

"Teatime, then?"

Vanessa laughed and nodded. He knew the routine by now. "Yeah, tea. Come help me make it?"

"Of course," he replied as she slid out of his lap and he stood up.

Vanessa sent the visitor code to Caia before heading to the kitchen. This particular Watcher and Companion always wanted tea and biscuits when they returned because they'd had nothing to eat or drink while they were down, and while they had tech to keep their bodies stable with hydration, they still craved the real thing when they woke. Grace usually made them something small to eat, like soup or a sandwich, to get them by until the next actual meal because she didn't expect Vanessa to cook for them and she'd said she'd feel strange asking Vanessa to do so.

Vanessa filled the electric kettle and flipped it on while Drew, who'd helped her with this task enough times to know her methods, grabbed the teapot and two cups. Vanessa fished the biscuits out of the cupboard and arranged them on a plate while Drew busied himself setting up cups of tea for himself and Vanessa separate from the pot they were making.

***

Upstairs, Euan opened his eyes, finding himself in darkness but able to feel Grace beside him. Neither moved, taking a moment to readjust before sitting up because a return was always a bit disorienting. Next to him, Grace rubbed her forehead, and he didn't need to see her face to know there was a grimace on it from the headache she always had when she came back. Euan slid his fingers into her hair and started massaging her scalp, hearing her sigh in relief. It was a small help, but he was more than aware of how she felt whenever they returned and was happy to alleviate it at least a little.

"Are you two ready?" Caia asked from outside.

"Aye," Euan replied, and a moment later, the curtains parted some just to let in a small amount of light.

"Vanessa is getting things ready, and Dr. Fraser is here."

Euan smiled and shook his head. He couldn't blame Drew for coming to see his girlfriend every chance he got; he'd have done the same thing. "Thank ye, Caia. Love, will ye be well enough for company, or shall we have Caia send a message to clear out?"

"It's fine," Grace murmured. "I don't mind him, and he rarely stays long after we come down. He's courteous that way, and I don't want to force Vanessa to kick her boyfriend out. She gets to have a life, too."

"Aye, she does, and it is kind of ye to remember it and make sure she does," Euan said as he kissed her cheek and slipped out of bed, offering her his hand. "It is likely they will just go up to her room anyway, or ye and I can go to the study for a bit."

"I'm honestly very willing to just go upstairs to bed and let them have the house," Grace replied as she took the proffered hand and got out of bed.

"That is another option, certainly." Crossing the room to the basin of warm water Caia always put out for them, Euan splashed some water on his face and sighed.

"Where did they send you this time?" Caia asked.

"1940s London," Grace said. "We had to stop someone from giving bomb schematics to people who wanted to use them to bomb the shelters from the inside."

"Oh goodness! How horrible! I am glad you succeeded, then."

"So are we," Euan said. "I was getting quite tired of the bombs at night."

"There were bombs?"

"Aye, the Germans dropped bombs on London from planes for months."

"People can be so terrible to each other," Caia said, her eyes sad as she frowned. "It never ceases to amaze me the cruelty we are capable of."

"There is naught pleasant about Nazis; that is certain. Nae the old ones and nae the new ones either."

Euan saw Grace's brow knit at the very mention of the new crop of extreme right-wing domestic terrorists popping up all over the world and inserting themselves back into politics. Times were dangerous everywhere, but at least they were rather safe from it in such a remote location. She picked up her clothing, handing him his, and they changed from the mission linens to make it look like they were coming back from a trip. Once they finished and felt ready for it, Caia made a quick transport to move them down to the garage and left from there. Suitcases were hidden inside to help with this deception, and these were collected before the two of them walked the short distance from the small building where the cars were parked.

"Here we go," Euan whispered when they reached the back door, and Grace nodded for him to go ahead. Opening the door, they stepped inside. "We are home!"

Vanessa appeared from the kitchen and waved to them. "Hey, guys, welcome back! Everything went well?"

"Yes, thanks," Grace said with a smile that belied her exhaustion. "Glad to be home, though. It was pretty loud where we were, so it'll be nice to get a good night's sleep finally."

"Aye, I agree," Euan groused.

"The tea is ready and waiting," Vanessa said as she walked with them into the kitchen.

"Thank ye," Euan replied, nodding to Drew at the table. "Back again, are ye?"

Drew laughed and looked down for a moment. "Aye, cannae stay away from my lass too long. Ye know how it is."

"I do, indeed. At least I have the good fortune to work with mine, so I dinnae have to be away from her at all." It wasn't always true, but true enough in this circumstance.

"Hi, Grace," Drew said.

"Hey, Drew," Grace replied before she winced from the continuing headache. "Ugh, man, I can really use that tea."

"Are ye all right?" Drew asked. "Ye seem to always have a headache when ye travel."

"Oh, I'm fine. Travel takes a lot out of me, and flying will often give me a headache. It's just stress headaches, nothing to worry about."

"Aye, that can certainly happen. I'm sorry ye are one of the unfortunate people who have to deal with that."

"Could be worse. Could be migraines."

"It could, and aye, that'd be worse."

Euan sat down at the table, followed by Grace, and he immediately poured her a cup of tea. In went the milk and sugar before he placed it in front of Grace, along with the plate of biscuits. She could make her own cup, of course, but he liked to do it for her when they returned, and she had no problem letting him. Grace always came first in his mind, and to him it was his primary job as her husband to always look after her, making sure she was well and seeing to her welfare before his own. It wasn't that he thought she was too fragile or inept to care for herself, he knew she could, but it made him happy to take care of her in small ways. He knew Grace was aware of it and allowed the gestures because she knew it made him happy to provide them. She'd once said to him that it was almost as if, without Lochiel, he'd needed someone else to serve, and the person he'd chosen was his wife. Euan agreed wholeheartedly, as everything he did for Grace he did without thinking. To him, it was as natural as breathing, another form of service, albeit one he vastly preferred to his previous life. Grace flashed a grateful smile at him and took a sip, sighing happily before picking up the aspirin Vanessa had set at her place and washing them down with another sip of tea.

"Has everything been quiet here, Van?" Grace asked.

"Yep, fine as usual. Euan, your mom wants you to come to dinner. I told her I'd let you know when you got back."

Euan nodded. "Thank ye. I am sure that meant ye as well, both of ye."

"I will nae object," Drew said. "Yer mum's cooking is great, and there's always pie."

Grace laughed. "So true. Aileen has loved making fruit pies since she learned to bake them."

"Where did ye go this time?" Drew asked.

"Cannae tell ye that, I am afraid," Euan replied. It was the standard line and let people decide what they wanted.

"They're totally spies," Vanessa quipped and Drew choked on his tea, coughing. Vanessa patted his back as she laughed.

"Ye are joking, right?"

"Nae entirely," Euan said, his small smile mischievous. "We just have to leave it there."

Drew stared at them for a long moment, then shook his head and looked at Vanessa. "Ye see? People can still surprise me."

"Not hard with this crew," Vanessa replied.

"Aye, that is very true," Euan said, though he knew if things became more serious, Drew would be brought into the secret as well. The truth couldn't be hidden from him forever, and it was more a matter of *when* they'd tell him rather than if.

The sound of the door opening and closing made them all look over at the hall before Mal walked in. "Oh, ye are back then! Excellent! Hey, Drew."

"Mal," Drew said with a nod.

"How was London?" Vanessa asked.

"Eh," Mal replied as he dropped into an open chair. "Oh, tea!" he exclaimed as he reached out to grab the pot, but Vanessa slapped his hands before he could get far. "Ow! Christ, what was that for?"

"That's *theirs* because they just got home. Go make your own."

Grace covered her mouth and laughed, but Euan didn't bother, having a hearty laugh at his brother's expense. "Serves ye right, ye mannerless heathen."

"All right, all right, *fine*." Mal groaned, purposefully overdramatic before getting up to put the kettle on again. "If I could go to London without running into Mara, though, I'd be happy."

Grace made a face. "*Her* again?"

"Ach, aye, but then she works at UCL so there is nae much I can do about it."

"Is that nae yer ex, Mal?" Drew queried.

"Aye. The same one who accused me of shagging my brother's wife in a crowded pub."

Drew rolled his eyes. "Aye, because that seems likely."

"Because if he had done so, he would nae have been alive for her to accuse," Euan said.

"That too," Drew said. "Ye dinnae seem the kind of man who would tolerate that."

"No, nae from anyone, but especially nae my own brother."

"I would just like to point out that this is not, nor has it *ever* been, a concern," Grace said.

Drew laughed, as did Euan. "I would nae think so. Dinnae worry, Grace."

"I can beat her up for you, Mal," Grace joked.

"Ach, I would have loved it if ye did, but I dinnae think I would want to bail ye out."

"They'd have to catch me first."

"Fair," Mal said, nodding. "Fair."

"What were ye after in London?" Drew asked.

"I'm doing work with some of the railway digs and the things they're turning up as they go."

"Oh, I read about that! They're finding some really interesting things, are they nae?"

"Aye. Well, interesting if ye like skeletons. Which I do."

"If ye need help with trying to figure out causes of death or the like, let me know. It'd be fascinating to work on."

"Aye? I will keep that in mind. They are always looking for people willing to do forensic examinations."

"Are ye nae worried about digging up the dead?" Euan asked.

"Nae really, and we rebury them elsewhere."

"Still," Euan countered. "I would worry about restless things and whatever project ye were doing." To him, digging up a grave was something you just didn't do. Though Mal always argued that it wasn't the same, he hadn't been able to convince Euan yet.

Mal pulled off the kettle and poured the water into another pot. "Has nae been a problem, and we take great care of them, I promise."

"Next thing ye know, they will be digging people up at Falkirk and Culloden," Euan said.

"In the future, maybe," Mal said offhandedly.

Euan dropped his cup, spilling tea on the table. Grace grabbed a towel and started mopping it up, and Mal immediately looked guilty while Drew studied Euan with curiosity.

"I did nae mean they would any time soon. It is nae even something anyone is considering. If they did do it, it would be centuries from now."

"How many?" Euan asked. "How many centuries are acceptable before ye dig them from the ground to study? It has already been nearly three, after all."

"A lot more than that," Mal said, his tone gentle. "We haven't even touched places we know are 500 or more years old. They're only now working with the Roman and the Norse settlements here, and that was 1,000 years ago."

Grace took Euan's shaking hand from his lap, covering it to help center him. He was mostly past it, they both were, but the mention of digging up his friends touched a nerve.

"He didn't mean anything by it, love," she said.

"Why does it bother ye so much, Euan?" Drew asked. "It seems a strange thing to be upset about so far past."

"I just dinnae think war dead should be dug up, is all. Those are our ancestors, Drew. Yers as well as mine. They more than earned the right to be left alone."

Drew nodded. "I tend to agree with ye. Nae sure there is much to learn that we dinnae already know. We know what weapons were used, what the injuries were, what the makeup of the forces was. It was all written down, whereas things with the Norse and the Romans were less so. It seems unnecessary."

"It does *now*," Mal said. "But we dinnae know what someone several centuries from now might want to know about those who rest there. Discoveries are happening all the time."

"So, what did Mara do when you saw her?" Grace asked, switching the topic.

"Oh, she glared at me for a while, but that's about all."

"Nothing too bad then," Vanessa said.

"Nah," Mal answered.

"We should finish our tea and let these two relax. They just got back after all," Vanessa said.

The other two men nodded, and Mal headed upstairs with his tea while Drew went up with Vanessa.

Euan sighed. "Thank ye for covering for me, love."

"Anytime," Grace replied, kissing his cheek. "Anytime."

CHAPTER 3

While Vanessa showered and got dressed the next morning, Drew headed downstairs for a cup of coffee. He'd ended up staying the night, knowing he could leave from the lodge and still make his night shift with plenty of time to spare. A strange sound caught his attention as he exited the room, his brow furrowing as he continued down the stairs, and he stepped out in just enough time to see Grace duck and back up as Euan swung a sword at her, seemingly *very* intent on trying to hit her.

As Euan came down at her from an angle, Grace pulled up her own blade and blocked it as she stepped to the side and let it slide down and off as she moved away from him. This put Euan's back to her and opened him up, and she tried to take advantage by swinging at him as he hustled forward just fast enough for her to miss before turning back to face her. He charged her, and Drew watched as she ducked, held up her blade to block his strike and turned her body into his hips, then pushed up, which sent him up and over her. He landed on his back with a thud and a small groan as Grace brought the tip of the sword to his throat.

"Grace! No!" Drew shouted at her.

Grace, surprised by his interruption, looked over at him in confusion. "What?"

"Don't do it! I know he was trying to hurt ye, but —"

From the floor, Euan laughed, and Grace stepped back away from him as he sat up. "It is fine, Drew. We were doing a bit of training indoors, as the weather keeps us from the yard now."

"Training? Christ, ye looked like ye were trying to hit her!"

"I was. She will nae learn anything if I dinnae challenge her, and as ye can see, she is perfectly capable of holding her own," Euan explained as he moved from sitting to standing. "Dinnae think for a moment she was nae trying to hit me, too."

"Sorry to have scared you," Grace said, smiling. "I suppose someone should've warned you."

"How in the hell are ye doing that and nae getting hurt?"

"Skill," Euan said. "Skill and very blunt weapons. Though, I suppose if ye landed on it, that could be bad."

"Ye think so?" Drew snipped, the doctor in him coming out in his irritated tone.

"It was my own fault there. That sort of thing happens, but it would certainly have been me dead if we were really fighting. Very well done, my love."

"Thank you," Grace said, a little smile of pride on her lips. "Euan's an excellent teacher if you want to learn, Drew."

"Aye, from what I understand, more than a few of the Fraser men were deadly with a broadsword."

Drew raised an eyebrow, intrigued by the prospect. "I've heard the same. Ye would really teach me?"

"Aye, I would be happy to. A bit of a lost art, so the more of us who know it the better, as far as I am concerned. I promise nae to hurt ye. . .at least nae *too* much."

Drew chuckled and shook his head. "I may take ye up on that, actually."

"Vanessa would like it," Grace said, shooting Drew a mischievous look.

"Why does that nae surprise me?" Drew asked, his chuckle turning into a laugh.

"At least you don't have to worry about the walk of shame this morning," Grace said.

Euan looked confused but Drew only laughed harder. "Aye, I have had to do that one a few times, and it is never pleasant. I figured ye would nae be at all surprised to see me here in the morning."

"Certainly not," Grace said, shaking her head and laughing.

"What is a walk of shame?" Euan asked, still puzzled.

Grace stifled her laughter and looked at him. "It's when you spend the night somewhere with someone you really didn't intend to, and you sneak out of their bed, room, and house early in the morning to walk home in the clothes you went out in."

Euan blinked and then laughed. "Oh! Been there."

Grace scoffed and rolled her eyes as he laughed.

"As it seems we are done practicing, we should have breakfast," Euan continued, which spurred Grace to pass him her sword.

"Aye, that was my thought too, and why I came down," Drew said as he headed toward the kitchen.

Euan joined them in the kitchen after putting the blades away and sat down as Grace started digging through the refrigerator for ingredients to use for breakfast.

"Hey, Euan, may I talk with ye a moment?" Mal asked as he walked into the kitchen.

"Aye, of course. Excuse me," Euan said to Drew as he stood up and followed Mal into the study, shutting the door behind them.

Drew was quiet for a moment, not having been left alone with Grace before. "I really liked that Icelandic album ye have. Vanessa played it for me," he said.

"Yeah? I love them. Their harmonies are just beautiful, don't you think?"

"Absolutely. I was telling her I'd have to pick it up for myself."

"I'm always happy to introduce new music to people," she said as she cracked eggs into a bowl.

"I will admit to being perplexed by yer varied tastes, however."

Grace smiled and shrugged. "Can't deny that one. I have music for varying moods."

"Vanessa did say that. She also said ye weren't what ye seemed."

Grace paused for a moment and looked up from the bowl, fixing him with an expression he couldn't read. "Did she?"

"Aye, but somehow that part does nae surprise me. Ye strike me as a person who does nae let everyone see ye."

At his explanation, Grace shed the previous look and returned to cracking the eggs. "Not untrue, but I prefer for it to be my choice as to who knows what about me."

"Like yer penchant for trying to stab yer husband?"

Grace made a small sound of amusement. "He likes it."

"That does nae surprise me either."

"I suppose I *am* a bit reserved," she admitted. "At least until I get to really know someone. Force of habit."

"From yer work?"

"No, at least not really, though I'm sure there's a bit of that, too. It's more a childhood thing."

"Ahhh," Drew said, nodding in understanding. "I have seen my share of that, unfortunately."

"Have you? That's less than ideal."

"Aye, more than I would like. Children coming into A&E with all manner of injuries, giving the most ridiculous excuses about how they got them, and it breaks my heart. Sometimes I can extract the truth out of them and get them to safety, and other times I can't."

Grace stopped for a moment, though she didn't look up. "I wish I could say I wasn't intimately familiar with that."

Drew's face mirrored the sadness in Grace's voice. "Ach, Grace, I'm sorry to hear that. I wish ye could say that, too."

"I'm one of the lucky ones, really. My grandparents took me in and raised me to keep me safe. They're the ones who sent me to school."

"I'm glad ye got out."

"Me too, but I'm mostly okay now, thanks to Euan and my little family here."

"Ye do have quite the collection, but they're all good people and that's important."

"It is, and Euan has been a tremendous help."

"As ye were to him, from what I understand."

"I did my best."

"When I met him and he learned I was a doctor, he mentioned he was seeing a specialist for PTSD, but that he found ye helped him far more than therapy did. Ye gave him stability, love, and acceptance.”

“As he did for me. We’re a good match, the pair of us.”

“Aye, ye are, though I feel that’s still a gross understatement. I can only hope Vanessa and I are as happy as ye two.”

Grace raised an eyebrow, glancing up at him. “That sounds a bit serious.”

“A bit soon, I know, I just —”

“You feel it.”

“Aye,” he replied, regarding her with the same curious expression she’d earlier offered him. “How did ye know that?”

“That feeling and I are on *very* good terms. Euan told you how long we knew each other before he married me, right?”

“No, actually.”

“Three weeks.”

“Ye are lying to me now.”

“Absolutely telling the truth.”

“Wow. It seems like the two of ye have known each other for years.”

“Well, we’ve been married almost two years now, so technically we have.”

“But more than that.”

“That’s why things went the way they did. It felt right, like I’d always known him. It was the most terrifying and exhilarating thing I think I’ve ever felt, but I don’t regret any of it.”

“I have nae told her.”

“You should.”

“I dinnae want to scare her off, though.”

“You won’t, trust me. Do it when it feels right to you, but don’t hold back just because you think she won’t take it well. She will, and life is far too short to worry about hiding your feelings. I would think that you of all people know that better than most. You see it every day, don’t you?”

“Aye, I do. I see heartbreak and regret and love. I see people trying to tell someone how much they meant to them before that person leaves the world forever. I see anger at God, anger at the person responsible for their pain, anger at anything. I've always thought to myself that I never wanted to be in that moment where ye regret all the things ye felt but never said before it was too late."

Grace, having stopped what she was doing to simply listen to him, responded with a tiny nod of affirmation. "I thought that might be the case. So, if you never want to be in that moment, why are you opening yourself up to the possibility by staying silent? If you want to be with her, tell her. If you love her, tell her. If you want more, tell her."

"As I said, though, it has only been a few months —"

"You're far more worried about what everyone else will say than what she will," Grace said, cutting right to the point. "But why? They aren't you. This isn't *their* life; it's *yours*. They can think it's too fast, they can think whatever they want, but it's your choice to make and not theirs. Only you know what you feel."

Drew, taken aback by not only how well Grace cut through his excuses, but also how well she was reading him, found himself at a loss for words. At the same time, he was confused about why he was opening up to her in the way he was, though he had no intention of stopping now that he'd started. Talking to her was like talking to his oldest friend, the one who would call him on his crap when needed, just as she was doing now.

"Ye are right about all of it. It's just a bit difficult to stop worrying about that sort of thing when I know she will hear it from others. I don't want her to be hurt because someone comments on how fast it all happened."

"Do you love her?"

"I —"

"It's a very simple question with only two possible answers."

"Aye, I do."

"Then what does it matter? Vanessa is tougher than that and

is more likely to tell them to kiss her arse than she would be to slink off to a corner and cry."

Drew couldn't help but laugh. "Ye are so right; she would."

"Do what feels right to *you*, Drew. Don't worry about everyone else. Trust me when I tell you that, in the end, none of it matters. Someday your family will tell your story, and they'll talk about how you were so happy together and wasn't it romantic that you just knew you were meant for each other so fast? Do you think they're going to be like, 'Oh, well, he should've maybe waited a bit longer because ye know his friends did nae like it?' No, they won't."

Drew laughed harder now at her dead-on accent. "Christ, ye are savage, aren't ye? There is a bit of a logistics issue, too."

"Is there?"

"I live and work in Inverness. She lives here. I come as often as I can and she comes to see me when ye are home, but I know she cannae move to Inverness."

"No, that's true. She can't."

"Logistical problem."

"Logistics can always be overcome with some thinking. I never let them get in my way, trust me. So, your options are thus: stop dating her, don't stop dating her and move and commute, or don't stop dating her and move and transfer to the hospital in Fort William."

Drew opened his mouth to reply but closed it again, remaining silent for a moment. He could certainly do any of those things, any of them but one. There was no way he was going to stop dating Vanessa. "Hmm."

"I suppose it would all depend on how attached you are to the hospital in Inverness or if you're up for a promotion or something. It's not that long of a drive, really, and you do it all the time now anyway."

"It's definitely something to think about, that is for certain. I can see why Euan said what he did about ye helping him if yer conversations were always this way."

"Something like."

"Ye really are a puzzle, Grace."

"Depending on what you choose, you might just get handed some missing pieces that will make everything far clearer."

Drew eyed her curiously, then shook his head. "Can I help ye with something?"

"Actually, yes! If you could get the kettle on, that'd be a help."

***

In the study, Euan and Mal sat across from each other, Mal looking uncomfortable. After a long, awkward silence, Euan finally spoke. "What is wrong with ye? Why are ye acting so strangely?"

"I just wanted to say I'm sorry for what I said yesterday. I was nae thinking about it, and it was inconsiderate of me."

"Oh," Euan said, following it with a sigh. "I dinnae blame ye. It is different for ye, ye see it differently, and I try to remember that. It is just the thought of disturbing all of it that bothers me."

"I would nae worry about it. As I said, there's no reason I can think of to do so, and they have mapped the ground with sonar so that any digs avoid the gravesites."

"Did they? What does that do?"

"It uses radio waves to send a picture back that shows ye what might be there. The waves will bounce off objects beneath, and that creates the picture. In this case, they could see the large areas that could only be the mass graves there. That will make sure they dinnae dig anywhere near it because they have no desire to disturb those men either."

"That is good to hear," Euan said, sitting back in the chair. "I wish I did nae react to it at all, but I still do."

"Ye still will for a while, I'd expect. It's nae as if it's gone away for ye because ye will always remember it. Ye are still in treatment for it, aren't ye?"

"Aye."

"The only difference now is that it does nae haunt yer every word, thought, and deed, and most of the time ye dinnae even think of it."

"Most of the time. It was nae true so much on this last mission."

"Why? Where did ye go?"

"London during the Blitz."

"Christ, really? I mean, ye would think they would take that sort of thing into consideration."

Euan gave a gentle shrug. "They sent us because we're good at what we do, and they needed us. This is never about me or about her. We did well enough even with the bombing. We were a bit rattled but otherwise fine. I think that would have been true even if we did nae have the past we did."

"What was the mission?"

"Had to stop a lad from giving bomb schematics to Nazi operatives who planned to use them to bomb the shelters in the underground."

"Holy shite!"

"Aye," Euan said, chuckling at Mal's reaction. "We stopped it, burned the schematics, and got the lad to safety. Oh! But then Grace did something amazing."

"What did she do?"

"Well, as we were taking the lad out, his friend showed up to collect the plans. He talked too much, and Grace insulted him."

"Nae surprised."

"Should nae be. Anyway, the idiot stabbed her." Mal gasped, and Euan held out his hands to calm him. "I know what ye are thinking, but remember, we cannae be harmed while we are working. So, she pretended it hurt her, then laughed as it healed right in front of him. While he was distracted, she broke his arm and nose and then knocked him out. It was a thing of beauty."

"Remind me to never make her angry."

"I would nae, honestly, and I am married to her."

"And yet ye trained her in swordplay, too," Mal replied with a wry smile.

"Aye, and she is excellent at it. She scared the hell out of Drew and surprised me by sending me over her shoulder this morning. Drew thought she was going to kill me."

Mal placed the palm of his hand against his face and shook his head. "Poor Drew. Does nae know what he has gotten himself into."

"I dinnae think he is that upset by it."

"What do ye think about that anyway?"

"About Drew and Vanessa?"

"Aye."

"Same thing I thought about Mam and Father."

"Really?"

"It will get there, maybe sooner than we expect. I introduced them for a reason."

Mal raised an eyebrow. "Do ye know something from The Council?"

"No, they would nae tell me that sort of information even if I asked. It just felt like I should. A flash of a moment."

"When will ye tell him, then? About —" Mal said, gesturing to Euan.

"Nae until we must. The longer he does nae know, the safer we are in case it does nae go as I think it will."

"A good idea, but Drew is a good man and a good friend. He'd never betray ye in a million years. I've never seen him like this, though, and I tend to agree with ye. They will be happy together. Would ye let him live here?"

"We would have to because Vanessa has to be here."

"Aye, that is true."

"I like him a great deal. He is honest, kind, and compassionate. He also has an excellent sense of humor. Ye need that if ye are going to live with this lot."

"Aye, that he does, and he is also all those things ye mentioned. More than that, he has drive. He wants to help people in any way he can, and he is an amazing doctor because of it."

"As I said, he will be welcome here, at least by me."

"What do ye mean?"

"Well, ye are Vanessa's friend. I would go so far as to say that, aside from Grace, ye are her best friend. Things would change."

"Aye, but I dinnae mind it because of *who* is changing it. I've known him all my life, and I know he would nae try to curtail our friendship. He's nae that kind of man. Besides, he has nothing to worry about from me, and he knows that."

"Good," Euan said, smiling.

"Honestly, though. Look at him and look at me. I'm nae bad, but I dinnae compare to Drew Fraser in the slightest."

"Ach, ye give yerself too little credit, Mal."

"I would nae normally say that for anyone but him. Is it odd to get those feelings? Where ye just know things?"

"Sometimes, aye. They dinnae come often, so I tend to pay attention when they do."

From outside, the sound of Grace and Drew laughing together made Euan smile.

"How long are ye home for?"

"At least a week I hope."

"No rest for the wicked, is there?"

"None, and the more wicked ye are, the harder ye work and the less ye rest."

"No wonder ye are gone all the time. The two of ye together are about as wicked a pair as ye could find."

Euan laughed. "Damned right we are, and I would nae have it any other way."

CHAPTER 4

"Gracie? Can I borrow the Range?" Vanessa asked as she came into the study a few days later.

"Sure. Where are you headed?" Grace questioned as she looked up from her laptop.

Euan looked up from his as well with the same curious expression his wife wore. They were both assisting Mal and his colleagues on various projects whenever they could on identification, translation, or anything else Mal could send their way. The research credit was under Grace's credentials because they had to be, but Euan was a massive help for certain projects and periods.

"I wanted to go up and see Drew before you guys have to head out again."

"Oh! Well, you know where the keys are," Grace replied with a small smile before she turned her eyes back to her work.

"You're the best!" Vanessa declared, hugging Grace where she sat and bringing a laugh from her friend before she hurried out of the room.

"I know!" she heard Grace call out to her as she reached the back door.

Vanessa laughed and grabbed the keys from the board before she headed out to the garage. Sliding into the car, she plugged her phone into the USB port and adjusted the seats and mirrors before she started it up. With a shiver, she turned on the heated seats and steering wheel. She loved driving any of the cars here, particularly Grace's Aston, and had free use of them whenever Grace was out. The Aston, however, was not practical for the end of November. She'd need to get her own car eventually; she just hadn't done it yet.

She made sure she took it easy as she started down the drive to the Dark Mile. Ice was always a very real and constant possibility up here where the roads weren't as well-traveled. She'd seen more than a few slides off the road and had no desire to be one of them, especially in a car that wasn't hers. As she reached the motorway, she glanced at the map. At this time of day, it would only take her about 45 minutes to get to Inverness, especially with no snow to slow her down, and she settled in to enjoy the drive.

It was beautiful, as it always was, all forest until the road reached Fort Augustus and Loch Ness. The sight of the massive loch coming into view through the trees could still inspire a bit of awe in her and always reminded her of how lucky she was to live here and have the life she did. The steel gray of the water reflected the clouded sky, the wind whipping up small whitecaps to break the solid surface color. It was like a mood unto itself, sometimes matching the sky above but other times brighter with the sun or sometimes darker as if to rebuff the sun's attempts to make it look inviting.

As the trees and water gave way to the buildings and streets of a city, she couldn't help but smile. Drew's flat was located in the old city center, the building itself constructed in 1894. The carved stone cornices and the wrought-iron railings outside of the huge windows gave it an elegance one would expect from an old building, though by Inverness standards, it was fairly new. She found a place to park with little trouble, which was always a pleasant change, hurrying up the front steps and to the elevator, excited to see him and knowing he was probably going to bed soon. She knew he'd worked last night because he was on nights this week, and next week he'd switch to day shifts.

Vanessa knocked on the door, and when Drew answered it, he looked shocked to see her. "Vanessa. . .hi."

"Hey." His reaction bothered her and immediately put her guard up. "Is this a bad time?"

"I. . .um, aye. . .sort of —"

"Drew, what's going on?" Vanessa asked, surprised to see him stumbling over his words this way.

"Drew, dear, who is it?" a woman called from behind him.

Vanessa gasped, and she shook her head. "What the hell? Drew . . ." She couldn't finish because her heart was in her throat.

"No. . .no it's nae like that, please," Drew said quickly as the pain of perceived betrayal manifested in Vanessa's expression.

"Then what *is* it like?"

"It's my mother; she's here with my nan. I would never do that to ye in a million years."

"Then why are you acting so cagey?"

Before he could answer, his mother spoke again. "Drew, really, who is it? Either let them in or send them off so we can visit with ye."

Drew's sigh was uncustomarily heavy. "This was nae how I'd wanted this meeting to happen. I wanted to prepare ye first. Come in," he said as he stepped back to allow her access.

Vanessa came inside as he moved to let her in, but before she could make her way any farther than inside the door, he pulled her into a tight embrace, just holding her for a long moment. She could feel how tense he was, and it only made her more concerned.

"Hey, are you okay?" she whispered.

"No," he whispered in return. "I'm sorry."

"For what?"

"For making ye think this was something it was nae. I mean it when I say I would never, ever do that to ye. Sorry for ye having to meet her."

"What?"

"Ye will see," he said as he took her hand and led her around the corner into his living room.

In two chairs sat two *very* different-looking women. One of them, an older woman, seemed kind, her gray hair piled in a loose bun on her head and dressed in a comfortable jumper and loose pants. The other appeared exactly the opposite, dressed in a suit and heels, her hair pulled tightly back away from her face, making her look severe and unpleasant. She looked Vanessa up and down and raised an eyebrow.

"Mum, Nan, this is Vanessa," Drew said.

"Oh! Yer girlfriend!" the older woman said excitedly. "I've heard so much of ye, and I'm glad to finally meet ye! I'm Nora, Andrew's grandmother," she continued, holding out her hand to Vanessa.

"Nice to meet you, Nora," Vanessa said, shaking her hand with a smile.

"Do sit down, lass. Andrew has been telling me all about ye since he met ye."

"All good I hope," Vanessa said.

"Oh, aye. All good. I've been telling him to bring ye round, but he has nae had the time, he said."

"He's pretty busy, but then so am I. Coordinating schedules can get complicated. Hi, I'm Vanessa." She reached out a hand to Drew's mother, who looked at it but didn't take it.

"Rhona," she said, her tone as icy as her expression. "Drew's mother."

Vanessa pulled her hand back, feeling the snub keenly, and sat down. "Nice to meet you."

"I wish I could say the same."

"Mum!" Drew exclaimed.

Vanessa looked at her in surprise. "I'm. . .I'm sorry if I've somehow offended you already."

Rhona ignored her and looked at Drew. "Really, Drew? An American?"

"What has that got to do with anything?" Drew asked.

"Chan urrainn dhut fiù 's nighean Albannach a thoirt seachad? Aon agad fhèin?" Rhona said. *Ye cannae even date a Scottish girl? One of yer own?*

Vanessa frowned. "Why would you say something like that?" All three of the others looked at her curiously. "Yes, I understood you."

"Ye speak Gaelic?" Nora asked.

"Well, I understand more than I speak, but I'm learning."

"How did ye come by that, lass?"

"My best friend and her husband mostly speak it at home, as does his brother, and they're teaching me. *She's* an American, too," Vanessa said pointedly as she fixed her eyes on Rhona. "Though her husband is about as Scottish as you can get."

"Aye, that's true. I've heard them," Drew confirmed. "I did nae realize they were teaching ye. And ye are right; Euan is about as Scottish as they come. He's a Cameron," Drew said, directing the last to his grandmother.

"Ohhh, excellent choice yer friend has made," Nora said.

"You have no idea," Vanessa replied.

"And what is it ye do, Vanessa?" Rhona continued, this time in English.

"I used to work in television production, but now I work for the aforementioned friends."

"Doing what?"

"Anything they need me to do. I keep their lives running for them while they're working."

"So, ye are an assistant," she said disdainfully.

"I suppose so, but I don't mind it. It's something they really need."

"And what do *they* do?"

"I can't really discuss that. I'll just say they need to be away a lot."

Rhona scoffed. "Nothing good, then."

"They work for the government," Drew explained, seeming to feel the need to come to the defense of his friends.

"How convenient. So, yer American friend just happens to marry someone from Scotland that makes enough money to have an assistant. How *clever* of her."

"Whoa, hang on. I'm going to stop you right there," Vanessa said as she stood up. "Don't you *dare* say anything about Grace. You don't know her or anything about her. Let me enlighten you on something: she didn't just *happen* to marry someone from Scotland and come into money. What she had was *hers*. She earned it. *He* didn't have the money for an assistant; *she* did. She didn't marry him for money because he didn't have any. She married him because she loved him."

"Good for her, but that says nothing about ye."

"Oh, but it says *plenty* about your attitude and what your actual problem is. You seem to think I'm with Drew for money. I'm not; I make plenty of my own."

"I think she actually makes more than I do," Drew added quietly.

Rhona ignored him. "I think ye have other designs than just the one but designs all the same."

"Are you serious right now? Since you seem to think all Americans are ignorant and horrible people, there's clearly no winning. I'll tell you this, though: I'm not ignorant, and neither is Grace. I have a degree from UCLA and Grace has a master's from Oxford with joint honors, but I shouldn't have to justify myself to you. I love your son, and it isn't for his money or his country of origin or whatever other ridiculous thing you're thinking of. That's what you should concern yourself with. Is he loved? Is he happy? All it seems like you care about is whether he marries someone you think is suitable for whatever vision you have for him. That's clearly narrow, so there's no need for me to even continue talking to you."

Vanessa walked past Rhona toward the door as all three sat in shock before Drew stood up quickly. "Vanessa, wait . . ." he said as he hurried after her, catching her at the door. "I'm sorry. I didn't want this, and she does nae represent my feelings in any way. Wait for me outside, will ye?"

Vanessa nodded, her eyes still showing intense anger before she walked out and slammed the door behind her. Drew placed his hand on the door and closed his eyes, taking a deep breath and releasing it before he turned and went back to the living room.

"What is wrong with ye?" Drew asked, not bothering to hide his anger.

"Ye cannae be serious, Drew. An American who works as someone's personal assistant? A *rude* American at that, though I should nae be surprised, as most of them are," Rhona said.

"Again, what has her being American got to do with anything!"

"They dinnae understand the culture, where ye come from, and who ye are. She's here because it's trendy. She is with ye for yer name, Drew."

"My. . .what? That does nae even make sense!"

"Of course it does. Ye have seen all the Americans moving through Inverness suddenly, all of them curious about the Frasers."

"They would find plenty since it's the most popular last name in the city," he sniped. "If that's what she wanted, she'd have plenty to choose from. She did nae seek me out."

"Ye need to stick to yer own kind, Drew."

"I cannae *believe* I'm hearing this. Ye really are a piece of work, ye know that? Ye insult her from the start and then call her rude for standing up to ye. Ye don't care what I feel about any of it."

"Because yer 'feelings' are leading ye in an unsuitable direction. Ye need someone to look at it with a clear head for ye. She is a *nothing*! Ye are a doctor, a brilliant one, and ye should be with someone like ye."

"Like me? Another doctor? A Scot? Both? It does nae matter to me! I'm nae working on an alliance for land and money!"

"Again, she is someone's *assistant*. She's nae intellectually yer equal no matter what degree she has. I also very much doubt her story about her friend."

"Christ, ye are ridiculous! Ye don't know what she is intellectually because ye have nae spoken to her! As for Grace? Her husband is Mal's stepbrother, and everything Vanessa said is true. Grace does have a master's from Oxford. I have seen the diploma myself in their study. She does nae keep company with stupid people."

"Dinnae speak to me with that sort of language, Andrew! I am yer mother!"

"No!" Drew shouted, finally losing his cool. "Ye are nae! Ye may have given birth to me, but ye did nae raise me. Ye abdicated that duty to Nan while ye went off to look after yerself when Dad left ye.”

Rhona gasped and then fixed an angry glare on her son. “How *dare* ye,” she hissed.

“How dare *ye*! How dare ye come into my home, insult the woman I love for no reason, and try to tell me how to run my life! What, ye think I did nae know Dad left ye? I heard and saw how ye treated him. Even now, ye only acknowledge *I* exist when it suits ye and when ye can brag to yer idiot friends about how I’m a doctor.”

“She is already rubbing off on ye with her rudeness! Ye never would have spoken this way before!”

“Actually, she is giving me the strength to finally stand up for myself against ye. She’s right: ye don’t get to decide for me; no one does. I don’t care what ye think of her or of anything. I am *done* caring.”

Rhona looked at Nora, who was smiling at Drew. “Ye are nae going to let him speak to us this way, are ye?”

“He is speaking to *ye*, nae me,” Nora replied. “*Ye* have earned this, nae me. Oh, but this was years in coming, Rhona, and I knew someday it would. Our Andrew has discovered just who he truly is and who he came from, and they are behind him now, giving him a voice. Now he is telling ye he has had enough, and ye would be wise to heed him.”

“What does that mean!”

“Andrew, love, if yer mother persists, what do ye plan to do?”

Drew looked at Nora but refused to look at Rhona. “Whatever I want. I dinnae have to speak to her or even have her in my life.”

“Ye see, Rhona? What is more important to ye? Yer snobbishness or yer son?”

“It should nae be a choice I have to make.”

“Ach, ye just did,” Nora said, shaking her head. “Andrew, ye do what ye must, what feels right to ye. I will love ye the same. Ye are a Fraser through and through. It’s in yer eyes and the way ye stand now, ready to fight for what ye love. Yer kin are within ye and making themselves known."

Rhona stood up. "Is this what ye are deciding then, Andrew? That ye don't have to listen to me?"

"Get out," Drew growled, finally looking at her. Rhona looked surprised by his tone of voice, at once dark and full of quiet anger. It was one he knew she'd never heard from him before. "Ye are no longer welcome here."

Rhona grabbed her bag and stormed out, which made Nora laugh. "Ach, good for ye, lad. It is about time."

Drew rubbed his face with his hands. "I'm sorry, Nan. I will give ye a ride home."

"Dinnae be sorry for a moment for doing what ye had to, what ye should have done years ago. She may be my daughter, but she has always been a snob. Why do ye think I took ye, hmm?" Nora stood up and placed a hand on his cheek. "Yer a good lad, Andrew. Ye deserve to be happy, and it does nae matter who it is with. I quite like her; she had the fire to stand up to yer mother straight away."

Drew chuckled a bit. "I had a feeling she would."

"Ye go out and talk to her. I will be fine here, and we can discuss rides later."

Drew nodded and went downstairs to find Vanessa, running through all that had just been said. For him, it was less the shock of her having told his mother off and more what she'd said: she loved him. They'd not said that to each other yet. Knowing which car she'd have, he found it easily. She unlocked the door for him when he knocked on the passenger side window, and he got in and shut the door, sitting there in silence.

"Your mom is a jerk," Vanessa said, breaking the silence between them.

"Aye, she is. That's why I told her to get out of my house. I have no intention of speaking to her again."

"What? Drew —" Vanessa said as she looked over at him, her surprise clear.

"No, I needed to do it. I should have done it a long time ago. This was the final straw for me."

"But. . .she's your mom."

"Technically, aye, but it was my nan who raised me and nae her. She likes to try to control me so that she has something to brag about."

"I'm so sorry."

"Don't be," he said, looking up at her. "But ye surprised me a bit."

"I shouldn't have gone off on her like that. I'm —"

"That's nae what I meant."

Her expression turned curious. "Then how?"

"Ye told her ye loved me."

Vanessa blinked a few times. "Oh. I did, didn't I? Well, I do. It wasn't a lie. I mean, I know we haven't said that or anything and —"

Drew smiled at her. "I love ye, too." Vanessa looked at him, wide-eyed and speechless. "I was talking to Grace the other day and . . ." He hesitated. "I should have said it to ye sooner because I felt it sooner."

"Why didn't you?"

"I was worried ye would think it was too soon."

"Unless it was the day after I met you, then that's probably not true."

Drew laughed and shook his head. "Nae quite. I remember sitting across from ye at that sushi place we went to a couple of weeks later and thinking how beautiful ye were, how lucky I was to be out with ye, and how glad I was that I went to the gathering and met ye. I felt so changed by the experience there and then by ye. Then I thought about how I knew I was sitting with the only woman I would ever need. It is a strange thing to sit across from someone when ye just feel it in ye that she is what ye want for good."

"Wait. . .Drew, what are you saying?"

He bit his lip nervously. "That I want to marry ye eventually."

"Oh my God," Vanessa whispered. "Are you joking?"

"Why would I joke about something like that?"

"But. . .your family . . ."

"The only one whose opinion I want is for it. The question is: Are ye?"

"Not if you're doing it just to spite your mom."

Drew couldn't help but laugh. "Infuriating her would be an added bonus but nae the reason."

"Hang on," Vanessa said. "Drew, are you asking me to marry you?"

"Kind of, aye. Doing a poor job of it, though."

"Kind of?"

"That's nae what I meant. I meant that I'm trying to say that, but it isn't really coming out how I would want it to and I'm very sorry for making a mess of it."

Vanessa smiled a bit. "Then ask me."

"Ye dinnae feel it is too soon?"

"Does this look like the face of someone who thinks that?"

"Fair enough." He sat there for a moment and then started laughing. "I dinnae know why I can't say it. I *want* to say it. Christ, this isn't romantic at all, is it?"

Vanessa laughed with him. "All right, fine, I'll rescue you: yes."

Drew grinned. "Well, there ye have it then."

"I expect a proper proposal at some point."

"What will that consist of so that I dinnae forget anything?"

"Jesus, you are such a doctor. You need lists and steps."

"Truth. Diagrams and illustrations are also helpful," he replied with a teasing smile.

"Just actually saying the words at some point would be adequate."

"I can do that. With the big shiny ring and all that."

"God, please no."

He looked at her curiously.

"Simple is good. I'm not into that status symbol stuff. Besides, diamonds are unethical."

"Noted. I suppose I should look for a place in Fort William."

"Are you still going to work here?"

"Aye. I have a pretty good spot in the department right now. I can always transfer later."

"I have a feeling you won't need to look once they find out."

"Who?"

"The family."

"Oh? Ye think they'll let me join ye there?"

"Pretty sure, yep. Especially since you're marrying in."

Drew laughed again. "Ye make it sound like I'm joining the mob or some dynastic family."

Vanessa just smiled.

"Wait . . ."

"I can't say. Not yet. It isn't the mob, though, and nothing illegal. I promise. They'll tell you everything."

"Who will?"

"Grace and Euan. It'll probably be very soon, as in the next time they see you."

"Should I be nervous?"

"No, not at all. In fact, I think you'll come away from it with an entirely new outlook."

"I'm intrigued. Anyway, Rhona is gone. Come up and talk to Nan? She liked ye."

"I'd be happy to," Vanessa said as they both got out of the car to head back upstairs.

"Nan," Drew called out as they entered his flat. "I brought her back."

"Excellent! Come round, come round," Nora said as she stood up. This time, she welcomed Vanessa with a hug.

"I'm sorry for her behavior, lass. I dinnae know where she gets it from. It is nae as if she grew up in some manor house to have such airs."

Vanessa laughed and returned the hug. "People can get pretty strange sometimes about how they see others."

"Sometimes, and sometimes they're just stupid," Nora said with a small shrug, which made Vanessa laugh harder.

"I think I'm going to like you."

Nora chuckled. "When ye are as old as I am, ye find plain speaking is more efficient. Though ye have no trouble with that yerself already."

"No, I don't. That's the Southern California girl in me. I don't take that crap."

"As ye should nae. I have always wanted to go to California," she said with a smile.

"You'd like it! It's pretty crowded, but if you're only visiting, it's fine. Grace is from California, too."

"Ah, yer friend! She sounds like an interesting character."

"She is. I hope you get to meet her."

"I'll make sure she does," Drew said with a smile. "I think they'd get on well."

"So," Nora said, looking at Drew, "what time of year are ye picking? As soon as ye can or later?"

"Nan, how —"

"I was nae born yesterday, Andrew," she said, cutting him off. "I already knew what was in yer mind and yer heart. Ye never would have fought back so hard if that wasn't yer intent, and all yer mother did was drive ye to move it up."

Drew looked at Vanessa. "Have nae gotten so far as planning."

"Well, what does she want? What about her family in America?"

"Nothing big," Vanessa said quickly. "That's never been a thing for me. I'd love for just my immediate family to come, and we could have something small, outside."

"That'll suit Andrew then. Ye have never been for flash and always outdoors if ye could be."

"Summer it is then," Drew said with a smile.

"Do ye have a picture of yer friends?" Nora asked. "It has been ages since I've seen Mal Cameron."

"Oh! Totally!" Vanessa fished her phone out of her coat pocket. "This one is my favorite," she said as she pulled up a picture of them from the gathering. In it were Mal, Malcolm, Aileen, Euan, Grace, and then Vanessa. Euan was in his uniform, and all of them were smiling with genuine happiness.

"Ach, look at how he has grown! And Malcolm! Still as dignified as ever. Who is this?" Nora asked, pointing at Aileen.

"Aileen, Euan's mom and Malcolm's wife. The one in the uniform is Euan, and Grace is next to him."

"Oh goodness, would ye look at him! He looks very handsome in that kit, and Grace looks lovely. They are happy; ye can see it."

"They are."

Nora swiped the picture before Vanessa could stop her and then raised an eyebrow. "Well. If that is how ye first saw Andrew, I am nae surprised ye are here now."

Vanessa looked over at the phone and saw it was a picture of Euan and Drew in just their kilts after the last shinty match when he'd come back with Grace. "Oh," she said with a laugh. "Yeah, well."

"I dinnae blame Grace, either. That is one gorgeous Cameron lad."

"Nan!" Drew said, though he was clearly amused.

"I am old, nae dead, Andrew," she said as she handed the phone back to Vanessa, who was laughing harder now. "Now, ye should take yerself to bed because ye have work tonight. Vanessa and I can get to know each other over tea."

Drew nodded and stood up. "We can leave early so that I can give ye a ride home first."

"That'll be fine. Off with ye now. Vanessa, lass, let's put the kettle on."

CHAPTER 5

"He did it," Grace said, looking up from her phone as she sat in the kitchen with Euan having afternoon tea.

"Hmm?" Euan replied, his mouth full of a biscuit.

"Drew. Vanessa just texted me. He asked her."

Euan's eyes widened, and he swallowed quickly. "Already?"

"Guess so. Vanessa says she has a story to tell us about how it all went down, so I have a feeling something happened."

"I am nae surprised he *did*, just surprised it was *now*."

"I'm not."

Euan eyed her, his suspicion plain. "What did ye do?"

"Nothing!"

"Oh no. No, no. Ye did *something*. I can tell by the look on yer face. Ye still think ye can fool me, Wife?"

"No, I didn't! I just answered honestly when he asked me questions while I made breakfast the other morning."

"About this?"

"He asked!"

Euan narrowed his eyes. "Nae sure I believe ye."

"Well, you can ask him yourself since you think you know me so well," Grace said, lifting her chin in a small show of defiance.

"Ye can be sure I will," Euan replied, smiling in amusement over her offense at the very suggestion she'd done anything improper.

Grace scoffed and rolled her eyes, causing him to laugh.

"I suppose we should figure out what we are going to do with them, then," he went on once he'd gotten his laugh down to more of a chuckle. "I dinnae think they can both live in her room."

"No, at least not long term, but the two rooms down here are much larger. One of them would probably work fine."

"Aye," Euan said with a nod.

Before Grace could say anything else, a mission notification came through, and she sighed. "Damn it."

"Must be something big if they are calling us back already."

"Yep," Grace replied, re-opening her text messages so that she could send one to Vanessa. "I'm telling her she can wait to come back until he goes to work. Mal's here; he can hang out until she gets back."

"Aye, I will go tell him," Euan said, getting up from the table and going upstairs to find his brother.

Grace stood up as Caia came in. "Already?"

"I know, I really am sorry," Caia said. "This mission is one no one else can do. It *must* be you."

Grace's brow furrowed in concern. "Really? That sounds dire. Any idea as to why?"

"No, but that is what the Councilwoman said."

"How very odd."

"I know, it really is, but I am sure they have a reason. They always do when it comes to the two of you."

"Yes, I know, and I think that's what concerns me most about this sudden callback," Grace said as she left the kitchen and went upstairs, Caia beside her. Euan joined them at the landing as they headed for the mission room.

"Whatever it is, we must get you ready quickly because they said it was urgent to get you on the ground."

"That is nae normal. What is this about?" Euan asked as he gave her a wary glance.

"I really do not know. If I did, you know I would tell you."

"Caia told me the Councilwoman said it had to be us and no one else, and that's why we've been called back early."

"I dinnae like the sound of that," Euan said, moving quickly alongside them, both sensing the urgency in Caia. "At all."

When they entered the mission room, Caia shut the door behind them, waiting in the hallway for them to change, and they wasted no time in getting into their linens. Grace brushed and braided her own hair, as well as Euan's, then knocked on the door to let Caia know they were ready.

"This one might be longer than usual, or it might not. We're ready with extra supplies to keep your bodies hydrated and the like while you are down in case that happens," Caia explained as she came back inside.

"Got it," Grace replied as she and Euan climbed onto the bed.

"Good luck, you two, as always," Caia said.

As Caia closed the curtains, Euan reached out and stroked Grace's cheek. Even though they were going together and always did now, it was part of their routine for him to show her a last bit of affection. It was never certain they'd be together once the mission started, and sometimes it was all they'd have to last them through the entirety. Grace covered his hand and squeezed it gently.

"Ye ready?"

"Let's do this."

The two lay down next to each other and closed their eyes, the transport immediate and seemingly more abrupt than normal. They took a moment to adjust before opening their eyes and looking around to find themselves in a small alcove off a long gallery. Grace knew what period they were in before the briefing even started just by looking at what Euan was wearing. With his beautifully embroidered blue velvet and silk doublet, Venetian hose, and a matching soft hat, she knew they were in the 16th century. Blue seemed to be The Council's favored color on him, and whenever they used it, he made an even more striking impression than he normally did when he entered a room. The collar and cuffs of his shirt were intricately blackworked, his long hair tied neatly at the base of his neck. Though the fashion of the time was short hair, he always preferred to keep his as it was. At his hip rested a rapier, a symbol of his status and station.

Grace herself was in a gown of rose-pink brocade, the sleeves beneath made of white silk and embroidered with flowers, the same as the kirtle that showed through the parted brocade skirts in the front. The chemise she wore was also blackworked, her hair tucked into a silk embroidered and pearled caul. On her feet were velvet slippers, further proof of their status because they had enough to use such costly fabric for shoes when most couldn't afford to even *look* at it. Evidently, they were not coming back to this period in their former roles.

The incoming briefing halted any further examination of themselves and their surroundings. England, March 1571. There were several targets, which was unusual in itself. Francis Walsingham, William Cecil, Roberto Ridolfi, Thomas Howard, the Duke of Norfolk, Mary, Queen of Scots, and the Queen of England herself, Elizabeth. Their mission was to prevent the success of the Ridolfi plot to assassinate Elizabeth and place Mary on the throne with a new husband: the Duke of Norfolk. Grace heard a sharp intake of breath from Euan when Mary was shown to be part of it; the former queen of Scotland whose son would eventually become the joint ruler of England and Scotland and would later lead to the very rebellion Euan would fight in. She looked at him in surprise, as even *she* couldn't have anticipated this, and it was clear in an instant why The Council had said it could only be them. This was larger than anything they'd ever done, and just *one* slip up would mean failure. This was, however, the perfect place for Euan's skills, and he'd need all of them if they were going to succeed.

"Christ," Euan whispered. "This is immense."

"Yes, it is, but we can do this. It is why they sent us."

"She will know us."

"I know."

"What do we tell her?"

"The truth," Grace said.

"What! Are ye mad?"

"Euan, she very much believes in the occult. We show up

13 years later and haven't aged a day; what do you think we could tell her that she would not suss out? She will believe me when I tell her."

"I trust ye," Euan said. "Where should we start?"

"With her. Once we have her on side, that will get us the access we need to Cecil and Walsingham."

Euan nodded and stood, extending his hand to help Grace up. Focusing on Elizabeth would help them find her, and they walked through the maze of palace corridors until they drew near to where she was. The sound of music drifted out of the great hall, as did laughter and the sound of clapping hands. Grace took a moment to steady herself and then assumed the proper posture, one of her hands resting gently at the front of her waist, the other sitting atop Euan's extended hand, her face placid. Nodding to Euan, she allowed him to lead her into the room, her eyes scanning the occupants as they blended into the crowd. The queen sat on a small, raised dais at one end of the room as her courtiers danced to the music being played by the court musicians. Her dress was, as expected, elaborate. Jewels and pearls covered the velvet she wore, each finger adorned with a ring. She was, by now, almost 38 and far from the young woman they'd known the last time they were here. She rested against the back of the chair, surveying the dancers while trying to seem interested, but Grace could tell she wasn't.

Moving them through the crowd of people, Euan strategically placed them at the foot of the line of dancers, where Elizabeth was sure to see them, and it took less than a moment for her to do just that. She shot up from her seat, staring at them as if she didn't trust her own eyes, and her action brought everything in the room to an immediate halt. Fixing her eyes on them, she stepped down from the dais and walked a few steps toward them, drawing the eyes of everyone else in their direction.

"Grace? Cameron? No, it cannot *possibly* be."

Acknowledged, they lowered themselves before her. "Your Majesty," they said in unison.

Elizabeth gasped and covered her mouth. "It is! Oh! Rise, please, and let me look at you!" A murmur broke out amongst the courtiers who were now wondering just *who* these people were to garner such a reaction from their queen. Grace and Euan rose, smiling at her. "Heavens, you have not aged a day! Blanche!"

Blanche Parry stepped down from the dais at her queen's command and came to her side, lowering herself and then rising. "Your Majesty."

"Look who has come to court! Mistress Evans and Master Cameron. And dressed so beautifully, too! Come, we must speak at once, and you may tell me where you have been all this time! Ladies," she said as she turned to address her maids of honor and other waiting ladies. "Please remain here."

Grace and Euan reverenced her and then followed her as she swept from the room, reverences and bows moving like a wave before her. Blanche fell in behind them, and as they crossed the great watching chamber to enter the queen's private rooms, people stared at them once the queen had passed. The doors to the presence chamber were opened by her guard and she strode through them. As they shut behind the small party, Elizabeth turned around to face them.

"Blanche, would you be so kind as to wait outside and instruct everyone that I am not to be disturbed?" Blanche lowered herself, rose, and then departed. The three of them stood looking at each other for a moment before Elizabeth let out what seemed like a relieved sigh and hugged Grace tightly. "It is *such* a relief to see you."

Grace returned the affection, though it surprised her. "Is it?"

"I sent for you both when they sent me to Hatfield, but word came back that you could not be found, and I feared the very worst for you."

"What did ye fear?" Euan asked.

"That Mary discovered your assistance to me and had her dogs do away with the both of you," she said with a small frown. "It broke my heart to think of it. You had both been such a great help and comfort to me when I was with you."

Euan chuckled. "Well, they could have *tried* but they would have found it difficult, I assure ye."

Elizabeth looked at him, her gaze questioning. "How is it you have come here? And how in the world do you look just as you did when last I saw you? It certainly looks as though you either were not a stable hand or have taken a great step up in the world without my knowing."

"That explanation I shall leave to my lovely wife," Euan said.

"Your . . ." Elizabeth began before her lips settled into a wry smile. "Well, seems I was not wrong after all."

"No, ye were nae," Euan said with a small, amused smile of his own. "But it was certainly nae as ye thought. She was my wife even when ye knew us."

"A secret marriage!"

"Yes, but not for the reason you think," Grace said. "Your Majesty, how safe is our conversation here?"

"Reasonably so, I would assume, as these are my private rooms and everyone else is back where you found me."

"Is there any chance anyone could overhear us?"

"This is court; there is *always* a chance."

"Is there a safer place?" Euan asked.

"What is this about?"

"We will tell you all, but we need to be sure we are not heard. That is of the *utmost* necessity."

Elizabeth studied them, trying to decide if she should trust them before she gestured to follow her without saying a word. They crossed through into the privy chamber, the room where Elizabeth slept, and she opened another door, signaling wordlessly for them to go inside. It was a small room, but they squeezed into what Grace realized was a prayer closet. This would be the safest place, as prayers were sacrosanct, and no one would dare listen in.

"Well?"

Euan looked at Grace and nodded to her. "Go on, love."

"Your Majesty, when you were young, did anyone ever tell you fairy stories? Tales of strange happenings and beings of all sorts?"

"Of course. Blanche is Welsh, after all."

"Did she ever tell you a tale about beings called Watchers?"

Elizabeth laughed. "Yes, I think she did, actually. What has that to do with anything?"

"Your Majesty, that story is true. There really *are* Watchers."

Elizabeth stopped laughing and looked at Grace with a bemused expression. "Come now, Grace, what kind of story is this?"

"It is not a story, or at least not a false one. I am a Watcher, and that is why I am here."

Elizabeth's expression went from amused to irritated in an instant. "That is ridiculous, and if you are simply going to tell me lies, you can remove yourselves from my presence and my court."

Grace sighed. "If I am lying, tell me, how did I know the things I told you? How did I know to tell you to draw lines in the empty spaces of your letters so that no one could add words that were not your own? How did I know Mary would not be queen long, that you would take the throne without a rebellion, and that you would be strong and loved? How did I know to tell you to have faith even though things would seem bleak?"

Elizabeth's eyes widened for a moment. "How do I know you were not being given that information by others?"

"Because you know full well that every communication, every person in and out, all of it was being monitored. If I was being fed information to give to you, why would I not just tell you so? I was on your side if you remember. It was I who had you avoid the Wyatt Rebellion. If I was meant to betray you, I would not have done so."

Elizabeth shook her head, not able to truly comprehend what she was being told. "Are you really telling me you are both otherworldly beings here to help me?"

"Aye," Euan said with a small nod. "That is precisely what we are saying."

Elizabeth scoffed. "I cannot believe you."

"The marquess of Winchester grows quite old, his time is coming to an end, and you are already thinking about who you want to have replace him. It would be yet another office for Lord Leicester."

Elizabeth stared at Grace.

"Oh, yes, I know. I know a great many things others do not. I know about the letters you passed with him in the Tower. I know what they said."

"How?"

"Because they still exist. Because I read them. Those same letters you keep hidden in a casket in a locked drawer. The ones you read when you feel especially bitter about not being able to be with him as you wish you could be while you dream of what could have been. 'My Eyes,' you call him."

Elizabeth gasped, and it made Grace smile.

"You know very well I could not have read them now, from where they are hidden, and they had not been written yet when last I was with you."

Elizabeth's face paled as she looked between the two standing there. "You are not lying to me," she whispered.

"No," Grace replied.

"How is such a thing possible?"

"It is complicated and something I really cannot tell you about because there are things you cannot know for a good many reasons," Grace explained. "Just know we are here to help you and not harm you. We always were."

"That is why you said she was your wife even when I knew you," she said to Euan.

"Aye, it is. For the sake of our mission at that time, she had to pretend otherwise. It should make sense to ye now, that moment when I told ye I could nae give ye what ye were considering asking me for."

"Of course. You were already married, and that is why you looked at her the way you did."

"Aye. It is hard to pretend ye dinnae love someone when ye do."

"I know the difficulty of that charade far more than I would like to," she replied. "Why are you here now after all this time?"

"To save your life," Grace said, keeping her tone gentle.

"What!"

"There is a plot against yer life, and we are here to make sure it does nae happen. For that, we will need yer help," Euan said.

"Who plots against me?"

"Mary —"

"The so-called Queen of Scots," Elizabeth finished, not bothering to hide the bitterness in her tone.

"Yes," Grace replied.

"What is she about this time?"

"What she is always about: the English throne."

"Am I safe now?"

"For now," Euan said. "And we will work to keep ye that way."

"What do you need from me?"

"Access," Grace replied. "We need to speak to Walsingham, to Burghley, and of course, to you. We can work with the other two to expose the plot and end it."

Elizabeth nodded. "You will have it, but you will need more than that if the plotters are working with Mary. Last time the vipers were amongst our own court. No, you will need a title, or you will not gain access to their company."

"A title, Yer Majesty?"

"Yes. Do you really think any of the conspirators will speak with you if they think you are a simple stable hand?"

"I suppose that *is* true, aye."

"It cannot be too high, or they will be suspicious," Elizabeth said, almost to herself. "Though I would very much love to give you the highest one I could think of just to watch them burn."

Euan and Grace both laughed.

"A knighthood will have to do."

"As ye wish it."

"Good. Come," Elizabeth said, opening the door and ushering them out of the prayer closet. "I do hope I can hear more about you and your work when there is less danger.”

“I will tell you all I am able, I promise,” Grace replied.

“I will hold you to it. Now, we will do this publicly because they all need to see it.” She stopped and looked at Euan. “I realize now that I do not know your actual name, Cameron.”

“Euan,” he answered with a small smile.

“Somehow it suits you,” she said before she turned and continued walking. “Open!”

The doors of the presence chamber opened immediately, and they made their way out, back toward the great hall with Blanche once again behind them. As before, the wave of bows and reverences went ahead of her as she made her way to the dais, but as she reached it, she turned to face her court.

“It is our great pleasure to welcome such friends to our court and within our power to choose to reward them for such dedicated service to our person. Master Cameron, would you present us your sword?”

A gasp rippled through the courtiers as the request made it clear what the queen intended to do. Euan pulled the sword from its sheath, saluted Elizabeth, then presented the hilt to her as he bowed. She took it from him and regarded him with a small smile, and Grace knew it was the enjoyment of being able to remind Euan of the power she held over him here, no matter who or what he might otherwise be.

“Kneel,” she commanded him, the room falling silent as he obeyed her. Turning the blade to the flat, she touched it first to his right shoulder and then to his left. “We do confer upon thee the rank of knight for all thy great services and deeds unto us, both known and unknown. You may rise, Sir Euan.”

CHAPTER 6

As the monitor intoned its shrill, flat whine, the medical team turned their eyes to the attending physician, who sighed and looked up at the clock. "Time of death, 22:36."

In near total unison, the entire group took a step back from the body on the gurney as Drew pulled the blood-stained sheet over the young woman they'd been trying so diligently to save. He was thankful that it shielded her from his sight for the moment, though it didn't prevent him from feeling that they'd failed — *he'd* failed — and tonight there would be another family in mourning. Walking to the edge of the room, he pulled the shoe covers off his feet, followed by his gloves — originally blue but now purple from the blood covering them — then the face mask and protective glasses he'd been wearing. Next came the surgical gown, all of it tossed into the biohazard bins as he went to the sinks to wash up before walking at a brisk pace to the lounge to change scrubs. Into biohazard went the previous ones and on went clean ones. With all of that done, he strode for the door, desperately needing fresh air.

As the automatic doors slid open with their customary science-fiction-like whooshing sound, Drew stepped out into the night, the shock of the cold air washing over him and cooling his overheated skin. He *hated* this part of his job, but it happened, and it never got any easier. He couldn't save everyone, he knew that, but that didn't mean he wouldn't try his hardest to do so. Unfortunately for the young woman in that room, his hardest and best hadn't been good enough; there had been too much damage done, and it was beyond anyone's scope to fix, save a miracle. He'd have to go back in soon — there were always more patients to treat — but for now he could take a few minutes to breathe, to regain his focus and control, to set it aside so he was ready for the next one. The problem this time was that the young woman had looked a bit like Vanessa, and the thought of it being *her* dead on that gurney made him feel panicked and sick in a way he hadn't experienced before. Maybe it was why he'd worked to save her far longer than he normally would've. It was his worst fear, always, that the ones he treated might one day be his own and he'd be unable to save them, and he didn't know a doctor who didn't share that fear. The worst patients to see, for him, were always children, though he was fairly certain that was true for almost anyone. Women in situations like this were the next worst.

Squatting down, he rested his head in his hands, closing his eyes. He wanted to scream, but he couldn't, and he honestly wasn't sure if he'd feel any better even if he could. Moments like these made becoming a GP seem a welcoming thought, but he knew he'd miss the rush that came with emergency medicine, that high he always got when he pulled someone back from the brink of death.

"Drew?"

Lifting his head, he stood slowly and looked back to see Vanessa. "Hey," he said, his voice low from trying to contain his emotion. "What are ye doing here?"

From the look on her face when she saw him, it was immediately clear that she could tell something was wrong, and he was both glad she could read him and scared that she knew him so well already. "Drew, what happened? Are you okay?"

"Aye. Aye, I'm fine," he said, attempting a smile he knew was far from convincing. He felt as though he were in a daze, and his eyes probably had that glazed-over look to them that he'd been told about by others when they'd talked to him after moments like this one. "Just needed a moment after my last patient."

Vanessa frowned. "I hope they're okay."

Drew shook his head in answer to her question because it was all he could do. If she'd seen the floor of the room he'd just been in, she'd know in a second why he was this way. There hadn't been a clean spot on it by the time they were done.

"Oh, sweetheart . . ." she said.

"Aye. I did my best, but it was nae enough. Nae this time."

"You did your best; that's all you can do. Sometimes it's just too much to overcome."

"Does nae make it easier, and I hate it every time it happens. I still remember the first one; though, in truth, I remember all of them. Ye wonder if ye really did all ye could, if ye missed something. Her family is here, and I'll have to tell them." He paused for a moment. "She reminded me of ye a bit," he said, his voice cracking despite his attempt to hide it.

"Drew, what can I do to help you?"

"There is nothing ye can do, nae really, at least nae now. At home maybe, but . . ."

"But not here."

"Right."

"You can't talk about it here, can you?" she said, recognizing the point he was trying to make with his non-specific answers.

"No, I cannae."

"I brought you some dinner," she said, sweetly changing the subject as she held up a bag. "They told me I could find you out here."

A small smile passed across his lips. "Thank ye, that was sweet of ye."

"Thought you might be tired of hospital food."

"It's nae that bad actually," he replied with a chuckle as he began to come back to himself a bit, shoving away those moments to try to forget them.

"I hate to do this, but I have to go home. I can't stay like I'd planned because Grace and Euan got called back early."

He frowned but nodded. "I hope everything is all right."

"Yeah, should be, but it must be something big if they're cutting short their rest period. Mal is there now but I know he's going back to London soon, and I never know when they might come back. Maybe come over when you're off?"

"Aye, I will. If anything, it's where I need to be tonight. With ye. Come back inside with me? We can talk for a few minutes in the lounge where it's warm."

Placing a hand on her lower back, he guided her through the doors and back inside to the doctor's lounge, where she put the bag in the fridge before hugging him tightly, a gesture he returned as if he were starving for it, his entire body tense. She'd only ever seen him outside of work after he'd had time to relax a bit, but that was not now, and he knew he'd have some explaining to do later about why he'd seemed so distant even though he didn't want to be. If he had his way, he'd leave with her right now to spend the rest of the night in her arms on the settee by the fire.

Kissing the top of her head, he smiled. "Ye be safe on the road back. Text me when ye get there so that I know ye made it safely, please?"

"Of course."

"Thank ye. Right, I need to go do one of my least favorite parts of my job."

Vanessa stroked his cheek. "I'm sorry. I'll be waiting for you. Call me when you're turning off the motorway."

Nodding, he gave her another kiss before he turned and walked out of the lounge with her. She trailed behind him, heading out the way she'd come, squeezing his hand for a moment as they approached a windowed room where two people sat on a couch. When she let go of his hand, he opened the door and stepped inside. The couple stood up immediately when he entered, looking at him expectantly.

"Mr. and Mrs. Buchanan?"

Both nodded in silence.

"My name is Dr. Andrew Fraser; I was the attending physician treating yer daughter."

"Is she all right?" the woman asked nervously, a pleading in her eyes that he hated to see when he had bad news.

"No, I'm sorry. We did all we could, but she did nae make it. There was just too much damage done."

The mother screamed, crying hysterically as she reached out and clutched Drew's arms. Her husband collapsed into a chair and sobbed in utter anguish.

"No! It's a mistake! It cannae be true! Please, tell me it's nae true!" she shrieked.

He took her hands in his, giving her a human touch amidst the hell she'd just been thrown into. "If I could say that, I would, I promise ye. If I could bring her back, please know I would."

She completely fell apart then, her cries mixing with screams of pain, and Drew held her up, giving her someone to hold on to in this moment where her husband was just as mired in grief. It was contact with the person who'd spent the last moments with her beloved child, as if she could absorb those last precious seconds by some sort of osmosis. It wasn't enough, it would never, and could never, be enough no matter what he did. These were the moments that stuck with him, the screams that lived in his subconscious, echoing through his skull in the darkness of sleep and plaguing his dreams, yet somehow, he'd have to leave this room as though none of this had ever happened so that he could go on to the next patient. He was never sure how he managed it, wasn't sure how any of them managed it, but somehow, he did.

It was dawn when Drew finally emerged from the hospital and shuffled to his car. Dressed in street clothes now, he was exhausted but far too amped up to worry about falling asleep. He hadn't had another death on his shift, and he was grateful for that. He'd pulled every one of those close cases back to the living, and he was proud of that; it at least helped him not dwell on the one. Once inside, he buckled in and found some music to listen to before leaving the hospital and the city behind him. As he watched it recede into the distance in his rearview mirror, swallowed up by the trees along the motorway and Loch Ness, he breathed a sigh of relief, feeling a weight lift from his shoulders. Soon enough he'd be with Vanessa and able to forget all of it, a sort of sanctuary he felt almost desperate to reach.

The drive was quiet and traffic free, and he called Vanessa as directed when he turned off the motorway. As he arrived at the lodge, she appeared at the front door before he'd even parked, looking sweetly tousled in her pajamas, safe and sound. Getting out of the car, he walked toward her, saying nothing, grabbing her hand to pull her back into the house after him. He didn't stop, moving them quickly upstairs to her room. Vanessa looked surprised as he shut the bedroom door, but he didn't give her long to think about it before kissing her. He needed this, needed her, needed to feel alive and know she was, too. Vanessa didn't protest, instead helping him out of his clothes between the almost demanding kisses he was giving her.

As they lay together afterward, she had her head on his shoulder, tracing patterns on his chest with a fingertip as he held her close to him. "I'm sorry," he whispered. "I just needed to —"

"Shhh," she said, cutting him off. "I get it, and it's okay. It isn't like you forced me; I was perfectly willing. You'd never do that."

"No, I would nae, but I still should have seen to ye a bit more than I did."

"You did just fine, trust me."

"I'll take yer word for it."

"I saw you tell the family," she said in a quiet voice.

"Aye, and that is one of the worst parts. What do ye say? What *can* ye say that makes any of it easier? There is no gentle way to tell someone their loved one is dead, and it's even worse when ye have to tell them it's their child. They will always say ye have the wrong person, it must be a mistake, beg for it to be a mistake, but it is nae. It never is."

"I can't imagine having to do it. I don't think I could."

"I wish I didn't have to."

"What happened?"

"She was stabbed to death by her ex-boyfriend. She had a protective order, but he ignored it and broke into her flat. He was waiting for her when she got home and ambushed her. I did everything I could, but the damage was too much. She was alive when she got to us but barely, and I think she knew she was nae going to make it. She was able to tell us the name of the person who did it, and ye know the worst part? This happened in front of their six-year-old daughter because she was coming home from work and had just picked the wee lass up from the child minder's. Her last thoughts, her last words, were panicked pleading to take care of her baby, begging us to tell the wee one how much her mam loved her, asking us over and over if she was safe. We could give her that comfort, at least, and she lost consciousness then like she was holding on just for that. We kept her going and tried whatever we could, but. . .he stabbed her twenty times. Twenty. Do ye know what that can do to a body? It just quit. Honestly, it was a small miracle she lasted as long as she did. Now there is a woman dead and a wee lass out there who will be forever scarred by watching her father violently murder her mother, and for what? His own ego."

Vanessa's lower lip was trembling, tears pooling in her eyes. "That's horrific. Why would someone do something like that?"

"I wish I knew.

"That poor baby. At least she can go to her grandparents, and they have something left of their daughter."

"Aye, but that is likely cold comfort for all of them. None of them will ever be the same, that child least of all.

"How did you know he stabbed her twenty times? Did the police tell you?"

"No, I counted them. I had to."

"Oh, Drew, that's awful. I'm so sorry."

"So am I, but it's what happens. It's part of my job. At the same time, I think: How can ye feel sorry for me? How can *I*? I'm alive; she's nae. I feel sorry for *her*, for her family, for her bairn, for everything she will never do now and everything they will never experience together."

"You still had to be there. You saw it, you had to deal with the moment where you knew that despite your best efforts, it was too late. I feel sorry for *that*, and I can only imagine how hard that must be on you. I know how empathetic you are."

"They tell ye to focus on those ye did save, and I do, I just..." he began before he broke down in tears, unable to say more.

Vanessa sat up and pulled him into her arms to just hold him. He knew she couldn't truly understand what he was feeling, what he felt every time this happened, and some nights those moments were far more frequent than others. She rocked him gently and stroked his hair, crying with him because his pain was so raw. He couldn't count how many times he'd cried like this, alone in his bed after a shift, when there was only silence and emptiness with plenty of time to feel every second of it.

"I love you," she whispered. "It's okay."

After about 10 minutes, he'd calmed down enough to speak again. "I'm sorry. I shouldn't. . .we aren't supposed to —"

"Drew, you can talk to me. It's all right, I'm not going to tell anyone, and you need to let it out to somebody."

"I don't want to burden ye with it."

"You aren't, so stop. You *have* to talk to me. I've seen what keeping it inside does to people."

"How?"

"I had to watch my best friend lie to everyone about who she was and what she did for three years. She only just finally told *me* when I came to visit in the spring. I watched her withdraw from everyone, live in her own head because she couldn't tell anyone what she was doing."

"I'm nae sure that is the same."

"It is. You feel like you can't tell anyone because it might make them unhappy, but you really need to get it off your chest. You can tell *me*, Drew. If I'm supposed to marry you, then you need to let me in and talk to me. It'll never work between us if you don't."

Drew nodded. "I'll try."

"Did you lose anyone else on your shift?"

"No. Close, but no. I managed to get them all back with us."

"See? One family is hurt, but think of all the ones who aren't, all because of what you did last night."

"I want to save them all, but I know that's unrealistic. Does nae mean I will nae try."

"And you *should* try. That's all that can be asked. You know you did everything you could."

"I did. Honestly, I probably stuck with her longer than I should've, but like I said, she reminded me a bit of ye."

"That must've made it worse."

"Aye, a bit." He sighed as he lay back down. "Thank ye for the sandwich, by the way. It was quite good." He had to change the subject, and he knew she understood that.

"I'm glad."

"How long are they gone for this time?"

"Hard to say. It usually isn't long, but they said this one might take longer."

"Do ye mind if I just keep coming here?"

"No, I don't, and I'm sure no one else would either. I'll double-check with them at the next check-in, but I already know the answer."

The affirmation sent relief through him. He had no desire to be alone, because alone with his thoughts meant alone with the nightmares that could sometimes come with them. Nightmares where those he loved replaced those who'd died, and he couldn't do anything to save *them* either. Nightmares of the patients he'd lost coming back to drag him down, angry that he hadn't done more. These were all things Euan understood well, and Drew realized they might need to talk about how Euan coped because it just might help him do the same. For now, though, the only thing to drag him down was sleep.

CHAPTER 7

After knighting Euan, the queen ordered rooms to be made ready for them near her own. There'd been some grumbling about this, but no one could or would go against the queen. Grace thought it fortunate that some were empty so that no one had to be moved out of a space they'd previously been occupying. That was the kind of disruption that would start them and their mission off on the wrong footing and require a great deal of hard work to undo. The Council had placed trunks belonging to them with the palace staff, and those had been immediately placed in the assigned space once the order had been given.

As the doors shut behind them, Grace took stock of their accommodations, making note of varying areas where walls might easily have eyes or ears to keep tabs on their movements and conversations. The rooms were spacious and well-appointed, accessed by a set of double doors that would place any visitor into a space that was, essentially, a presence chamber. This was where they would entertain guests or spend their own leisure time if so desired, but they'd be fools to expect any sort of privacy here. There was a large fireplace in the center of one wall, with a set of chairs and a table near the hearth, a much larger dining table with several chairs across the room, a writing desk, a bureau, and a few other pieces of furniture. The bedchamber was on the left side of the room, separated from the main area by a set of doors. Inside, there was a massive bed with curtains around it, a wardrobe, and a small fireplace to warm the room.

Grace went to the windows that lined the back of the room,

the thick velvet curtains pulled back to let the daylight in. Pushing herself onto the stone seat so that she could look out, she saw that their windows overlooked a garden, and she was thankful it wasn't the Thames. Such a view might be fine now when it was cold, but if they were here when it got warmer, it wouldn't be. For now, snow covered the ground, and she couldn't help but think of how lovely it would be to walk there when the weather improved.

This wasn't the first time she'd been in this particular palace, and it likely wouldn't be the last, though it had changed some in the interceding years since she'd last occupied space amongst the English courtiers. For a fleeting moment, there were the echoes of former laughter and conversation, memories of the fear in the faces of others as their fates played out on history's stage. Whispers, tears, heartbreak, intrigue, with some of it relegated to pages in history books, but so much of it known only to her as the last living person to have borne witness. In the next moment, she felt Euan put his arms around her waist from behind, interrupting her recollections, and she smiled. He always had a knack for knowing when she was lost in her many pasts and just how to pull her back from them.

"Well, well, well, what do ye think of this turn of events, Lady Cameron?" Euan said, immediately switching to Gaelic in case they were being watched, as he normally did. No one here would understand it, and it ensured the privacy of their conversations.

Grace laughed at his use of the title, switching her own language. "Is it as strange to say as it is to hear?"

"Aye," he replied, laughing. "Can ye believe it? Me, an English knight."

"Why not? You are as good as any other, if not better," Grace countered as she turned to face him, sitting down on the seat so that he could join her there. "Granted, you are not *exactly* from the same country, but I am not sure it matters to her."

"That is probably true. I have a feeling it ruffled a good many feathers, though."

"Good. It will make them want to speak to you and find out who this man is that he should be so honored so quickly and so publicly. In fact, I think that was the whole point. It would be highly unlikely we could even get *near* Norfolk if we did not have a title."

"Ah, he is that sort, is he?"

"They are *all* that sort," Grace grumbled.

"Do ye think I could keep it?"

"Keep what?"

"My knighthood, of course. I earned it!"

Grace laughed again and shook her head. "I do not think anyone will take it from you, but you certainly could not claim it at home. They are not hereditary, so you could not pretend to have passed it down. Besides, how would you even explain that?"

"Aye, that *is* true, but I can tell the family, can I nae? I cannae wait to see Mam's face."

"Aileen! Imagine what Malcolm will say!" Grace then gasped. "Oh. Oh, Euan. Imagine what *Lochiel* would say. You, a knight? You would be his equal. . .no, you would outrank him. He would lose his *mind*."

At her comment, Euan laughed so loudly and so hard he could scarcely breathe. "Lochiel! What *would* he think?" he got out between laughs. "He would be shocked, perhaps angry, perhaps both. That he would have to treat me as an equal would infuriate him, that I would outrank him would make him apoplectic. I wish I could see it; in fact, I would pay The Council to let me find him and have the satisfaction of telling him. Ach, I would love to see his face."

"And to think, you were made so in order to disrupt a plot led by the Stuarts, the same family you would fight a rebellion for to restore them to the English throne."

"Aye, well, there is some question as to if they led it or were just part of it. All the same, it is nae *her* turn, now, is it? They must wait their turn."

The statement only made Grace laugh more, and Euan wiped tears from his eyes as he tried to stop laughing. When he finally had a moment of composure, he took Grace's hand and kissed it. "Thank ye for that glorious picture, love. I appreciate it; it will make me laugh for weeks to come."

"You are *very* welcome. So," she said, a sly smile forming on her lips. "I have my very own knight, do I?"

"Aye, ye do, though I think things got a bit turned around."

"How so?"

"I am supposed to save ye, nae the other way around. Also, I was nae wearing armor or anything white, but *ye* were."

Grace chuckled and shrugged. "A fair observation, but you were not a knight yet when I saved you."

"Good point, clever lass. I must say, however, ye look gorgeous in that gown. The colors suit ye."

"Thank you, though I had forgotten how restrictive these could be. They are made less for function and more for fashion. You look handsome, as always."

He smiled at her before standing and pulling her up with him, drawing her into his arms to hold her close. Closing her eyes, Grace rested her head on his shoulder, soaking in the moment. She'd become so used to his presence on missions that she was glad she'd never go alone again. When he was there, it felt as though no one and nothing could hurt her even though it wasn't necessarily something she had to fear while working anyway. There'd yet to be a recurrence of Divergent intrusion — something for which she was exceedingly grateful — but if there were, at least they'd immediately know what to do. The fear of it, the worry, faded further and further into the background with each mission they worked and returned from safely.

"I think I shall very much enjoy calling ye Lady Cameron and hearing ye called such," he said as he caressed her cheek. "It is no less than ye deserve, even when we go home."

"And it was no less than you deserved for everything you did the last time we were here, whatever those things were."

"I have no intention of telling ye what those were either, and I think ye are fine with that."

"I am. There is a reason I do not ask you."

"And now, after everything, ye know ye have even better cause nae to ask me because ye know what I can do and what I have done. At least this time I dinnae have to pretend ye are nae my wife."

"That is certainly a good thing."

"I swore she was nae going to believe ye for a moment there."

"Yes, that was a bit more difficult than I expected, but she came around in the end."

"Mentioning her letters to Lord Leicester was genius. I would nae have thought of it, but then again, I never studied her."

"No reason for you to have done, I suppose."

"Nae really, no."

"Shall we unpack and see what we have been sent?"

"Aye, we should settle ourselves in. I have a feeling Caia was right. With so many involved, this will be a long one."

Grace pulled herself from his arms and crossed the room to the first trunk, opening it to find her own clothing. There were gowns of velvet, brocade and silk, kirtles with embroidery, pearls, and natural stones, matching slippers and more practical shoes, some lined with fur for the winter. Linen and blackworked chemises, decorated cauls, stockings, dressing gowns, cloaks, and any other thing she might need. A smaller trunk contained varying hats. In the next trunk were suits of wool, velvet, and linen, along with jerkins made of leather for Euan. Hose, hats, boots for riding, shoes for court, more shirts with the delicate blackwork his current shirt bore. Weapons, night clothes, a small trunk of hats, gloves, and all other things a man of his station might require. All of them were beautifully made by Council Wardrobe and station appropriate.

"Ah, good," Grace said. "We have a few hours to refresh ourselves before we have to change for the private supper with Her Majesty, so I am glad we have found our clothing to air out."

"Aye," Euan agreed as he took a knee and sorted through the contents of his wardrobe trunk. "Ye realize this supper will likely include Cecil and Walsingham?"

"Perhaps, but we will see."

From within another trunk, Euan produced books, parchment, quills and ink, decanters for wine and whisky, cups, table linens, eating sets, and a few things that were decorative in nature. In the final trunk were thick and luxurious blankets to keep them warm on these still frigid nights, more for appearances than anything else. As the pair of them unpacked and put things away, some of the palace household came in to light the fires and make sure all was satisfactory before departing.

The summons to supper was not long in arriving, nor was the escort assigned to take them there. The escort, made up of the queen's own guard, moved in silence, leading them on a strange route. Grace glanced over at Euan, knowing this wasn't the way they were meant to be going. The expression he wore told her he was more than aware of it, his posture showing him to be ready for any possible attack on them. Before long, they stopped before a set of doors, one of which was opened for them. As they stepped inside, the door was immediately shut behind them, leaving them in a darkened chamber that Grace recalled as being where the Privy Council met.

"Please, sit down," a smooth yet chilling voice intoned from a dark corner.

In the next moment, the speaker emerged from the darkness as if he were part of it. Tall and dressed in black, the man looked stern, his gaze sharp and calculating, observing and noting everything. The spade-shaped beard he wore only added to the seriousness of his expression, and there was no question as to who stood before them. Sir Francis Walsingham was the queen's spymaster and for good reason. He was exceptionally good at what he did, sussing out intrigue and treason wherever it might try to hide. Nothing escaped his notice, and anyone who tried would find themselves quickly outmatched. Employing an extensive network of spies that spanned the whole of the country and every major European court, Walsingham had his finger on the pulses of a million plots, ready to snuff them out at just the right moment.

Grace lowered herself, and Euan bowed. "Sir Francis," Grace said.

He nodded and gestured to the table, and both took a seat as directed. "I understand from Her Majesty that you have need of a meeting with me."

"Indeed. Was the reason made known to you?" Grace queried.

"Yes, which is why I am meeting you *here* and not at supper. It would be best if you were not seen meeting with me; it could arouse suspicions amongst those who plot."

"It sounds as though ye already know who it is," Euan said.

"I have an idea, certainly. I also know you are here to assist me."

"We are, and we know *precisely* who it is," Grace confirmed.

"Do you now?" he asked, arching an eyebrow in interest.

"Norfolk plots with Mary against the queen. *Again.*"

Walsingham smiled, but even that normally benign expression seemed cold and almost devoid of any sort of actual feeling. "Indeed, he does. You are cleverer than you seem, Lady Cameron."

"I am a great many things more than I seem, Sir Francis."

"We shall see about that," he said, studying her in a way that made her almost uncomfortable. "However, here is what I need from you: I need the both of you to gain his trust and admittance into his society. You must find out what he knows, who is aware of his plans, who assists him, and how. Sir Euan, as a countryman of Mary's, you should be easily able to convince Norfolk and his conspirators that you are for her."

"Aye, I could if that is what is needed."

"It is. You, Lady Cameron, will be under a bit more suspicion, as you are both a woman and English. They will expect you to support the queen and you must convince them otherwise."

"How should we convey information to you whenever we may have it?"

"Let the queen know you need to see me, and *I* will find *you*."

"Surely ye need more than our word as to what we find?" Euan asked.

"I need whatever you can give me as proof of what they are planning. But," he said, looking at them with a suddenly sharpened gaze, "I *am* rather interested in why you have suddenly reappeared after so long away."

"You wonder if we are to be trusted, you mean," Grace replied.

"I do."

"We heard mention of a plot amongst those in the North who still support Mary's return to the throne. We came to warn Her Majesty."

"I dinnae have a taste for what my country is becoming, Sir Francis," Euan added.

"Understandably so. You both have an opening to reel him in after what happened today. He will want to get to know who you are, to discover your loyalties, particularly as Sir Euan is from Scotland."

"As soon as we know of anything, we will tell you."

"Good. If anyone asks why you were here in this room, it was to discuss your new knighthood."

Euan nodded, and the two of them stood, giving courtesy to Walsingham with a bow and a curtsy as he faded back into the darkness from whence he'd come. Outside, the escort waited for them, leading them back a different way than they'd come to confuse anyone who might be watching. The route placed them before another set of doors, these having guards posted outside who opened them to let the entourage inside this inner sanctum. When they entered, they found Elizabeth sitting at a table with a guest whom Grace wasn't surprised in the slightest to see.

"Ah! There you are at last," Elizabeth said as the two of them paid her courtesy. "I take it your first introduction went well?"

"Yes, thank you, Your Majesty," Grace replied. "All is set."

"Excellent. My Lord Leicester, these are the two I told you

about, the ones who were with me before I was questioned about Wyatt."

Robert Dudley, the Earl of Leicester, was a tall man, at least for the period, with dark eyes and dark hair. His shoulders were broad and seemed even more so in the high-necked doublet he wore and the ornamental chain that stretched from one shoulder to another across the front of it. He was, at this moment, the closest person to Elizabeth aside from Blanche, his position in her favor earning him more than his share of tax revenues, monopolies, lands, titles, and any other gift she could bestow. If anyone wanted to get near her or closer to her ear, they needed to get through *him* first, and one word from him could destroy someone's career at court. With all this power at his disposal, the man had his fair share of enemies, none of them shy about their feelings in that regard. His expression, at present, was friendly and open, though Grace was sure it could be otherwise if needed. Much like Euan's.

He smiled at them as they turned to pay him courtesy. "I have heard you spoken of fondly many times. You are the one who taught Bess the sword, are you not?"

"Aye, m'lord, that was me," Euan said.

"I should very much like to test your skill sometime."

"I would be happy to oblige ye."

"I look forward to it," he said before he looked at Grace. "Lady Cameron, a pleasure to meet you at last. The giver of excellent advice on how to keep oneself alive when treachery abounds."

"And I am very glad she followed it, my lord."

"As am I," he said as he continued to look at her, a strange expression on his face.

"Robin, why do you stare?" Elizabeth asked.

"She reminds me a bit of Amy," he replied, his voice momentarily distant before he shook his head. "Apologies, Lady Cameron."

"None needed, my lord. I understand; grief can be a powerful thing that comes to us unexpectedly even years later."

"How true," he said.

"Do sit down," Elizabeth ordered, a slight hint of irritation in her tone at the mention of Leicester's long-dead wife, the reason she and Leicester could never marry.

Euan and Grace took their seats at the table, surveying the offerings. They didn't need to eat or drink, but they could when they needed to pass as normal people in moments like this one. Grace looked over the selection and picked up the wine from in front of her, taking a sip. It was a fine wine; one she was happy to taste while not having any of the effects.

"Have you settled into your rooms?" Leicester asked.

"Aye, we have, m'lord. They are fine rooms, and we feel quite fortunate to have them," Euan replied. "Thank ye, Your Majesty."

"I wanted to keep you near our person in case anything might happen, Euan," Elizabeth said. "Please forgive my dropping of titles and pretense. We have known each other far too long for that, and it gets tiresome when one is alone with friends."

Euan chuckled. "I cannae be offended by ye declining to call me something I was nae known as before an hour or two ago."

Leicester laughed. "Well said, Euan. Please, call me Robert," he said before Euan nodded to him. "It *is* quite the surprise, however, to have a Scotsman knighted in the English court."

"Aye, well, when one does nae like what their country has become, then what? Surely ye dinnae stay to defend those ye feel are wrong."

"Some do, for how else do you steer your country in the proper direction once more?"

"With all due respect, I will leave that for the politicians. My talents dinnae lie in diplomacy but in war. If it should come to that, I will be happy to lend my sword, but as it is nae there yet, I will do what I can from here."

"That is fair," Leicester replied. "I suspect you would be the sort who would prefer to beat some sense into a person rather than bother trying to negotiate with them."

"Nae necessarily, but sometimes that *is* the best and most expedient option," he replied with a wry smile before taking a drink of his wine.

"Quite," Leicester said with a similar expression.

"I wish it was something I could do," Elizabeth mused.

"Oh, now, I do seem to remember you being an excellent aim with a hairbrush," Grace replied.

Elizabeth laughed. "Touché, Grace. Though I never did manage to get *you*."

"I never gave you any reason to try."

"That does not mean I did not consider it."

"Whatever for?" Grace asked, eyebrow raised.

Elizabeth flicked her eyes to Euan and then back to Grace, and Grace laughed in understanding.

"Ah, I see. Well, that would not have won you any points, to be sure."

"Likely not, you are right," she answered, a sly smile crossing her lips.

Euan and Leicester looked at each other, slightly confused, and then shrugged. "Should I make sure to have a hairbrush handy at the next Privy Council meeting, Bess?"

Grace choked on a sip of her wine as she started laughing and coughing at the same time, which made Euan laugh at her and earned him a glare from Grace. "Better a supply of them rather than just one," Grace coughed out. "I would feel terrible for the page who had to fetch it after each throw."

Leicester laughed loudly, as did Elizabeth. "You are a witty one, Grace," Leicester said.

"I tell her that often," Euan quipped.

"I could simply stand beside you and hand them to you from a basket," Grace said as she stopped coughing. "Oh, look! Here is one for Burghley for saying something stodgy. Come to think of it, he might need his own basket, as we would quickly run out just on him alone. One for Pembroke, for his arrogance. Perhaps if you hit him enough, he will deflate. Ah, there goes Knollys again, on and on about the joys of Puritanism; here is a brush."

Elizabeth clapped her hands as she laughed so hard it

brought tears to her eyes. "Oh, that would be brilliant. I can imagine their faces."

"Be sure to tell me what day you plan to do it so I am conveniently absent," Leicester said after he stopped laughing.

"I would never throw one at *you*, Robin."

"You lie," Leicester said with a half-smile. "You would if I offended you enough."

"Then I suppose you should be sure you do not offend me so much, hmm?"

Grace pressed her lips together to stifle a small laugh, and Leicester shook his head.

"It is good to be in your company once more, the pair of you. I always did find you infinitely amusing," Elizabeth said.

"Perhaps because, unlike others, we treated ye first as a person and nae as a princess," Euan offered. "Neither of us hesitated in being honest with ye."

"No, you were unfailingly so. I always knew I could get sound counsel from either of you, untainted by politics or the desire to gain anything."

"We had no need of gain," Grace replied.

"Oh, that is clearer now more than ever. You already had far more than I could ever dream of."

Leicester looked at them curiously. "How so, Bess? They had not even a title when they served you, unless you are saying they had a hidden fortune somewhere."

"They had each other, for a start," Elizabeth said, her voice betraying her calm exterior. She knew those words would eat at Leicester, and by his expression, it was clear they'd hit their mark. "Otherwise, they are far more well-traveled and educated than I had even realized."

Well-traveled. That was one way of putting it. "Our job was to protect you. We certainly could not have others knowing we were not quite what we seemed," Grace countered.

"Que pensez-vous qu'ils auraient fait s'ils découvraient? S'ils avaient su que nous travaillions contre la rébellion, vous auriez été gravement en danger," Euan added. *What do you think they would have done if they found out? If they had known we were working against the rebellion, you would have been in grave danger.*

Elizabeth gasped, and even Leicester stared at him, eyes wide. "You speak French?"

"Oh, aye. And others, too. As Grace told ye, we are nae as we seem."

"My God," Leicester said quietly. "You truly are not, are you? You are right that such knowledge would have put Bess in terrible danger."

"Aye, it would have, and so we played our parts carefully. But if ye are surprised by me, Grace might kill ye."

"Euan," she replied, nudging him.

"What? Ye have accomplishments ye should be proud of. Ye are as well educated as anyone here."

"Is she?" Leicester asked, looking at Grace curiously, as did Elizabeth.

"I have had the privilege of an extensive education, yes," Grace replied.

"That would be a different thing for a woman than a man," Leicester said.

"That would be true in ordinary circumstances, but that is not the case with me. As Her Majesty does, I have a command of several languages, both written and spoken. Mathematics, classical theory and writings, philosophy. . .all the same things you are likely schooled in, my lord."

Elizabeth smiled with appreciation at another woman in her orbit who was as schooled as she was and not ashamed of it. "And yet it is often said women cannot handle the rigors of such an education."

"I would say it is quite the opposite. We can sometimes handle it better than a man."

Leicester laughed and shook his head. "Such women are more the exception than the rule."

Euan raised an eyebrow. "A strange opinion to have, m'lord,

when ye will nae allow them to show ye otherwise. It makes ye wonder what we, as men, fear by letting them do so. Do we fear they will prove us wrong? Exceed us?"

"Certainly not," Leicester replied. "There are simply things they cannot do, and their talents are best used for their homes. With the exceptions of a few, of course, but God has ordained them to be so."

Grace wanted to roll her eyes but refrained, sitting back and pretending to drink her wine instead. Euan, however, laughed. "I assume ye believe this applies to all areas of men's pursuits?"

"Indeed. A woman cannot fight a war; they are too fragile, too emotional for such a task. They want to *preserve* life, not take it. There are things we can do that they cannot because of physical strength. It is the way things are."

"Oh, I think ye would be surprised."

Grace smiled into her cup. They both knew that, in their own time, women were perfectly capable soldiers.

"I think I would not be."

"Would ye care to test it?"

Elizabeth looked at Euan, intrigued. "How?"

"Grace, love?"

Grace looked over at him, confused for a moment, before understanding what he was asking of her. "If you really wish me to."

"Oh, I think I would," he said with a crafty smile. "However, Lord Leicester would have to agree to fight ye and nae be scandalized when ye remove that bodice to give ye the room ye need."

"Are you *really* suggesting that Robin challenge Grace?" Elizabeth asked, incredulous.

"Aye. If he truly believes what he says, he has naught to fear."

Elizabeth looked to Leicester. "The offer has been made, Robin. What will you choose?"

Leicester smiled, clearly not feeling threatened. "I think I would like to see this, for I do not believe Lady Cameron could best a man in any sort of combat."

"Is that so? *Any* sort?" Grace queried as she put her wine

aside, irritated now by the very insinuation that she *couldn't* do it.

"Let us start with this one, love," Euan said, checking her impulse to beat the man to within an inch of his life when he took her up on the offer, as he knew she'd want to. "If he requires further proof, ye can offer it then."

"I will not need to remove my bodice. Just the sleeves," Grace said, standing along with Euan, who deftly untied the laces holding Grace's sleeves to the bodice and pulled them from her arms. Leicester did the same, rising from his seat and unbuttoning his doublet.

"Have ye a rapier, m'lord?"

"I do, of course, and as these are my rooms, I will be but a moment to fetch it," he replied as he disappeared.

"Grace, are you quite sure of this?" Elizabeth asked.

Grace only smiled as Euan handed her his weapon. He gave her a small nod, which she returned as Leicester came back with his own rapier. She needed no verbal encouragement from Euan, as anyone doubting her was always sufficient incentive. Elizabeth stood up from the table and joined Euan at a safe distance.

"Are you sure about this, Lady Cameron?" Leicester asked.

Grace turned to him, her face placid. "Of course."

"Very well. I will be sure to take a bit of care."

"No need," Grace replied as she took up her position. "It proves nothing if you do."

Leicester took up a position opposite Grace, and the two of them watched each other for a long moment before he made the first move, a feint thrust toward her midsection to test her out. Grace easily and immediately parried it away, looking at him with an annoyed expression. He smiled and then quickly brought in an actual strike to her left, down toward her shoulder. Grace met him easily and shoved his blade away hard as she stepped back. She brought her own in for a slash at his midsection, which he barely moved away from in time because he'd not been expecting it. He looked at her in shock as Euan smiled behind his hand.

The next series of moves were quick, and Grace met each one with a parry and attack of her own. An overhead strike was caught by Grace, who shoved her guard toward his blade and away from her, as she immediately brought it around her head and at his side. He moved away from her, trying to get to her back, but she turned with him so that he couldn't. As he tried to come down at her neck again, Grace stepped to the side and let his blade come behind her back and slide off her own. This put him off-balance in his forward movement, and the moment he turned around, he found the point of Grace's blade at his chest.

She held it there, staring him down as he raised his hands. "Well, well, well. You really *are* not what you seem, are you? Very well played, Lady Cameron."

Grace lowered her blade and took a step back, curtsying and then rising with a smile. "Thank you."

"Perhaps *now* you will not underestimate a woman so quickly, Robin," Elizabeth said as she returned to the table, her tone as full of supreme satisfaction at Leicester's humbling as her expression was.

"Who taught you?" Leicester asked Grace.

"I did," Euan said, his expression one of pride. "As ye can see, there is naught fragile about my wife, or any woman really. Perhaps there are some, but *they* are the exception. Women are stronger than any of us give them credit for. The things they must endure are things we would never dare. What is a sword to them, what is battle, compared to the giving and sustaining of life? Their agonies are daily suffered without recognition because it is expected of them. We take it for granted. They put up with us and all our foolishness while at the same time birthing and raising our bairns. What do they get from us for all of it except to be told they are less?"

Grace turned to look at Euan, surprised to hear him speak so eloquently on the topic, while Leicester looked at him in curiosity.

"Well spoken, Euan. It seems you chose well, Grace," Elizabeth said.

"I did," she replied as she smiled at him. "I truly did."

CHAPTER 8

When they returned to their rooms after supper with Elizabeth and Leicester, Euan pulled Grace into his arms before the doors to their rooms were even shut. To see her best the man in such a way had him thinking of only one thing. . .and that was how quickly he could free her from the layers of clothing keeping her from him. Once he had them both undressed, he sat her on the edge of the table and knelt before her to show her *exactly* what bearing witness to such a thing had done to him and just how *she* was going to benefit from it. Grace gasped, her hips arcing away from the table before he wrapped his hands around the tops of her thighs and pushed her back down. Dropping her head back, she ran the fingers of one hand into his hair, clutching it tight whenever he did something that particularly pleased her. Euan continued until she was skating the edge, and he felt he couldn't take it any longer before he stood and pulled her hips into him, groaning at that first contact with her. Kissing her neck, he placed a gentle bite on the tender skin and moaned in her ear, knowing how mad for him it always made her, and found that this time was no exception. There was nothing sweet or gentle about this, nothing quiet, just unabashed enjoyment of each other until they both found their release.

Kissing her shoulders as he caught his breath and came back to senses, he rubbed her back and felt her shiver, letting him know how sensitive her skin still was — always a sign that he'd done everything right and she was just as happy as he was. Stepping back, he lifted her from the table and set her on her feet, guiding her to the pillows near the fire so that they could lie down there and enjoy the warmth. After he covered them with a blanket, Grace rested her head on his chest and closed her eyes as he absently stroked her hair. At home, they might fall asleep this way, but there was no chance of that here, and this would be their last moment of peace for who knew how long.

"Ye were magnificent in there tonight. I am proud of ye."

"I have an excellent teacher, as it turns out."

"Ah but teaching only takes ye so far. Ye knew he would underestimate ye, and ye took advantage of it. By the time he caught wise, it was too late. Ye have the mind for it, as I do."

"I am glad I will not need to use it as you did, however."

"Ye can never be sure, and that is why I taught ye. Well, *one* of the reasons."

"The other was so you had someone to train with."

"Aye," he said, chuckling. "I will admit there is a bit of selfish reasoning on my part."

"I do not think I have ever heard you speak so passionately about women's equality before."

"Does nae mean I did nae feel it."

"It is very modern of you, and I am sure you did not feel that at home."

"I had no other experience I could base it on there. Now I have ye, Vanessa, The Council, and all the other women in the world doing things people have long told them they should nae or could nae. Nae only doing them but also doing them capably and sometimes far better. How could I see any of that and nae realize men are stupid to believe ye are the weaker sex?"

Grace laughed and placed a small kiss on his chest. "If only they all thought the way you did."

"Leicester may now."

"I think he is more likely to hold on to his belief of exceptions. He knows no other way and will never see another to shake him from it."

"That he could look at his own queen and still think such a thing baffles me."

"Exception."

"Proof that if ye give a woman the means to succeed, she will."

Grace sighed. "That is far truer than you realize."

"Aye. So, what should our plan be?"

"For tomorrow? Get ourselves a meeting with Norfolk, I would imagine."

"What of the wider scope?"

"There are so many players that the only thing we can do is work it as it comes once we begin. There is no good way to strategize this, not yet."

"I have a feeling I will be sent to her."

"To Mary? Yes, likely, as you would be the obvious choice once you ingratiate yourself with them."

Euan frowned. "More time apart."

"I know," she replied with a soft sigh. "But this is what it is. Perhaps we will get an extended break after this so that we have some time together."

"I hope so, since we were called back early this time."

"I will do my best to keep my ears open amongst the ladies and the household to see what, if anything, any of them know."

"Wise. If anyone would know of anything happening, it would be the household. They see all."

"I feel this mission suits *your* skills far more than it does mine."

"No, because those skills are yers, too. Ye are just as good at this as I am, if nae better, if I am honest. I was thinking earlier when we were with Walsingham that I had nae noticed that yer accent and speech patterns had turned English because ye had done it so smoothly. I swear to Christ if ye had been with me at the time, perhaps we would have won the war. The two of us together would have been hard to stop."

"It would be fun to find out, would it not?"

"Aye, but we will never know, and that is fine by me. I would nae want ye anywhere near any of it, no matter how safe ye would be. Having ye there once was *more* than enough."

"Why not?"

Euan shrugged. "Why? Naught good happened there, so what is the point of going back to any of it? If it is just to satisfy a passing thought, I have no interest in it. They would nae send us there anyway."

"That is true, on all counts. It is much more amusing to simply imagine it."

"Though I do have to wonder how ye would participate. Ye saw how Lochiel treated ye when ye tried to warn him; do ye really think he would have let ye come along?"

"I am not sure I could have passed for a man."

Euan laughed. "No, I dinnae think so, for yer features are far too delicate for that, but if I had known ye and known what ye were capable of, I would have found a way. I will admit, however, that with the amount of power we would have wielded there together, the sheer control we would have had of everything and everyone, it would have been damned near impossible to resist the temptation of using it to take it all."

"Somehow, I am not surprised that you would try, and I am certain you would have successfully smuggled me into the Cameron regiment if you *had* tried. I also cannot fault you for taking the thought of what we could achieve together to its natural conclusion. It is something I have often wondered myself: what are we capable of together when there are no limits?"

"God only knows, but I dinnae think anyone is in any sort of rush to find out."

"That is certainly true; but let us return to a more realistic scenario that does not involve us wreaking havoc on the world. Maybe I could have gone in a male mission body to make it easier for you to get me in."

"Aye, though for me, having ye there would have been a wee bit selfish and nae only because ye would have been of great help. I would nae have wanted to be away from ye for so long," he replied with a smile. "And if ye *had* shown up in a male body, I dinnae know how I would have handled that."

"Had your first make-out session with a man, I would guess."

Euan laughed hard. "Aye, probably."

"Seriously, though, I would not have wanted that either, to be apart so long. I am glad I have no reason to send you off to battle and wonder if you will ever return."

Euan stroked her hair. "Ye will nae *ever* have to wonder that. Ye will always know where I am, and most times, it is right beside ye."

"Yes, but even though I know you are safe when we work, I still worry when you are away. I cannot understand why, but I do."

"I think it is natural for ye to do so. I worry about ye, too. As we have seen, things *can* go wrong and make us vulnerable. Even if it did nae, ye would still worry because ye love me. Ye cannae reason with emotion, love. Emotion does nae know the difference between mission and non-mission."

"You are right about that. I do not know how any of them did it."

"Who?"

"The women in the clans who sent their men away for months at a time with no word as to whether they were alive or dead. I know women throughout history have done so, and even now people send their loved ones off to war, but at least now they know quickly if something has happened. I do not think I could do it."

"If ye had to, ye could. Ye would be surprised at what ye could endure if that was what had to happen, if ye knew no other way of things. Ye would do as they did and pray there was never a war to take us, and if there was, that we stayed safe and came home. Ye must do it when we work, when I am gone from ye for weeks at a time. It is the same thing."

"But I know you are coming back."

"I am gone all the same. Ye tell yerself I am coming back to ye to get through it, and ye do what ye have to do until I return. Rationally, ye know I will return to ye because there is no way

I could nae, but yer heart always holds that fear. Ye send me off to war constantly, but it is a different kind of war. It is the same thing, Grace. Ye do it, and ye dinnae even realize."

"I suppose I do. I had never thought of it that way."

"I have, if only because I now face doing the same every time we work. I leave ye alone, leave ye to fight whatever battles come yer way without me. While I know ye will be fine, there is always the part of me that worries ye will nae be and I will nae be there for ye. I must trust ye, have faith in The Council, and know that ye and I will always come back together in the end."

"Would you have been able to do the same if we were back at your home and I had to go away to war?"

"Honestly? No. There would be no chance I would let ye go alone into something like that. Nae because ye could nae do it, but because I would nae want ye to. If ye were to perish, I would want to be there with ye. I saw too many of my kin die with no one there to comfort them."

Grace sighed and stroked his chest. "We are lucky it is not something we will ever face."

"Aye, we are, and I will never deny that."

"But back to the task at hand," Grace said, shifting the topic away from even the *thought* of either of them dying. "This is going to be tricky; I am sure of it. They might admit you more easily, but I will have a bit more trouble."

"Ah, but ye have one thing others dinnae."

"What would that be?"

"Ye have yer beauty and yer charm. In times like these, playing on such a thing will get ye far. I know ye hate it, but sometimes that is the best option."

Grace made a face. "Doing so always makes me feel like a bit of a whore."

"Are they paying ye?"

"What?"

"When ye flirt and smile and charm them, are they paying ye for it?"

"No."

"Then ye are naught of the sort. Besides, I have known a good number of lasses doing such work, and they are far more powerful than anyone would think."

Grace leaned up on an elbow and looked at him curiously. "Is that so?"

Euan laughed and shook his head. "Dinnae look at me like that, as though they very *notion* scandalizes ye. I will be honest with ye and say that I did partake more than a time or two, but that was nae a bad thing then. We all did. There was nae a man I knew who had nae been to such a place at least once."

"I should not be surprised but —"

"But ye are. That is because in the modern world it is seen as dirty, something beneath people, something only unfortunate people need to resort to. It is nae so and never has been. There *were* those types, of course, but ye found just as many men who did nae need it in that sense."

"Like you."

"Aye, like me. When I was just a fumbling lad, Malcolm and the others got together to buy me some. . .instruction. Even Lochiel assisted them in it. A good many of us learned that way, and *ye* certainly benefit from that experience. Sometimes, when we were away, the lads would go, and I would join them. During the war, if we found ourselves in a town with such services, we availed ourselves of them because we missed the touch of another and wanted to remind ourselves that we were still human. In Edinburgh, one of the houses even assisted me in my planning."

Grace was silent, but he could see the conflict in her features. It had been different then, expected, and while she understood what he was saying, there was the innate bias he'd pointed out. He'd done all of it before he'd ever known her, and The Council had made sure he was free of any consequences of those actions before she'd even regained consciousness.

"You are right. It was different for you," she said after a time. "When you were in Edinburgh, did you —"

"Aye," he replied, openly and honestly. "But nae in the way ye think. I did nae pay them; they did it because they wanted to, same as anyone else."

"So, as if they had just met you somewhere?"

"Right." Euan reached out and tucked some hair behind her ear. "I will nae lie to ye, but I also will nae be ashamed of it. I did naught wrong."

"No, you did not. I just —"

"Ye are fighting against what ye know, what ye have been taught to believe. Deep down ye knew this about me, Grace. It was a part of life, and it was done openly by all of us. It is only different now because it has come so close to ye. From all yer study, ye knew this was something treated differently than it is now."

"The perils of being married to a man from the past, I suppose."

"It does nae sully ye by association."

"I did not think it would."

"I promise ye there is nae a nobleman here who has nae done the same and more than once."

"I absolutely believe that," she agreed before she frowned at a thought. "Would you again? Now?"

"No," he answered without hesitation. "And there are many reasons for that, chief amongst them that I love ye and ye are my wife. I get all of that from ye and have no need of others. There is also the knowledge of what such a thing means *now*. It would, in the eyes of everyone, make me unfaithful to ye, and I would never put ye through that."

"Would it make you unfaithful in your own?"

"Aye, it would. It is why I never would have anyway. Even if ye had married me in the past, I never would have done it again. I also never would have sought that out with anyone else."

"What do you do in situations like that when we work? I am sure you must go to such places when you are with other men. What do you do?"

"Let them think I am doing as they are, when really, I am just sitting upstairs with the lass and conversing quietly.

Sometimes we have a drink, giving her a break for the time she is with me. They appreciate that, appreciate being treated like a whole person. We also make the occasional noise, so they think I am up to it."

The thought of it made Grace laugh. "And they do not tell the others you did nothing?"

"Of course nae. We have an understanding, and her silence is paid for."

"What reason do you give her for your lack of participation?"

"Ye," he said, causing Grace to smile at him. "Ye have naught to fear. Nae ever."

"This is why you say I should do what I must?"

"Aye. There is no shame in it. I am nae, however, saying ye should offer them anything in the way of affection."

Grace laughed. "So you *do* have a boundary after all."

"Ye are damned right I do. Nae that I think ye would anyway."

"Ugh, no."

Euan laughed loudly at her reaction. "That is my lass all over. Ye have such high standards."

"I simply do not care for idiots or traitors."

Euan raised an eyebrow.

Grace, realizing what she'd said, went wide-eyed and pale. "I mean. . .well. . .not. . .not all of them?"

"Nae all of them."

"I. . .I would not consider you a traitor because you did not believe in it anyway. Besides, it was only seen as treason by those who were loyal to the Hanovers."

"Did nae make me any less guilty of treason before the law."

"You were an outlaw, too!"

"Somehow that makes it better because. . ." Euan watched as she tried to think of what to say before he started laughing at her. "I am teasing ye. I knew what ye meant by it."

Grace rolled her eyes and shoved him, which only made him laugh harder. "Damn it, Euan!"

"Ye care for at least one traitor," he said with a grin.

"I do. I suppose that makes me one, too?"

"Maybe a little. Nae sure it counts two-hundred years on, however, although to other Scots it might make ye a heroine."

Grace chuckled and shook her head. "I am fine, thank you."

Euan rubbed her back. "Sometimes I wish it could always be this way."

"What way?"

"Just ye and I, happy and peaceful, laughing and talking."

"It would be nice, would it not? But we have a job to do just as everyone else does. We make it possible for them to be like this while we cannot."

"Which is why I enjoy these moments when we get them."

"Then again, were we not this way, we never would have met, and we could never do this."

"Mm, that is fair."

"Do you know what makes me feel lucky at this moment?"

"No, what?"

"Knowing that I do not have to do what Elizabeth must. I do not have to live my life without the man I love being truly mine. I am not sure I could."

"Aye, ye dinnae, and ye could nae, which is why ye made the choice ye did. I would make the same choice."

"You could not give me enough of anything in the world to be a queen."

"Christ, no. Ye would hate it with every shred of yer soul and beyond. Far too much attention for yer taste."

Grace laughed and shook her head. "I would. Come on, let me brief you on all our targets so you know what to expect."

CHAPTER 9

A summons from Elizabeth arrived mid-morning, calling for Euan alone. Kissing Grace goodbye, he let it linger, knowing the mission had now truly begun and everything after this moment would change for God only knew how long. There was no telling if he'd be sent off to do something immediately, away from her and on horseback for weeks to get to wherever the mission required him to go, and it was something they were both keenly aware of. It was precisely why they often took the night before to simply spend time in each other's company, as they'd done the previous night.

Euan wended his way through the palace to the queen's rooms, where he was immediately admitted into her presence chamber. Elizabeth emerged from the privy chamber and looked him over appraisingly, earning her a small smile from the man who still looked every bit as she last remembered him, when she'd been a young woman wondering what it would be like to be Grace. Even now, it was clear from the way her eyes lingered as she took in his appearance that part of her still very much did. He was, of course, just as off limits to her now as he'd been then, and nothing she could do would ever change that. It allowed him to be a bit freer with his flirtation toward her now, though, because he knew she was very aware of it.

Euan bowed to her. "Good morning, Yer Majesty. How may I assist ye?"

Elizabeth bid him rise with a slight wave of her hand. "I would like you to attend me at the Privy Council meeting today.

It will give you a good introduction to those you should know."

She was choosing her words carefully, lest there be any ears to carry them back to the conspirators, and Euan nodded in understanding. "If it pleases Yer Majesty, I would be happy to attend ye there."

Elizabeth held out her hand to him, and he took it and kissed it with another bow before he held it and escorted her out of the presence chamber. "Did you rest well, Sir Euan?"

"Aye, quite comfortably. Thank ye, Yer Majesty. The rooms we occupy are more than adequate."

"I shall say that Leicester was quite animated when you left us." Euan chuckled. "Was he now?"

"Your wife bested him in swordplay; how could he not be?"

Euan's chuckle became a laugh. "Aye, she did, but that was because he underestimated her. He already believed she could nae do it and that made him vulnerable. Should they try again, I am nae sure the outcome would be the same, though it might be."

"You truly train so much with her?"

"Oh, aye, we most certainly do. I dinnae give her quarter because she is a woman or my wife. She must know how to fight back when someone is really after her; otherwise, it is a worthless skill."

"You are truly an enigma."

"If ye think so of me, ye ought to spend more time with Grace."

Elizabeth smiled. "I think I might. Knowing what I do now, I have *so* many questions."

"I know she will endeavor to answer them as truthfully as she is able."

The phrasing made her look at him curiously, but she was smart enough to know she couldn't question him on it now. "You are about to find yourself in the den of the vipers. Be wary," she whispered.

"Dinnae fret about me, for I have dealt with far worse," he replied with a conspiratorial smile. "Worry about keeping yerself safe and yer guard up. Let us do the rest."

Elizabeth gave a small nod as they approached the doors to the room Euan and Grace had been in with Walsingham just the night before. The guards posted at the doors opened them to reveal fifteen men sitting at a long table. All of them stood as the doors opened, though there were some curious looks as Elizabeth entered with Euan as her escort, but none of them would speak a word about it. Near the head of the table, Leicester caught Euan's eye and smiled at him. Euan gave him a nod of greeting and helped Elizabeth into her seat before he bowed and backed away as the doors to the room were shut.

"Well, gentlemen, here we are again. As you have all noticed, and some of you likely take exception to, our newest knight has escorted me to the Privy Council. It will be a fine introduction for him to be present here and learn not only who you are but also where you stand on matters. Shall we proceed?"

"I, for one, welcome Sir Euan to the meeting and hope he finds it informative," Leicester said. "There may be areas where his knowledge will lend an entirely new perspective."

"But he is a *Scot*, not English, and thus should not be present when we discuss matters that may affect his country," one of the men said as Euan raised an eyebrow.

"Are you suggesting he would be a traitor after he was just knighted by Her Majesty for his prior service to her, Pembroke?" Leicester asked.

"I am saying it should always be a consideration for anyone."

"That is *quite* the insinuation," replied another, whom Euan instantly recognized as Norfolk. "Shall we consider *you* a traitor then?"

Euan considered his statement rather funny based on what the man was currently involved in. He actually *was* a traitor, but he was playing the game well. It would be difficult to outwardly suspect he was anything but a loyal subject.

"*I* was not recently imprisoned in the Tower under suspicion of it," Pembroke said.

"Enough!" Elizabeth commanded, raising her voice and

changing her tone to one that instantly silenced the room. "I will have *none* of this foolishness! I assure you that Sir Euan is a loyal subject and would harbor no such ideas, no matter his country of birth. Lord Burghley, proceed."

Burghley looked at Euan nervously and then back to the queen. "There is the question of the former Scottish queen."

"What of her?" Elizabeth asked in an irritated tone.

"She still asserts her claim to the Scottish throne as regent for her son rather than his current regent, the earl of Mar. She wishes English recognition and help for her claim, as well as a loosening of her captivity."

"She should know that her people no longer want her after they rejected the mediation put together for her restoration. Her son is king and in his minority. I am not sure what she expects from us except an army, which is something we will *not* provide her."

"Perhaps we should ask Sir Euan what her people want, as he is one of them," Pembroke sniped.

"I cannae speak for all the people of Scotland, m'lord, but I *do* know that she has ruined her chances there beyond repair. The murder of her husband and the alleged forced marriage to Bothwell stripped any goodwill she may have had left. Nae that the regents are any better, which is why they keep dying," Euan replied, his tone cool as he fixed a look on Pembroke that dared the man to press him further.

"Are you suggesting the regents are meeting their ends due to their positions?" Burghley asked.

"I am nae suggesting; I am telling ye. It is the way of things there. If ye abuse yer position, others will nae hesitate to remove ye from it if they think they can do a better job. I am nae so foolish as to believe ye are nae fully aware of that, m'lord. She may still have supporters, but nae enough to make sending an English army into Scotland worth it."

"And what about you? Do *you* support her?" Pembroke asked, much to the clear irritation of everyone else.

"Am I in Scotland?"

"No."

"Is it she who sits in this seat and upon the throne out there?" Euan asked, gesturing toward the closed doors. "Did she knight me yesterday?"

"Of course not!"

"Then that ought to answer yer question, dinnae ye think?"

Leicester hid a smile behind a hand, and a couple of the others turned laughs into coughs.

"Are we now finished with questioning loyalties so that we can get on with the business of ruling a country?" Elizabeth asked, her aggravation with Pembroke plain. "What is next?"

"The Treason Act to be sent to Parliament, Your Majesty," Burghley said.

"You have it ready for my review?"

"Yes, Your Majesty."

"Good. Let me see it."

Euan remained silent for the rest of the meeting, no one else daring to risk the queen's ire by questioning Euan and his loyalties. When the meeting was released, Leicester was drafted to escort the queen back, purposely leaving Euan alone. Pembroke brushed past him, bumping him with a shoulder, and Euan rolled his eyes while shaking his head. Having now met all the men Grace had mentioned hitting with hairbrushes last night, he fully understood the desire and wished he'd possessed some so that he could've done so in her place.

"Do not mind him; he is an idiot," Norfolk said as he fell into step alongside Euan.

Euan bowed his head for a moment and continued walking. "Yer Grace. He makes it clear he does nae care for me, that is for certain."

"You are stealing his attention."

"How so?"

"You are all the things he wishes he was," Norfolk replied with a small shrug.

"Perhaps."

"You handled yourself well today, I must say. I would not have expected it from you."

"Aye? And why would that be?"

"You speak quite eloquently for someone who only recently came by a title."

"Appearances can be deceiving, but I gather yer assumption comes from my country of birth being what it is?"

"I do not have anything else upon which to judge you."

"Ye are more than welcome to change that whenever ye wish."

"I will admit that you intrigue me, Sir Euan. Perhaps you would be willing to join me for dinner."

"If that is yer wish, I would be happy to. It will be good to meet others here, as it can be a bit lonely with only yer wife as company, can it nae?"

Norfolk laughed. "Very true. It *is* hard to have intelligent conversation with women."

Euan hated himself for saying it, and Norfolk's agreement with the sentiment only made Euan feel worse about having spoken the words at all, the bitter taste of them burning the tip of his tongue like acid. He hated denigrating Grace to anyone even if he didn't mean it. It always felt as though he was betraying her in some small way, making her a lesser being so that he could fit in with the smaller-minded.

"At least on certain subjects, aye."

"Unless it is about breeding or running a household, they have nothing of any use to say. Come, the meal should be waiting."

Euan bit back the answer he wanted to spit at Norfolk, following him to his rooms in silence. As the two men entered, he looked around to familiarize himself with the surroundings and where things might be secreted away. These rooms were far larger than the ones he occupied with Grace, but he realized, of course, that it was because this man was a duke, ranking just below the queen in precedence. If the monarch had sons, they would often be named dukes upon their birth, just as it had been with Cumberland, the one he'd almost killed. He rather wished he could just kill this one and get it over with so that they could go home, but those days were behind him. *Almost* behind him, anyway.

As Norfolk gestured to the table, Euan took the indicated seat. "Dinnae ye think the queen is of more use than that?" he asked, picking up the thread of their previous conversation.

"Do you?"

"Nae really. I feel she is indecisive at times and can be a weak leader," Euan replied, knowing the man was testing him and that he needed to play along despite what his true feelings may be.

Norfolk regarded him curiously. "And yet, just a moment ago, you were praising her."

"Ah, but that was in public. We dinnae all say what we truly feel when in public, and ye know that as well as anyone."

"Too true," he replied as he sat back in his chair, still looking at Euan. "Though you accepted a knighthood readily enough."

"Who would nae if such a thing were offered to them?"

Norfolk chuckled, but the sound was dark and anything but friendly. "You truly are not what you seem, are you? You *do* support Mary then."

"I support whoever will do the best for me, my prospects, and my fortunes. Right now, that is our current queen. If that should change, well . . ." Euan said, offering a small shrug.

"A man of like mind. How refreshing."

"I think all men here are after what they can get."

"They are, but not many are willing to be so changeable in their loyalties. Would it surprise you to know she had supporters here?"

"Nae at all. I have heard she can be quite charming."

"There are those of us who feel she is the rightful heir."

"I am aware of it. Why do ye think I am here?" Euan chose the words carefully, knowing that Norfolk wouldn't take them the way he truly meant them.

"How do I know I can trust you?"

"How do I know I can trust *ye*?"

The two men sat looking at each other for a long moment in a silent impasse before Norfolk spoke again. "I suppose we have no choice, do we? There is no way of knowing for sure."

"No, there is nae."

"We may be of some use to each other, you and I."

"I was hoping ye would say that," Euan replied with a small smile, though it was cold at best.

"And what of Lady Cameron? Where do *her* loyalties lie?"

"They lie where I tell her they should. She knows her place and does what she is told."

Norfolk's laugh was as sinister as it was soft. "Ah, to have such a beauty under one's control is a rare gift indeed. She could be of use to us, too."

"She could be. I would be more than happy to bring her to ye whenever ye wished to meet her."

"Very well. What brought you into my cousin's service in the first place?"

"Rebellion," Euan replied as his lips curled into a mischievous smile.

"Indeed?"

"Aye, Wyatt was plotting a rebellion, which ye well know. I had an interest in making sure he did nae succeed, though I did want her sister off the throne. I was well aware the plot was a disaster and that I needed to keep her away from it until a better opportunity presented itself. Mary saved us the trouble by dying, however."

Euan's irreverence about the former queen brought dark laughter from Norfolk. "She did, certainly, and not a moment too soon. My cousin is more pliable and less willing to act decisively when it comes to the Scottish queen, which only helps *us*. I am sure you saw the same when she was just a princess."

"For someone who has had so much death in her life, it is nae surprising that she hesitates to be the one to now deal it."

"I suppose so, but we can and will use that to our advantage."

"There are plans already?"

"Not exactly, at least not yet, but I think you could be of great help in formulating them. You would be handsomely rewarded for the effort."

"How would ye guarantee it?"

"Because it would be in my power to give once I was king."

Euan raised an eyebrow. "Ye mean to marry her yerself then?"

"That is one plan."

"Bothwell would take issue with it as her current husband."

"He can take issue all he likes, but he *will* get out of my way or his head will be on a pike for all to see. He is a clever man, and I am sure he will see it my way."

"Did ye nae just get out of confinement for the same plan, Yer Grace?"

"I did, but there is more to this one. As I said, such favors would be mine to bestow upon those who were loyal and assisted us. A higher title for you, perhaps. Money, monopolies, political power, lands. There are so very many options."

"Very well," Euan replied as he picked up a glass of wine and held it up in a toast. "God save the Scottish queen."

CHAPTER 10

As Euan returned to his own rooms after his dinner with Norfolk, he slammed the doors shut after he'd entered, reminding himself to breathe. Resting his hands on a table, he closed his eyes and tried to tamp down his rage, though his fingers curled into fists all the same. Norfolk was *precisely* the kind of man Euan despised, a far more sinister and dangerous version of Strickland and some of the other leaders he'd dealt with in the past. The man knew how to play the game and he knew how to play it well; it was the only reason he was still alive. That alone made him a dangerous opponent that couldn't be trusted or expected to act predictably and made Euan's job all the more difficult. That he'd needed to disparage his own wife to win this traitor's trust infuriated him, and it made it clear to Euan that Grace's treatment by Norfolk within this plot would be harsh at best. He hated the very thought of it and often felt as though she bore the worst of it whenever they worked; that it was sometimes because of him made that guilt heavier. It amazed him how unaffected she was by all of it because he knew if their positions were switched and he was the one constantly treated in such a way, there would be scars he couldn't hide.

"Euan?"

The sound of her voice brought his head up, and he looked over at her. He felt a sense of relief in seeing her there, still untouched by what was to come. "Hello."

"Are you all right?" she asked as she slowly approached him, concern written on her face. Able to read him like a book after so long, she knew the answer to the question just by his posture and her asking him was only a formality.

He gave a small shake of his head, gesturing for her to come to him. When she reached him, he pulled her close and wrapped his arms around her, taking a moment to let her presence calm him, as it always did. The smell of her hair, the scent of her skin, and the feel of her heart beating against his chest as he held her were all strong balms for his sizzling temper or frayed nerves. After a short time that way, he led her to a chair and sat, pulling her into his lap.

"We are in," he whispered into her ear in Gaelic. He wanted no one to hear anything said, not even in another language. "I just dined with Norfolk."

Grace looked at him and smiled. "That was fast. Well done," she whispered in return, switching her speech to match his as always, following his lead.

"This is going to be awful for ye."

"Why do you say that?"

"He thinks women are worth naught unless they are breeding or running a household. He asked where yer loyalties sat, and I was forced to tell him ye placed them where I told ye to because ye knew yer place. I am *so* sorry."

Grace's expression darkened before she shook her head in resignation. "I am not surprised."

"Ye know how much I hate doing this to ye."

"I know, but this is what the attitudes of the time are and what we must deal with. I cannot say with any ounce of truth that I was not expecting this somewhere deep down."

"He wants to meet ye, as he feels ye can be of some use."

"Oh, I am sure he does," she murmured, her sarcasm plain no matter what language she was choosing to speak at that moment.

Euan placed a gentle hand on her cheek and turned her face back toward him. "Ye know I dinnae mean anything I say when I do this. Please, tell me ye do."

"Of course I know," she replied, her former expression softening when faced with his desperation for her reassurance. "You are doing what you must, and I understand that. I know how you really feel about me, and I can feel how much turmoil even the thought of this brings you."

"I hate myself for saying any of it. It is like poison on my tongue," he said before he sighed.

"But you must drink the poison left on your tongue and dripped into your ear so he thinks you can be trusted, no matter how it might erode either one."

"Aye, I must, and each time I do, I will be looking forward to the moment when they realize they have been betrayed and ye had a large part in it. The looks on their faces when the realization hits will be a glorious thing to behold."

"And you *will* get that satisfaction, as you always do."

"I know I shall, and I will savor it just the same as I would were it the first time I saw it. I long for it because that means it is over and I can take ye home. Home is where ye can be yerself once more and I can prove to ye that none of what was said was true."

"You do not need to prove it, Euan. I know it is not."

"Nae to prove it to ye but to *myself*. I need to redeem myself in my own eyes for spending so long tearing ye down."

"Tell me what happened. What is his intent?"

"To place Mary on the throne, which we knew. It is exactly the plot ye described. I have nae yet discovered what will bring about its success."

"We will; there is time for that. What did he promise you for your help?"

Euan chuckled a bit. "Everything he could think of. Money, power, lands, a higher title, and monopolies. I know damned well he has no intention of actually giving me any of those things if he succeeds, but it does nae matter anyway."

"What do you think he would do instead?"

"If he were smart?"

"If he were you."

"Are they nae the same?"

"Smart is not nearly adequate enough a term to describe you, in my opinion."

Euan smiled and shook his head. "He would kill me and make sure anyone else who knew of his plot was dead. Once Mary is queen and he is king, he would have no use for us, and we would know the truth about how he came by his newfound position."

"Is that really what *you* would do?"

Euan gave a nod. "It would be the only way to be sure those who could unseat ye with the truth cannae do so. Is it nae how such things have always happened?"

"Yes, it is, though he could also use a different tactic and keep those so loyal to him appeased by giving what he had promised. He would then have a loyal circle around him."

"In an ideal situation, aye, but it is more likely they would see him gone for their own schemes or continue asking for more and more to keep their silence. There is no such thing as loyalty amongst traitors, and once the door is opened for such machinations, others will take advantage of it. This is something the Scottish regents are currently learning the hard way and something the queen's father learned the hard way, too."

"I am so glad I do not have to deal with such things or worry about them."

"What do ye mean? Ye do; it is what ye spend an entire mission doing."

"Yes, but I mean as a regular person trying to run a country. At least here I have the benefit of foresight."

"If ye did find yerself in such a position, ye would be fine as long as ye were vigilant. Ye would be one step ahead of them, as I would be. They are nae as clever as they believe, ye know that."

"Again, you could not convince me to be a queen for anything. There is not enough of whatever it is to make it worth it."

"I think I would like to see ye as one, just once."

"Whatever for?"

"I would like to see ye dressed so finely, for one. Ye would be beautiful, more than ye already are."

"If dress is all you desire, we can do that somewhere that does not require me to rule a country."

Euan laughed; his mood lightened by her presence as it always was. "Aye, I suppose."

"What did you tell Norfolk about your aims?"

"That I serve whoever will do the best for me. As that seems to be him, I am happy to lend my support."

Before Grace could answer, there was a banging on their door. Euan immediately stood, Grace sliding from his lap and onto her feet as the doors were unceremoniously flung open without waiting for an invitation and two of Norfolk's household entered, followed by the man himself, the doors shutting behind him.

Euan frowned but bowed. "Yer Grace. What is this about?"

"I decided I would meet your lady now instead of waiting for her to be brought to me."

It was an obvious pretense to see if he could catch them out, and it irritated Euan all over again as Grace curtsied while Norfolk looked her over appraisingly. "If it pleases ye."

"It does."

"It is a pleasure to make Your Grace's acquaintance whenever he desires it."

"Did I speak to you? I suggest *silence* unless I do," Norfolk snapped, his tone as disdainful as his expression.

Grace looked taken aback by the immediacy of his hostility, but Euan didn't flinch. "I apologize, Yer Grace. She is used to the queen's ways."

Norfolk approached Grace, studying her, and she looked back at him fearlessly. "The queen's ways," he drawled derisively. "You shall have a new queen soon enough, *little pet*, so perhaps you should learn to be more restrained and less bold."

"She is not here yet, Your Grace, and so I must remain as this queen expects me to be."

He frowned at her and then looked at Euan. "I thought you said she knows her place and does what she is told? It seems that is not the case after all. Perhaps you should remind her."

Euan looked at Grace, her expression turning panicked. Euan knew exactly what Norfolk was suggesting and so did she. This was a test, a test of how far Euan was willing to go, how well he would take instruction, and Euan hated him for it. There was nothing he could do here, no way to save it or get around it. Worse, it was clear Grace was aware of *that*, too. He walked toward her, making his posture menacing and his gaze cold.

"Perhaps ye are right. I should."

Grace paled, shaking her head. "I am sorry. . .please. . .I did not mean to —"

"It is too late now," Norfolk said, cutting her off. "I wish to see you reprimanded for your insolence."

The pleading in her voice made Euan hesitate for a fraction of a second even though he knew he *had* to do this, and he wanted to run Norfolk through for forcing him into this corner. Grace took a step backwards to get away from him, and he wasn't sure if it was real or if she was playing the part she needed to play.

"Ye have insulted His Grace nae once but twice," Euan said, his voice taking on an edge of malevolence he'd never used with her before. "Ye know what that means for ye, dinnae ye? Nae only have ye displeased me but ye have also embarrassed me. Ye have tried to make me into a liar when I told His Grace ye were mindful."

The dark edge to his voice brought tears to Grace's eyes as she faced the realization that she was no longer dealing with her husband but the man he had to become to do the things he hated.

"I will not do it again," she pleaded, her voice frantic. I —"

She didn't get to finish before Euan did what Norfolk was expecting, delivering a slap so stunning in its intensity that it sent Grace to the floor, the sound reverberating through the room. If she could feel the full pain of it, it would be horrible, and he was thankful she couldn't. What *couldn't* be dulled was the emotional pain it brought them both, making him want to be ill as she remained on the floor, sobbing. Shoving it away, Euan stepped forward and grabbed her by the arm, hauling her up, his other hand grabbing a fistful of her hair and turning her roughly to face Norfolk. Her nose and mouth were bloodied, proof of the extremity of his violence, and her tears carried it down her neck in a river of pale crimson.

"Such a shame that a beautiful face must be so marred unnecessarily," he said as he reached out with a handkerchief to wipe some of the blood from Grace's face. "Though I consider it recompense enough. Well done, Sir Euan."

"Apologize to His Grace," Euan growled through clenched teeth, giving her a shake by the hair clenched in his fist.

"I am sorry, Your Grace, I will be more careful in the future," she said in an obedient yet shaky whisper.

"Good," Euan said. "Now, get ye to the bedchamber and remain there. This is nae over," he continued, shoving her toward the door so hard that she stumbled.

Grace hurried the short distance into the bedchamber, shutting the door behind her, and Euan looked at Norfolk.

"It seems you truly *are* willing to do what you must to get ahead in life, Sir Euan."

"To check her is nae to get ahead but to remind her she is nae the queen and cannae speak as though she is."

"Very true. Forgive my intrusion upon your time, sir. I shall look forward to meeting Lady Cameron when she is more. . .composed."

Euan bowed, and Norfolk walked to the door and out. Euan's hands slid into fists and clenched so tightly they shook as he tried to shove back that darkness in himself. He couldn't go to her immediately, just in case Norfolk's men were listening for it, but he didn't want to anyway. He was far too full of rage and self-loathing for that. He'd struck her, injured her, the sickening sound of it still ringing in his ears along with the sound of her broken-hearted sobbing. The blood on her had come from *his* hand, and it was something he'd previously never had to do for this work, not once. Dear God, he wanted to be the one to drop the axe on this man when all was said and done! Perhaps he could pay the executioner to make it painful as recompense for not being able to end the monster with his own hands.

Once he was sure they'd gone, he turned and hurried toward the bedchamber. Grace looked up with a frightened expression as he entered, unsure as to whether he was alone or had come to do her further harm, and to see it was like a knife in his heart. The blood on her face brought back flashes of those first moments after their return. Blood everywhere. *Her* blood. "Grace," he whispered hoarsely. "I —"

Grace hurried to him and threw her arms around him, hugging him as his knees gave out and they sank to the floor. Euan broke down and held her, though he could feel her shaking in his arms. That she was here at all told him she knew he hadn't wanted to do it, that he'd been forced into it.

"Shhh, you had to. I know you did. Shhh."

"I never. . .I cannae. . .God, forgive me!"

"I know, I know," she whispered. "I am all right."

"Ye are nae; ye are *lying* to me! I know ye are nae all right. I can feel it!"

Grace sighed. "It will be fine. I just need to reconcile it, that is all. Please, Euan, I understand."

"I am nae sure *I* do."

"You had no choice. He was testing you; we both know that."

"I *hate* him. I would love to go after him now and plunge a blade so deeply into his gut that his ancestors will die all over again."

"At least I barely felt it," she said softly through her own tears even as his continued.

"It does nae matter! Ye felt it in yer *heart*, and that is what hurts ye now."

Grace shook her head. "He came here to force it and he would have had you do something similar no matter what. Now we know precisely what we are dealing with."

Euan pulled back to look at her, the blood on her face making him feel that same sickness all over again. "I would never do this to ye, no matter what happened."

"I know, but I knew it was coming."

"Did ye?"

Grace nodded. "I was prepared for it but pretended I was not, as I should have. What I was *not* prepared for was watching you retreat into yourself to be replaced by the ugliest, darkest parts of you."

"I had to," he whispered. "I could nae have done it otherwise."

"I should have known that, but at the time, it did not register."

Euan sighed and stood, fetching the basin with water in it and a clean cloth, bringing it back to clean her face. His hands shook, the memories of doing this before still so strong they could take his breath away. "I hope he never asks that of me again."

"He might, or it might be worse. I will endeavor to make sure he does not have a reason to."

"If he asks worse of me, this mission will fail because I will murder him where he stands."

"You will not. Be reasonable."

"As far as I am concerned, that *is* reasonable. Thank God for the mission body. Ye have nae a mark on ye now."

"We will have to act otherwise for a day or two, at least."

"Aye. Ye will have to get Andy to leave some marks on ye." A daily reminder for him of this moment, but one that was necessary for the larger game. He wondered how long it would take him to recover from it. . .or if he ever truly could.

Grace gave a small nod and reached up to wipe tears from his cheeks. He still had no control over them, his heartbreak clear, though even if it hadn't been, Grace would've been able to feel it as he could feel hers. "We should reach out to The Council to update them. I am not sure much else will happen tonight, and if it does, we can do it again."

Euan nodded but said nothing.

"What did you mean when you said it was not over?"

His hand paused from wiping her face. "I dinnae know. Naught, really. Perhaps telling the both of us I would fix this somehow."

"While letting him believe you would punish me further."

"Aye," he said.

Grace cradled his face in her hands and smoothed some more of the tears away. "I love you. I promise I am fine."

"I am nae. I cannae forget the sound or the way it felt when I struck ye."

"Come lie down with me," she whispered.

"Let me undress ye so that ye can do so comfortably."

Grace nodded and stood, turning around so he could unlace the bodice. Before long, he had her down to her shift, the trappings of wealth in this life puddled on the floor at her feet. Euan followed her to the bed and lay down beside her, pulling her close to him. To his surprise, Grace kissed him, and he realized how desperate he was for that contact so he might erase what he had just done even for a moment. There would be nothing more than this, as they both were not in the right frame of mind for it, but this was all that was needed.

"I am sorry," he whispered against her lips. "Though that is nae even close to expressing what I truly feel."

"I forgive you," she whispered in return. "You did what was required of you, that is all."

Euan kissed her cheek and then settled back down beside her so that they could contact The Council together.

"Euan, Grace. What is the update?" Councilwoman Rochford asked as the connection opened up.

"Euan has made inroads with Norfolk, and things are proceeding well," Grace replied.

"He is a bastard," Euan said. *"He has already tested me and done so against Grace."*

"Yes, well, no one ever said he was a good man, and that is why you are there. I am glad to hear things are going well so far. We have a message for you."

"A message?" Grace asked.

"Vanessa has contacted us to pass on a request from her when we spoke with you."

"Is everything all right?" Euan asked.

"Yes, fine. She wanted to ask you for permission for Dr. Fraser to change residences."

Both Grace and Euan smiled. It was the kind of news they needed after what had just happened. *"Please tell her it is fine and to take one of the larger rooms downstairs,"* Grace replied.

"All they will need to do is shift things from that room to her former one," Euan added.

"We will pass the reply on to her. Good luck and keep us updated."

CHAPTER 11

The specialized ding on her phone caused Vanessa to immediately pick it up from where it sat on the small table beside the couch instead of ignoring it as she usually might. She was watching television with Drew, who was drifting in and out of sleep as he shifted from night shifts over to days. She unlocked it to read the message from Caia about Grace and Euan being safe so far, that things were going well, and they'd given permission for Drew to move in while they were away.

"Hey," Vanessa said, giving Drew a gentle shake.

"Hmm?" he mumbled sleepily, opening his eyes. "What's wrong?"

"Nothing, just got a message from Euan and Grace. They're okay with you moving in here while they're gone. We can have one of the downstairs rooms; we just have to shift everything from there into my room upstairs."

"Nice," he said, smiling. "I'll do it next week."

"Can't wait. I told you they'd let you."

"May have to get Mal to help me."

"I'm sure he will. I will, too."

Drew sat up and stretched. "Did they say where they were?"

"No, and they never would. They can't. The message isn't even actually from them; it's from their handler." It wasn't exactly how it worked, but it was the easiest way to describe Caia's role in terms Drew would understand.

"They have a handler? Ye make them sound like animals."

Vanessa laughed. "Their handler is the one who manages

their logistics, keeps in contact with them, collects their progress notes, and updates them on anything they need to know from the head office."

Drew looked at her curiously. "Are they really spies?"

"Something like that," Vanessa replied.

"Really?"

Vanessa shrugged. "I can't say more than that, but they'll tell you when they get back, I'm sure. I mean, you'll be living here, so I can't see how they'd be expected to keep it a secret. They *do* have to get permission, though."

"Sounds complicated," he replied as he leaned over and kissed her cheek. "But I like the idea of nae being away from ye."

"I'd offer to help you pack so that you could get here sooner, but I can't leave while they're gone, at least not for that long."

"That's fine. I dinnae think ye need to go through everything for me, and I can always see if Mal would be up for staying and helping. It is nae as though I have all that much. I suppose I will nae need my furniture."

"Some of it, maybe. We can decide which ones."

"All yer things are new; we should just use those and nae worry about hauling mine down."

"Do you want to go pick out which room we want?" Vanessa asked, smiling.

"I dinnae think I've seen the rooms down here, so, aye."

As Vanessa got up from the settee, Drew followed her. "They're across from each other, and I think they used to be for the staff to sleep in, so they're bigger. Multiple people to a room."

"Makes sense."

Both rooms sat at the back of the house, at the end of the hallway. One was next door to the study, the other set back a bit from the kitchen, and that was the one Vanessa entered first. There wasn't much in either room at the moment, but this one had been used as the spinning room for Aileen. All the tools had remained here when she'd moved in with Malcolm because there was more space and she could come work on it while visiting. It was larger than Vanessa's room upstairs with a window looking out onto the back garden and the woods beyond it. There was a fireplace to warm the room, just as all the other bedrooms had.

Drew looked around, nodding in approval. "This one is nice. I like the view," he said as he walked inside and peered into the closet, which was surprisingly large.

"Let me show you the other one," Vanessa said as she walked across the hall to open the other door.

This room was a bit brighter because of the two windows in it, similar to those in Grace and Euan's room a bit farther back upstairs, though it had the same view of Loch Lochy and the woods. It was the same size as the other, but this one had shelving built into the wall for books. A door opened into the downstairs bathroom, and though it would be somewhat communal because the others could use it if they were downstairs, it would mostly be used by the person in this room exclusively.

"Ah, this one is lovely," Drew said. "Look at the view!"

"And we have access to the bathroom right from our room."

"No one is using this?"

"Nope. I think there was talk of making it a children's room at some point, but that's not even a concern right now."

"I suppose if that happens, it will be dealt with as it comes."

"Probably, yeah. I mean, really, they're also able to add on to this place if they want to. I heard Euan talking about it with Malcolm before. The property goes back pretty far and out to the sides as well."

"So, they dinnae just own the house?"

"No, they own the land, too. I wouldn't worry too much about space."

Drew nodded. "I think this one will do nicely."

"I like this one, too. There's even room for your books!"

"I do have some of those," he replied, chuckling. "All boring medical stuff, though."

"I bet it isn't *that* boring."

"Some of it is, trust me."

"You'll have to teach me some stuff."

"Some stuff?"

"Doctor stuff!"

Drew laughed. "Ye mean first aid? Or actual treatments."

Vanessa joined him in laughter. "Um, both? I don't know."

Drew shook his head, still laughing. "I can teach ye some basic things, but that is about all. The rest ye would need to go to medical school for, and I dinnae think ye want to do that."

"Probably not. No need for me to go when I have my very own hot doctor right here."

"Do ye? Ye are dating other doctors, are ye?"

"I mean you!"

"I dinnae fit that bill, sorry."

"Yes, you do."

"Nope. Ye should get yer eyes checked. I am really warty and wrinkly, with a lot of hair in my nose and ears. I thought ye knew!"

Vanessa laughed. "If that's what's hiding beyond my eyesight, I don't think I want it fixed."

"I shall leave ye with yer illusions then," he replied as he placed his hands on her hips to pull her close to him. "But thank ye for the compliment."

Vanessa slid her arms around his neck. "Come on, you know you're hot, Drew."

"Actually, no, I dinnae. I have nae ever really thought so, but I'm glad ye do."

"Wait. . .seriously?"

"Aye. I always felt I sort of made up for it with personality."

"Uh, no. You had nothing to make up for. Were you bullied in school or something?"

"No, nae that I recall. I just did nae have many friends. I preferred books to sport. I like both now, so I suppose I evened out."

Vanessa regarded him curiously. "You were still attractive, I'm sure. Girls *had* to be flirting with you, I mean, even as an adult, right? There's no way they couldn't."

"Probably did, but it depends on when. If it was a patient,

I would nae notice. I had a job to do, and I'd never look at a patient that way. For the most part, I was too busy with school to date much. I did get around, don't get me wrong, but it was nae an all-consuming thing."

"Well, I'm here to tell you that you are. Even Grace thinks so."

Drew raised an eyebrow. "Does she? That's interesting, given whom she is married to. Fairly certain Euan is the lad most of us wanted to look like."

"She does. She told me when we started dating that you were really attractive, and she wouldn't know what to do if you walked into the room as her doctor."

Drew laughed. "Christ, to be honest, I don't know what I would think if I walked in and saw *her* either."

"Hey!"

"It is nae like that, stop it."

Vanessa chuckled. "I know. Grace is gorgeous in this really …" she said, pausing to think of the word, "otherworldly, kind of way. I'm not offended that you would think that, not at all. I know I don't have anything to worry about on either side."

"Ye are right, ye don't. Mostly because I dinnae really think of her that way. She is as ye describe her, and I can appreciate that beauty, but that's all. I know, as ye do, that she *definitely* doesn't think of me that way because Euan is the only man she sees. Nae to mention that I don't feel like dying by his hand if I ever tried getting close to her in that way."

A wry smile crept across Vanessa's lips. "He *would* kill you, that's true. But you're right; he's her everything. Interestingly enough, though, it wasn't his looks that drew her to him. That was just a bonus. They had an instant connection."

"I don't think I've ever heard the story of how they met. It wasn't something any of us asked when we met him."

"That's a story for them to tell," Vanessa replied, her voice softening.

"Whatever it is, it seems fairly intense judging by yer reaction."

"It is, but they're intense people. At least in the sense of the way they experience things. If anyone ever hurt her . . ."

"I wouldn't want to be there to find out what he'd do."

"You should be just as scared of her if the positions were reversed. Gracie isn't a violent person, but she'll also do anything she has to do to protect Euan."

"I can believe it."

"The good thing is, they feel just as deeply about their family and chosen family. I don't feel like I need to worry about much of anything."

"And ye shouldn't. Ye are with a good bunch."

"And with you, too," she replied with a small smile.

"I am part of that bunch now, am I nae?"

"I suppose you are, yes."

"And I could nae be happier about it," Drew said as he pulled her into a tight hug. "It's good to finally feel at peace. At home, with the woman I love, soon to be the wife I love, and just. . .being."

"Well, pretty soon I'll get to welcome you home properly, Dr. Fraser."

"Now *that* is a promise if I've ever heard one."

"You bet it is."

CHAPTER 12

A knock at the doors brought Grace's eyes up from the pages of the book she was reading. She felt instantly wary of who might be lurking outside of them but reminded herself that it couldn't possibly be Norfolk because Euan was with him and would've walked into his own rooms without knocking. Setting the book aside, she stood and smoothed her skirts out before going to the door to open it. To her surprise, a young woman stood there with a stack of linens in her hands.

"Good morning, Lady Cameron. I brought fresh linens for you. May I come in?"

"Yes, of course," Grace said, stepping back to allow her entry and shutting the door behind her. "I did not realize they were changed daily."

"Not for everyone, but Her Majesty insisted we do so for you, as she knows such a thing would be your habit."

"And she would be right. It is kind of her to think of it."

"Are you all right, my lady?"

"Whatever do you mean?"

"Your face looks quite painful. Did you have an accident?"

Grace reached up to touch her cheek, having forgotten about the marks they'd had Andy place there because she couldn't feel them. "Oh. Yes, I did, if you name that accident the Duke of Norfolk."

The young woman grimaced. "I wish I could say I was surprised to hear that, but I am not. You are not the first to meet with such brute force."

"No?" Grace asked, curious.

"Not at all. Most of the time, it is one of us, so I am surprised it was a lady close to the queen."

"It was not him who put these marks on me. That was Sir Euan at the duke's urging."

The gasp of shock was real and not feigned, something Grace found surprising. "He did that to you? I would never have expected that!"

"Why not?"

"Well, when we saw you together, you seemed so loving to each other, and we all thought it was wonderful to see a man in the higher ranks who actually loved his wife. How sad that it was not so."

Grace sighed as heavily as her heart felt. "He *does* love me, but the duke backed him into a corner because he did not like the way I spoke. He had no choice."

"A man always has a choice, my lady. He could have refused."

"If only that were true. What is your name?"

"Helen, my lady."

"It is a pleasure to meet you, Helen."

"And you, my lady. I will go change things out for you now."

Grace offered a small nod, and Helen departed into the bedchamber. Crossing the room, she looked into a mirror to see her face, and it looked every bit as painful as Helen had suggested it did. There was bruising around the corner of her mouth, but the worst was at her cheekbone, where there was a cut surrounded by purple bruising. That injury must have come from the ring Euan was wearing as part of his daily outfit in this period. Her eye, too, was blackened, but only a small amount. Seeing it brought tears to her eyes as she remembered the entirety of the moment, the way he'd looked and the way it had felt when his hand had collided with her face. There'd been a moment where she'd wondered if he'd actually be able to go through with it, and part of her had hoped he wouldn't, but she'd also known he'd have no choice but to do otherwise. The pain in his voice and in his eyes after Norfolk left was also gut-wrenching to remember. Though she'd assured him she was fine and wondered how scarred by this he'd be, she also speculated about herself. She wasn't as fine as she wanted him to believe, *needed* him to believe for his own sake. Her own sobs had been real, borne of the Grace who'd been struck by men far more times than she ever should've been. She reminded herself, as she'd so often done since yesterday, that it wasn't *her* Euan who had done this; in fact, it was Norfolk. Closing her eyes, she turned away from the mirror just as Helen came out of the bedchamber.

"Are you going to be all right?" Helen asked, concern written all over her face.

"Yes, thank you," Grace said.

"Is there anything else you need?"

"No, but I appreciate your asking."

"Very well. Good day, my lady," Helen said, lowering herself before turning to leave.

"Wait!" Grace said suddenly, causing the young woman to turn around and look at her curiously. "I actually see something wrong with the bed that I know Sir Euan would not like. Come with me, please."

Helen followed to the bedchamber, looking concerned about being accused of doing something wrong, but the moment she was inside, Grace took her hand and pulled her to a corner of the room, and Helen stared at her in mute shock.

"Tell me something, Helen," Grace whispered. "How much do you and the others dislike Norfolk?"

"More than there are words for, my lady," Helen whispered in return. "Why?"

"What has he done to earn your ire?"

"What has he *not* done is a better question."

"How so?"

"He sees us all as worthless, only there to clean his rooms, wait on him, and fulfill his every whim."

"Whims?"

"He would make whores of us, and whether we are willing

or not is of no consequence to him. If he wants you in his bed, then he expects you to be there, dragging you if he must."

Grace felt disgust and anger at the words. "He forces you to bed him?"

"He has succeeded with some. None of us want to serve him, and we tend to go in pairs if we must. He is cruel and ugly, even to his wives. We have seen him strike them, and he does not care who sees it."

"If I told you we could make him pay, would you help me?"

"Perhaps. What does that mean?"

"It means he would go away forever, never returning to prey on any of you again."

Helen smiled. "I am listening."

"I would need you and the others to look for any letters of a certain kind when you go to his rooms. I will tell you what to look for. Bring them back to me, and I will copy them, then give them back to you to return just where you found them before he is any wiser."

"That is all?"

"That is all, and I shall reward you handsomely for it beyond the satisfaction of helping him pay for his crimes against you."

"I will help, and I know the others will, too. Tell me what to look for."

"Anything written in French, anything with a seal on it that you do not recognize. If it does not look like words but instead looks like symbols or gibberish, bring it to me."

"What are you looking for?"

"Correspondence with Mary of Scotland or her helpers."

Helen's eyes went wide. "What has he to do with her?"

"He means to kill the queen and place Mary upon the throne, then wed her and become king."

"Filthy, traitorous cur!" Helen hissed. "I will never let him hurt Her Majesty, and I would poison him myself and go to the gallows with not a shred of remorse for doing my duty to my country and keeping him away from such power."

Grace grinned. "I do like your fire, Helen, and I quite agree."

"How shall we get these to you?"

"Bring them when you come to change the linens. I will copy them while you change the bedding and tidy up about our rooms, then you can carry the letters back out in the dirty laundry to be returned. I will bring you in here to converse so that we are not overheard."

"As you wish it, my lady."

"I want you to know this: No matter what you see of Sir Euan, he is nothing like it."

"What do you mean?"

"When he is with His Grace, he is playing a part, earning his trust. He is the most wonderful, loving man you could imagine any other time."

"But he struck you!"

"Because he had to, and believe me, he wanted nothing more than to strangle Norfolk with his bare hands. Watch him, and you will see."

"That is good to hear, as we all thought him so handsome when he arrived."

"And he is."

"Unless he is with that entitled pig."

"When he is with the swine, he must be the swine to lull it into a false sense of security. Only then will it make a mistake and seal its fate."

"Then I hope I get to see the truth in the end."

"So do I."

"When do we start?"

"Right now," Grace said, her lips curving into a wicked smile. "Let us begin braiding the rope he will use to hang himself."

CHAPTER 13

<u>APRIL 1571</u>

Grace hurried down the darkened hallway as quietly as she could, checking to make sure no one was following her. When she arrived at the door she sought, she knocked twice, waiting for the command to enter before she slipped inside and shut the door, immediately lowering herself in a curtsy to the men gathered there.

"Well, if it is not our little Lady Cameron. What brings you here?" Norfolk sneered.

"Your Grace, I have just heard that Baillie has been arrested at Dover. The books he carried in defense of Her Majesty, Queen Mary, and the ciphered letters were seized, and he was taken to the Marshalsea."

Norfolk slammed his hand down on the table, and Grace jumped, taking a few steps back and looking down at the floor. "Damn these incompetent fools! Do you know if they were able to crack the cipher?"

"No, Your Grace, it seems they were not. Lord Cobham conveyed the letters to the bishop of Ross and the Spanish ambassador, who created more innocuous letters to give to Burghley. We are safe for now."

"That does not solve the problem of my not getting what was intended for me, does it?" he replied, leaning in close to her face.

"N-no, Your Grace, but. . .I have the letter meant for you.

Lord Cobham sent it on," Grace said, producing the letter from inside a pocket and holding it out to him.

Norfolk looked at it and then at her, a sly but malevolent smile crossing his lips. "It seems you are less incompetent than some of the men involved here. *Very good*, little pet," he said as he plucked the letter from her fingers.

Grace looked at Euan as Norfolk turned his back to her. He sat at a table with some of the other men, but he was stone faced. "Your Grace, if I may —"

"You may *not*. See yourself from here and back to your rooms where you belong, Lady Cameron, for we no longer have need of you at this time. Go blackwork something or whatever it is that you women do."

Grace lowered herself in response, glanced at Euan again, and left. Her pace was swift, nearly a run, and she wasted no time opening one of the doors to their rooms and shutting it behind her. Leaning back against it, she let her guard down, placing her hand to her chest and trying to control her breathing. Norfolk was too much like Richard, and his treatment of her was pulling her back to that place far more effectively than she'd have liked. Most of her meekness toward him and in his presence was an act, but some of it wasn't.

"Are you unwell, Lady Cameron?"

Grace jumped, her eyes snapping open to find Walsingham sitting in a chair, and she sighed in relief. "I dislike interacting with Norfolk. He is unnecessarily cruel toward me, and it brings back some unpleasant memories."

Walsingham raised an eyebrow in curiosity. "I will admit I am not used to people looking relieved when they see me. Usually, it is something more akin to terror, so relief is a nice change."

"I have no reason to fear you, so why would I react any other way?"

"Are you sure of that?"

"Quite."

"And why is that, may I ask?"

"Because if I *did* have something to fear from you, it would not be you here now but a room full of the guard waiting to drag me off to a waiting barge on the Thames. As there is no such escort awaiting me, I can infer that you have no desire to kill me. At least not tonight."

Walsingham's lips twitched in something like a smile. "An excellent observation. You *do* intrigue me, Lady Cameron."

"Likewise."

"Is Norfolk actually cruel to you?"

"Of course he is. He has no respect for women in the slightest and sees us all as disposable. I am only here to be my husband's toy to control."

Walsingham rolled his eyes. "Why am I not surprised? I am sorry to hear he treats you thusly, but it is his mistake to underestimate you. He has no idea what you are truly capable of or how big of a hand you hold in his coming downfall."

"Yes, and it cannot come soon enough for my liking, I assure you."

"There is still a long way to go. We do not have letters from Mary yet, and that is what we need. We need to see her letter agreeing to it."

Grace's expression betrayed her aggravation. "That will be hard to come by."

"Is Sir Euan working toward getting them to send him to meet her?"

"Yes, but they have had no need of it yet. With this development, they may."

"You gave Norfolk the letter?"

Grace nodded. "He accepted it and dismissed me."

"Good, good," Walsingham replied with a dark smile. "In doing so he has drawn the trap tighter around himself and the others."

The door opened, and Euan walked inside, shutting it behind him before stopping short when he saw Walsingham and bowing. "Sir Frances."

"Sir Euan," Walsingham replied with a nod. "How do things go on your end?"

"Well," Euan replied. "They dinnae suspect me in the slightest, and as far as they know, Grace is so far under my control that she will commit treason right beside me."

"Will they send you to meet Mary?"

"Soon, and I may end up going more than once."

"Excellent. The letter Lady Cameron delivered was a copy of the one meant for him. We have a man with Baillie even now, trying to convince him to read the ciphered letters for us."

Euan came farther into the room and sat down. "Lord Lumley is involved, as are Pope Pius and King Philip. The Duke of Alba is the one who is meant to invade, though those negotiations continue. They are using a man named Ridolfi to finance the plot; he is a banker as well as a papal agent."

"Well done, Sir Euan. Keep up the good work, the both of you." Walsingham stood up and looked from Euan to Grace. "Your wife is a credit to you, sir. She excels at this work."

"I am well aware," Euan said, smiling. Walsingham nodded and departed without another word while Grace turned to look at Euan, her expression unhappy, and it brought him to his feet in an instant. "What is it?"

Grace shook her head and closed her eyes. "I am. . .he is so much like Richard at times that I cannot . . ."

"I can tell he frightens ye. Ye have no need to fear him, but that reaction is so ingrained in ye now that it comes without yer bidding. Yer reactions to him are real."

"Some of them, yes," she admitted, sighing. "But I *hate* when you are with him. You are someone else."

"I have to be."

"That does not mean I have to like that you are."

"No, it does nae, and I am sorry it grieves ye."

"What I want is your protection. For you to stand up for me, to not let him treat me the way he does, but that is the one thing I will not get."

Euan sighed softly. "I want to, God knows I do, but I cannae. The more he believes I am like him, the more he trusts me and the deeper into his confidence he draws me. If ye think, for even one moment, that I did nae want to rip him away from ye just now, then ye have gone mad. I hate to see him anywhere near ye."

Grace stepped forward and slid her arms around his waist, resting her cheek against his chest. "I just want my husband back," she whispered.

"He has never left ye. He is the one here with ye each night, happy to be himself again when darkness comes and he can spend it in yer company," he whispered in return.

It was late into the night now and their usual time alone together to be who they truly were and relax a bit. It was the part of the day they both looked forward to the most, the part where he recovered at least some of himself from the depths to which he needed to sink in order to fool Norfolk, the part where he got to be with his wife again while pretending none of this was happening.

"Fully back. I want to go *home*. We have been here a month already, and it looks to be several more still to go."

"I know, love, I know. So do I, but we knew this would be a long affair."

"I would not have minded if it were less demoralizing."

Euan stroked her back, letting her steady herself in the comfort of his presence. He knew without her needing to say it that it helped her to get her bearings and was what she needed now. "I understand perfectly well what ye are feeling: that mixture of fear, anger, and sadness. It was the same thing I felt in France with Lochiel. The difference is ye are unable to do anything about it, while I was."

There was a gentle knock at the door, and Euan turned to look at it curiously, releasing Grace to go to the door and open it. A young woman stood there with a pile of linens in her hands, and he looked at her in confusion. "Aye?"

"Good evening to you, Sir Euan. I have the fresh linens Lady

Cameron requested. I know it is late, but the request came at a terribly busy time. May I enter to change them for you?"

Euan looked at Grace but backed away to let her in as he saw Grace smile when she set eyes on the young woman. She lowered herself before Grace and then turned to walk into their bedchamber. Grace made a small gesture with her hand to Euan before she followed her inside.

Grace remained silent until Euan had shut the door behind him. "Helen, excellent to see you, as always. What have you got?"

Helen smiled and pulled two letters from the pile of linens, holding them out to Grace. "Exactly what you asked for."

"You brilliant girl," Grace said, grinning. "You will be handsomely rewarded for this before you leave tonight."

"Even if I was not, it would be worth it to see that dog shut forever inside the cage he deserves."

"What is going on?" Euan asked.

"Oh, I forgot you have not met, how remiss of me. Euan, this is Helen. She works as part of the household and has a *very* deep dislike for His Grace," Grace replied.

Helen lowered herself and smiled at Euan. "A pleasure to meet you at last, sir. Well, at least the *real* you. I have seen you with *him*, but Lady Cameron has assured me that is a part you are playing."

"It is," Euan said, nodding, not hesitating to trust her as long as Grace did.

"I can tell, for you look so very different now. More friendly, open, and relaxed."

"I am very much all of those things when I am alone here," he said, offering a gentle smile that was as genuine as it was disarming.

"Of course, sir. Most people here are not as they seem."

"Except for Norfolk, who is *exactly* as he seems," Grace muttered.

Helen laughed. "Yes, he is."

"Why do ye wish to help?" Euan asked.

Helen's laughter faded. "He wants to hurt the queen. We all know it. We saw how he treated his wives when they were here, and we see how he treats Lady Cameron, how he treats *us*. He dares not treat the queen that way because he cannot, but he would if he could."

Euan raised an eyebrow. "How does he treat ye?"

"As if we are nothing except people to clean up after him and warm his bed whether we wish to or not. He struck all of his former wives; we all saw him do it."

Euan closed his eyes and shook his head. "I am sorry for it. Have faith, for ye will be delivered from him soon enough."

"I know," Helen said, nodding. "That is why we are doing all we can to assist Lady Cameron. The sooner he is gone, the better off we all will be."

"Helen, I think you are suddenly faint," Grace said. "You should take a rest by the fire, and perhaps Sir Euan will pour you some spirits to assist you."

Euan gave Grace a confused look, but Helen understood the assignment. Turning and walking to the door, she stepped out into the main room and began to busy herself as though she were straightening things up before she stopped, shook her head, and braced herself on a table.

"Helen! Are you well?" Grace said as she came out of the room to check on her as though she hadn't just instructed the woman to do this very thing.

"I am feeling a bit faint, Lady Cameron, but I will be well. I will go back now."

"No, you will not! You must be exhausted, and it is my fault for having you come at such a late hour to see to a whim of mine. Please, sit and rest for a moment. Sir Euan, would you be so kind as to give this poor lass a drink to revive her?"

"Aye, of course," Euan replied, playing along even though he had no idea what was going on.

"While she recovers, I will finish the letters I was writing to our family," Grace said, walking over to the desk and sitting down.

Euan poured Helen a drink, helping her to sit down before the fire to wait. Crossing the room to where Grace sat, he looked over her shoulder. "What is that?" he asked, switching to Gaelic.

"Another nail in his coffin," Grace replied in the same.

"But these letters are coded. I cannae read them."

Grace turned her face up to him and smiled darkly. "I know, but *I* can," she replied as she held up a piece of paper with varying ciphers on it and watched Euan's jaw drop.

"Christ, woman! Where did ye get that? What do they say?"

"I will worry about that later. For now, I need to copy these so that Helen can return them."

Euan nodded, returning to keep Helen company as Grace began copying the letters. Taking a seat in a chair near her, she looked up at him. "I apologize for nae speaking in English around ye. I often forget when I am alone with my wife."

"I understand," Helen replied. "It is also safer for you with all the unseen ears," she whispered so quietly only he would hear it.

Euan winked and slipped onto the floor to sit beside her so that they could converse more easily without worrying about being overheard. "I thank ye for yer work. It is important."

"Sometimes there are things only household can get you. Such as extra linens."

Euan laughed softly. "Always good and appreciated."

Helen smiled. "I wish you could always be this way. It makes you more handsome."

"More?"

Helen blushed. "Well, yes. We all think so, but then you are with Norfolk and . . ."

"It makes me ugly by association."

"Yes."

"Cannae fault ye for that."

"Perhaps when this is all said and done, we will *all* get the treat of seeing the real you."

"Perhaps, though I cannae promise it. We may have to leave for our safety before then."

"I hope not but understand if you must."

"How did ye come by those letters?"

"Lady Cameron asked if we might look out for things like it and, if we found them, bring them to her. She would copy them and give them back to us to replace where we had found them so he would never know."

Euan smiled wryly. "It is a powerful thing when women work together to bring down a man."

"It can be, but you have to really be a monster for us to want to do so."

Euan laughed. "Aye, which is why I would never want to make an enemy of any of ye."

Helen laughed as well, the two of them continuing to speak quietly, with Euan getting Helen to tell him all the palace gossip while Grace worked, though she'd laugh if she overheard something in their conversation.

"How are you feeling, Helen?" Grace asked as she finished and stood up.

"Much better, Lady Cameron, thank you. I will collect the dirty linen for you and be off."

"Wonderful," Grace said, and shortly afterward, Helen emerged with the "dirty" linen. Grace placed one hand on the top of the linen stack, her other on the bottom. "Here is a small thank you for your trouble," she said, placing some coins into Helen's hand on the top of the pile while slipping the letters into her hand underneath it.

"Most appreciated, as always, my lady," Helen said, departing as Grace opened the door for her and closed it once she was out.

Without another word, Grace hurried to the desk, pulling out the papers and bending over them, her eyes darting between the letter, the cipher list, and the sheet she was writing on. There was no sound but the scratching of the quill, and Euan came back to the desk, watching her make quick work of the translation.

"Oh my God," Grace whispered.

"What is it?"

Grace looked up at him and then stood, pulling him down

as though she meant to kiss him but placing her lips near his ear. "It is her agreement to the plot. The letter is old, but it is still valuable. We needed that, and now we have it."

Euan pulled back with a loud gasp and stared at his wife. This was a lynchpin, and he knew it. It wouldn't end everything, but it was a large step in the right direction. Once he got over the shock of what she'd said, he shook his head and smiled at her.

"I swear to Christ, lass, if ye had been with me before, it would be the Stuarts on the throne now and nae the Hanovers. Ye terrify me sometimes."

"In a good way, though?"

"Oh aye, in a *very* good way," he replied, his lips curling into one of his wicked smiles.

Chapter 14

<u>July 1571</u>

The delivery of the translated letters to Walsingham had been the boon they'd been waiting for, and Euan could've sworn Walsingham had been tempted to kiss Grace when she'd handed them over. There were other letters intercepted and copied — some of them intercepted just before Norfolk's servants burned them to keep them out of the hands of those who might intend to do just what Grace was doing — but none quite so damning as their predecessors.

The next several weeks were spent in a flurry of secretive meetings, negotiations, and letters, with Euan and Grace moving amongst it all, keeping themselves steady and playing their parts in the madness. Euan hadn't yet, as was expected, been sent to Mary as an emissary because the letters using the typical go-betweens had been sufficient. . .until now. Euan, along with two of Norfolk's secretaries, traveled north to meet with the former Scottish queen. Euan was the obvious choice to go as a representative, and the secretaries were tasked with watching him and reporting anything they saw from him that might be amiss. Euan was, of course, very aware of this bit of machination and would give them nothing to report. He found them to be unpleasant men in general, and so the long journey had been spent mostly in silence other than conversation between Norfolk's two men. For his part he spent that same time wishing Grace was with him. He'd asked if she might come, suggesting that another woman may perhaps make Mary more comfortable, but was denied, and taking his leave of her had been difficult in the extreme. Something didn't sit well with him, but he couldn't put his finger on it and there was nothing to be done about it now.

When they arrived at the place where Mary was currently confined, they were met by the Earl of Shrewsbury, one of the wealthier English nobles who'd been charged with looking after Mary for the last several years. The cost of the queen's confinement had been shifted onto Shrewsbury to save the crown money, but the earl was being rewarded in other ways. Dismounting his horse, Euan bowed to Shrewsbury before approaching him.

"My lord Shrewsbury, I am Sir Euan Cameron, sent on the queen's business to see the prisoner."

At the sound of Euan's accent, Shrewsbury raised an eyebrow. "Is that so?"

"Aye, my lord, it is," Euan replied, producing a letter with Elizabeth's seal and signature. It was a ruse — a ruse Elizabeth was a part of — but it was the only way to get him inside to see Mary. Norfolk himself couldn't send Euan to her, but Euan had told Norfolk about having convinced Elizabeth to send him for this other errand.

"I see," he said, as he opened it and read through it before nodding. "Very well, do come in, Sir Euan." Euan and the two men with him followed Shrewsbury inside and up several flights of stairs to where Mary was being kept. "She is within, but I warn you to watch yourself with her. She has a way of playing with people."

"Aye, I have heard as much."

"I shall have a room made ready for you and your companions for the night."

"Most appreciated, my lord," Euan said, bowing to Shrewsbury before he departed. Turning to look at the other two men with him, Euan surveyed them with a hard expression. "Ye wait here."

"But . . ."

"Wait here," Euan asserted.

They frowned but backed away, and Euan knocked on the door, waiting for a response to give him leave to enter. When it was given, Euan opened the door and walked in, taking stock of the room as he shut the door behind him. Mary still lived lavishly, even in confinement, with her own staff of no less than 16 at all times. Several ladies stopped and looked at him curiously, but Euan ignored them and bowed to Mary, who was sitting in a chair next to another woman, the both of them working on a massive piece of embroidery.

"And who are you?" Mary asked, looking up from the tapestry.

"Madame. J'ai été envoyé par le duc pour vous parler. Ils pensent que je suis ici par ordre de la reine ursuper, mais je suis vraiment là pour lui." *I have been sent by the duke to speak to you. They think I am here by the usurper queen's order, but I am really here for him.*

Mary looked at him and then smiled, holding out her hand. "Very well," she replied in English as Euan took the offered hand and kissed it. "You may rise. Bess, I wish for you to go," she said to the woman beside her, who Euan now knew was Shrewsbury's wife, later to be known as Bess of Hardwick. "Go. All of you go," she said, waving her hand to dismiss the ladies and leave her alone with Euan.

Euan remained silent, waiting for the women to depart the room as ordered. It gave him time to study her, this former queen who was about the same age as his own wife. Though she was treated well, she was still confined, her time outdoors limited, which showed in her pallor.

"Go on, monsieur. It is safe for you to speak here."

"It is a pleasure to meet ye and be of service to ye, Yer Majesty."

"You are a Scot!"

"Aye, I am indeed," Euan replied, his smile mischievous.

"Sit you down, monsieur," Mary said, gesturing toward a chair near her, an order he immediately obeyed.

"Thank ye, Yer Majesty."

"What is your name?"

"Sir Euan Cameron, Yer Majesty."

"A knight as well?"

"In England, Yer Majesty." Mary regarded him with immediate suspicion, but Euan smiled. "At the duke's suggestion so that I might have at least some station to meet ye. He could nae very well send a commoner to ye."

"No, he could not; you are right. And what message do you carry?"

"He would like me to tell ye all is ready and imminent. Yer liberation comes soon," he replied as he pulled another letter out and handed it to her. "From his own hand to yers."

Mary took the letter and tucked it away for later deciphering. "What else should I know?"

"The Duke of Alba stands ready and yer supporters mass even now. Ye will be conveyed to London where ye will wed His Grace and plans can start for yer coronation."

"And what of our cousin?"

"She will be dealt with before ye arrive. Ye need nae worry about her."

"I do not wish to be seen as having any part in her murder."

"Ye will nae. I will make sure of that."

"It is to be you who deals the blow?"

"Aye. Appropriate, no?"

Mary smiled but tamped it down almost immediately. "When should I expect this?"

"Within two months. The end comes soon, and yer patience will be rewarded."

"Will it be you who comes to fetch me?"

"If ye wish, it could be."

"I think I should like one of my own countrymen to lead me triumphantly into London to take my rightful place."

Lead her triumphantly into London. Euan fought the urge to laugh at the suggestion. Another Stuart would also believe such a thing would happen, and it wouldn't. "I think that sounds grand, Yer Majesty."

"Where in Scotland do you come from?"

"The Highlands. Lochaber."

"Far from us, then."

"Aye, a bit, but we all know of ye and support ye. Yer treatment and confinement are unjust, and the regents are doing poorly. Ye need to return to power and unite us."

"I will be happy to, and when I do, I want you to go to Holyrood and bring my son to me."

Her son. James, the son who would eventually forsake her to become the heir to the English throne, uniting the two kingdoms under one crown and the start of the Stuart reign that would end in Euan's death and the deaths of most of those he'd known. How tempting it was to rid himself of these people before it could start, but he could never and would never do it. "I will do whatever my sovereign asks of me."

"I see you wear what seems to be a wedding ring. Most unusual. Are you married?"

"Aye, but nae for much longer."

"What do you mean?" Mary asked, frowning.

"Lady Cameron is English, Yer Majesty. When ye are returned to yer throne, she will have served her purpose. Will it nae be so tragic that after our great triumph she suddenly dies so young from a strange illness? I will be grief-stricken, of course, but able to find myself a proper Scottish wife."

To speak those words made Euan feel sick, but it was part of the game he had to play. He watched Mary's frown turn into a small smile, and it angered him to see it, the lack of concern for the life of another woman. "Of course you would. Perhaps you might find her in my own household."

"Perhaps," Euan said, smiling with pleasantness he didn't feel.

Mary stood, and Euan stood with her out of respect, watching as she walked to a table on the other side of the room. Lifting the lid on a small box, she took something out and shut the lid before returning to Euan. "I think you will find that the contents of this bottle will accomplish what you wish for with little inconvenience to yourself."

Mary extended her hand toward him, offering him a bottle that could easily be concealed in the palm, filled with a purple-colored liquid that looked as nefarious as she was hinting it was. He took it from her, resisting the urge to smash it on the floor before her. "I thank ye for yer magnanimous assistance, Yer Majesty."

"We should let the others return before suspicions get too high. I assume your excuse for being here is my expenses?"

"Aye, it is, so let us get down to our false business, shall we?"

***

Grace sat before the fire in their rooms, wrapped in a robe and staring into the dancing flames. It was silent, *too* silent, without Euan here, and she hated it. She wondered where he was now, what he was doing, if he was thinking of her and wishing he was with her as she wished she were with him. They'd known this was coming, that he'd eventually be sent to meet Mary, but that didn't make the separation any easier. She felt vulnerable alone due to the limited options placed on her because of her sex and her status in this period, and that didn't help matters either. Curling and uncurling a strand of hair around her index finger, she sang softly to herself in an attempt to break up at least some of the silence.

The court had moved palaces before he'd left, away from London and its penchant for summer pestilence. The outdoors and its fine weather beckoned but offered no respite from the loneliness she felt. Helen, in all her kindness, would come to dress and undress her and offer some evening companionship, which Grace appreciated a great deal. During the day, Grace would do her best to stay near Elizabeth and her ladies for the company, able to fill some of the space with idle chatter and gossip. Yet, when the night came again, she was alone with her thoughts and the longing for him that was so strong it was painful.

One of the doors to their rooms opened, and Grace sat up, turning around with a smile, expecting to see Euan coming through the door. Her smile faded, however, when she saw who it really was. Instead of her beloved, there stood Norfolk. She rose from the chair and curtsied but knew his presence here at this hour meant nothing good.

"Rise, Lady Cameron," he said as she recovered and stood there, eyes on the floor. "You were expecting your husband, I assume?"

"Yes, Your Grace."

"He has not yet returned and is, no doubt, spending some time amongst the future queen's ladies."

"What may I do for you, Your Grace?" she asked, ignoring his suggestion because she knew full well that Euan was doing nothing of the sort.

"I found my rooms too quiet, and the household is busy, so I decided to come and have you entertain me instead. It is not as though you have anything better to do."

"I am not . . ." she began, bristling at his insult but forcing herself to tamp down any display of temper. "Sir Euan would not like me to entertain you without him being present."

Norfolk laughed, shaking his head. "Do you think I care what *he* would or would not like? I do not. However, I know that he really would not care because he does not love you, little pet, but surely you know that."

Grace looked up, her countenance pained. She knew he was lying, but she had no idea what Euan had led him to believe and had to play it as such. "No, I do not know that."

"Then how sad it is for me to have to bring you such bad news," he said, walking over to her and gripping her chin in his hand to leave her unable to look away. "He does not love you," he whispered, his tone giving away just how much pleasure he was taking in hurting her. "He married you for one reason, and that was access to the English court. You have now served that purpose and are no longer needed."

"Are you saying he will leave me?"

"Leave you? Oh no, no; if he simply left you, then you would be in the way, an impediment. No, my dear girl, he plans to kill you."

Grace felt her heart skip as she gasped. Had he said that, or was it something Norfolk was making up? "No, he would *never* do that."

"He would, and he has told me so. He has even told me *how* he plans to do it. He is quite open about how he will rid himself of you and marry a Scottish woman."

Grace yanked her chin from his grip and shook her head, backing away from him. "No . . ."

"Yes, but there is a way you can save yourself. Become my mistress, and when Mary has served her purpose, *you* will be the next queen of England. I will order Sir Euan not to harm you and inform him you will now be in my care and thus no longer a burden to him."

"Your what? No! Please leave, Your Grace. You do not know what you are saying!"

Norfolk strode forward and seized Grace by the arm, walking her backward so swiftly she almost stumbled, until the table stopped their progress. "Who do you think you are, ordering me to leave, hmm? You can do no such thing. You have no power or command over me! Did you hear a request in what I said? I am *telling* you what will happen, not *asking* you."

"Let go of me!" Grace said, wresting her arm from his grasp to step away to the side but finding herself pinned. Though she wanted to strike him to free herself, she knew better than to do so or cause him injury, lest it ruin everything.

"I was trying to be kind, but I see I will have to do this another way."

Grace knew what he meant, and the horror on her face was real. "You cannot —"

"I can. I can do whatever I want because, you? You are *nothing*," he hissed before he kissed her forcefully. Grace struggled against him before he grabbed her hair and yanked her head back to kiss her neck.

"Stop!" Grace cried out, shoving him hard away from her and creating an opening for her to get past him.

She only made it a few steps before he grabbed her by the wrist and yanked her back, slapping her hard before throwing her face down against the table. Before she could move, he was behind her, holding her head against the table by her neck with one hand and grabbing at her clothing with the other in a way that let her know he'd done this before. "He has often talked about how sad he will be not to share your bed when you are gone, how beautiful your body is, and how pliable you are to his desires. I would like to find out how true it is."

"No!" Grace shouted as she threw an elbow backward to collide with his ribs. The hit made him let go of her, and she reached out and grabbed a knife from the table, spinning around and pointing it at him. "Do *not* touch me," she said through clenched teeth as she glared at him.

"Or what? You will kill me?" he taunted, smirking at her as he stepped forward. "I do not think you have the courage of that conviction."

Grace, however, met him in that step, the point of the knife pressing against his chest. "Are you sure you would like to test that theory?"

Norfolk looked down, stopped, and smiled. "I *do* like the fight in you, Lady Cameron. It seems he has not broken you as well as he thought, though I shall enjoy finishing the job for him."

Norfolk turned and walked out, laughing as he shut the door behind him. Grace stood there, breathing hard, stunned for a moment before she shook herself out of it and ran forward, shoving a heavy piece of furniture in front of the door in case he decided to come back. Once she'd barricaded herself inside, she sank to the floor, shaking as she sobbed uncontrollably. There was no doubt that he'd meant to assault her further, that he truly believed he would take her as a wife. Mary was destined for death at the hands of the man she believed would be her liberator once she'd made him king, her purpose served, and she didn't know the danger that awaited her in London.

"Euan, come back. . .please. . ."

CHAPTER 15

Something was wrong. Euan walked to the window of the room they'd been given for the night and pressed his hand to the glass, looking out at the road. Something was very, very wrong, and he couldn't get to her. The thought made him frantic, but there was nothing he could do except pray that Grace would reach out to The Council if she was in too much danger. He knew this would be an extreme measure and she wouldn't do it unless it was absolutely necessary, but he feared she'd wait too long to make the call because she felt she could handle it on her own. These were the times he wished he had Caia's ability to go between places in an instant, but even if he had it, he wouldn't be able to use it because he wasn't alone in this room. The other two would notice, and there'd be no way for him to hide it. Though he missed Grace terribly, he was now aware that something big had happened in his absence, and whatever it was had caused significant distress for her. He could feel it, feel the turmoil and the fear that swirled within his wife.

Closing his eyes, he rested his forehead against the coolness of the pane. "I love ye, be strong, I am coming back for ye," he whispered.

Euan had the party back on the road before dawn, planning to keep a fast pace and not caring if it made the others uncomfortable. Even moving as fast as they were, it would take them five days to reach London, and that was five days too long. The final day would be the longest and most grueling because he had no intention of stopping only 10 miles from reaching Grace. Both the men with him and the animals were exhausted by the time they reached the palace, the two secretaries barely able to keep their seats, but Euan was off his horse without a word, determinedly striding into the palace in search of his wife. No one and nothing would keep him from her now, not even the Devil himself.

Though it was late, and the halls were pitch black but for the pools of light created by the candles and torches placed along the way, he knew precisely where he was going. He'd still been here when they'd moved palaces, so the location of their rooms was no secret to him. When he reached the door, he went to open it but found it barred, which raised his level of concern. "Grace?"

As soon as he spoke her name, he heard something clatter to the floor, followed by the scraping of something heavy being moved away from the door, and when it opened, a tearful Grace was immediately in his arms. Holding her close to him, he backed her inside and shut the door behind him.

"*Mo ghràidh*, what has happened?"

"He . . ." she began, but she was crying too hard to get anything out.

Euan embraced her, rubbing her back as she sobbed into his chest. "Shh, my love. I am here now. I have ye."

"Thank God you are back! He cannot come now, cannot harm me with you back!" she said, the fear in her voice unmistakable.

"What do ye mean? Grace, tell me what happened."

"He came and he —"

"*Who* came?"

"Norfolk."

Euan felt the hair at the back of his neck stand up at the mention of the man's name. He'd come here when Euan was gone, on purpose, and there was no chance of the reason being anything but villainous. "Why?"

"Euan, he told me you did not love me, that you would kill me when all was said and done so that you could marry someone from Scotland because you had only married me for access to the English court." Grace panted between sobs. "He told me you were open about your intention to do so, that you told him how you would do it."

Euan sighed, shaking his head. "I did tell him that."

Grace looked up at him, her expression one of horror. "How could you do that?"

"It was a lie, ye know that. I would *never* hurt ye. It is all part of the game."

"No! It gave him leave to think he could come here and proposition me! He told me I could save myself from your plans by becoming his mistress, and once Mary made him king, he would get rid of her because she had served her purpose. He would then marry me and make me the next queen, telling you that you need not kill me for he would take care of me for you."

"What! Grace, I —"

"He struck me and tried to force himself on me!"

Euan went still, barely breathing. "What did ye say?"

"He *hit* me, Euan. He tried to force me to. . .but I stopped him by pulling a knife on him. He said he enjoyed the fight in me and would enjoy finishing the job."

Euan's eyes and expression darkened, his features becoming stony with pure hatred. He knew she was telling the truth; she'd never lie to him, especially not about something as serious as that. *This* was what he'd felt, her terror at what Norfolk had come here to try to do to her. She could only fight back so much because he was a target; they both knew that.

"I will kill him," Euan said, his voice terrifyingly calm and as dark as his expression as he turned toward the door.

"Euan, you cannot," Grace said.

"Can I nae? I dinnae care about rules right now, Grace. This is too far. Killing him myself will make sure he does nae succeed in his plan while saving the crown some money and time in the process."

"Euan, please —"

"*No one* touches ye in such a way. *No one*. I dinnae care who he is."

"He did not succeed."

"But he tried! He *tried*, and had ye been any other woman, he would have been successful. Ye and I both know he might have even been so with ye had ye been unable to reach a blade because there is only so much ye can do to fight back. He thinks he can lay hands on ye, violate ye, and take ye from me? No, I will make sure he never touches ye or anyone else again."

"You can do that by finishing the mission. We are so close now. You are back, so he will not try it when you are here," Grace said, trying her best to get his calmer mind to prevail over his fury.

With an angry snarl, Euan walked past her to the fire. She was right, he knew that, but he hated that she was. He couldn't do what he wished to do and ruin all the work they'd done thus far in the process. "I swear to Christ, Grace, if I could wield that axe myself, I would."

"I know," she whispered as she placed a hand on his back.

"This is my fault. All of it."

"What? No, do not say that."

"Aye, it is. Had I nae said to him what I did, he never would have tried this. He would nae have even gotten it into his head that he could get away with it. I am so very sorry, my love." He turned to face her. "I will nae say it again."

"You will say what you must to continue what you are doing, for if you change now, he will become suspicious."

Euan shook his head and turned away from her again, disgusted with himself. No matter what she said, he knew the truth. He'd done this to her with his attitude, with the things he'd said. It was those things that had made Norfolk believe he could move against Grace so callously and openly. He'd put her in danger because he'd acted and spoken without thinking of where it could lead, and he'd have to be more careful in the future. The end of this mission couldn't come soon enough.

"How did the meeting go?" Grace asked, trying to change the subject.

"Fine," he replied, his voice soft. "She believed everything I said."

"Everything is in place then."

"Aye."

Before another word could be spoken, the doors to their rooms opened. Grace immediately stepped behind Euan, who reached behind himself to secure her there as he felt her hands grip the back of his doublet like two tiny vices. "Yer Grace," Euan said as Norfolk walked into the room uninvited. He made no effort to disguise the dark edge to his voice and refused to offer the man any courtesy whatsoever.

"Sir Euan, welcome back. I know it is late, but I am *most* desirous to hear about your meeting." Taking note of Grace hiding behind Euan, he smiled, though it was pure malice. "Good *night*, Lady Cameron."

Grace began to take a step back, but Euan held her fast. "No. She goes nowhere."

Norfolk raised an eyebrow. "*You* do not give the orders here."

"Aye, when it comes to my wife, I do. She stays where I want her to stay, and right now that is here."

"Well, is that not sweet? A strange attitude for a man who speaks so openly about his plans once her purpose has been served."

"That is my own business, nae yers. Her purpose has nae yet been entirely served, and so she still belongs to me, no matter what ye might think."

"I do not know what this little *slut* has told you, but I feel I should remind you who you are speaking to. Let me be clear: I can do whatever I want because I am already the most powerful man in England, and soon enough I will be king. When I am, your wife will be mine, and I will get to enjoy her as you have. In turn, you will get what I have promised you and will no longer have to concern yourself with her."

"I have agreed to no such deal."

"You do not have to; she is mine if I say she is. I could have her right now, and you could do nothing about it but watch while I taught her the true meaning of subservience. I would be careful with your words and your attitude, Sir Euan. It would be a terrible shame if Walsingham suddenly found out what a traitor you are, do you not think?"

"If ye betray me, rest assured ye will go down with me."

"No, I will not, for I have bound you so tightly to all of it that it will be *you* they take down instead of me, Euan. *You* will be the example, the one choking as you hang from the gallows while they cut you open and allow your guts to spill out of you for the crowd's entertainment before they hang you in chains. I suggest you not risk it for a woman you do not even love."

"She is still *mine* until then, and while she is, ye will keep yer hands off her."

"I will not argue it with you further. Did the meeting go well?"

"Aye, all is set, and she has agreed to everything."

"Excellent. We can speak more in the morning about the details. Enjoy your. . .homecoming," he said with a smirk, his words dripping with sarcasm. "And do try not to break her; I prefer she have some fight left."

As he left the room and shut the door, Grace rested her forehead against Euan's back and sobbed even as his free hand tightened into a fist. He was going to enjoy watching Norfolk come crashing down and realizing just who was behind all of it.

CHAPTER 16

As July slipped into August, Euan did his part to ensure Grace was never alone if it could be helped. He didn't trust Norfolk to keep away from her, and they both knew that if he came for her again, she'd be as much at his mercy as she'd previously been. Neither of them had been prepared for such a brazen attack because no one had ever tried it before, and it wouldn't be a mistake they'd make twice. All the while, they continued to play their parts, with Euan still meeting with Norfolk and the other conspirators to go over letters received and advancing plans, while Grace and the ladies in her confidence continued their own efforts. At night, they'd compare notes to discover where the false leads were or to corroborate what had been heard or said. It was clear to the both of them that the time for action drew near, and they needed to be extra vigilant. Grace was certain that the change in outcome was down to the letters. Before, there were letters that hadn't been burnt as Norfolk had instructed, but it seemed this time they'd been more careful.

Grace sat at the desk, working on deciphering another letter that Helen had given to her, and that Grace had copied and returned. The only sound in the room was the scratch of the quill on parchment, as Euan had yet to return from the supper meeting with the others. Frowning, she stared at the page, drumming her fingertips while she thought. Some ciphers had changed, and she'd been spending a great deal of her time trying to figure them out. She whispered to herself as she studied it, trying to make sense of it, when it all suddenly shifted into place and her eyes went wide. It didn't say what she thought it did, did it? No, it couldn't possibly.

Grace bent over, transcribing it as swiftly as she could, and as the message came into focus, she gasped, the quill dropping from her fingers and the chair falling backward as she shot up from it. She needed to get to Walsingham, and she needed to do it now. Stuffing everything away in a secret compartment in case anyone came in to go through their things, she folded the letters and stuffed them into a pocket. Running to the door, Grace opened it and paused to cautiously observe who might be moving about the palace hallways. Seeing no one, she slipped out and shut the door in silence, keeping herself in the darkness that hung like a curtain near the walls. She wouldn't go far because there'd be too much of a risk of being seen if she did. Instead, she stopped outside of the queen's rooms, as there'd be nothing suspicious about Grace being there, even if it was late. The guardsmen posted outside recognized her, and one of them went inside to get permission to allow her in.

When he returned, he held the door open for Grace, who nodded in thanks. As she entered the presence chamber, Blanche was there to meet her. Grace curtsied to the older woman and then rose. "Mistress Parry, thank goodness. I need to see the queen, immediately, and I need someone to be sent for Walsingham."

Blanche frowned. "What is this about, Lady Cameron? It is late, and the queen is already in bed."

"It is about her safety. Please, you *must* trust me."

As soon as Grace mentioned Elizabeth's safety, Blanche went pale. Nodding, she turned and hurried into the privy chamber. Not long afterward, Elizabeth came out, wrapping a robe around herself and looking at Grace in alarm.

"Grace, whatever is the matter?" Elizabeth asked.

"We need Walsingham here."

"Blanche," Elizabeth said, needing to say nothing else for the woman to understand what was being requested. As the door shut behind Blanche, Elizabeth studied Grace. "You look concerned."

"Because I am."

"You have not been yourself lately."

"No," Grace replied, her voice quiet. "When all is said and done, I will explain why but not now."

"Where is Euan?"

"Still at the supper meeting he is attending with His Grace."

Elizabeth's expression showed her irritation at the very mention of Norfolk. "Of course he is."

"I hate it, too."

Elizabeth's face softened into something like pity. "He is not as he should be with you."

Grace shook her head. "He is not. He tries but —"

"But he is in too deep with them now, and the mask is hard to take off completely."

"That is part of it, but he is tired; we both are. We have been away for so long, and he grows weary of the ruse he must keep with the others because it is so opposite his true nature."

"I know it well. I hate to see him that way, and if I do, I can only imagine what it does to you. You miss your home and your family."

"Yes," Grace said with a small sad smile.

"Would you tell me about them while we wait?"

"If you wish," Grace replied, following Elizabeth to a set of chairs. "What would you like to know?"

"Their names, who they are, whatever you wish to tell me."

"Well, there is Aileen, Euan's mother. Malcolm is her second husband, and he has a son from his first marriage. He is also named Malcolm, but we call him Mal. My closest friend, Vanessa, serves much the same function for us as Blanche serves for you. She makes sure our household runs smoothly so that we do not have to worry about anything. She is to be married soon, and her intended's name is Andrew. He is a doctor."

Elizabeth smiled. "You are lucky to have so many so close to you. Do you all live in Scotland?"

"We do. It is beautiful where we live, and I wish you could see it."

"I wish I could see a great deal more than that of where you come from."

Grace chuckled. "I am not sure you would know what to make of any of it even if you did."

Elizabeth beckoned her forward, and when Grace got near, she whispered to her. "Tell me from when you come, Grace. I so want to know."

"Almost four hundred and fifty years in the future," Grace whispered in return, smiling as she watched Elizabeth's eyes widen.

"So far!"

"Yes," Grace said, biting back a laugh.

"There must be so much that is different, then."

"Very much. Women, though not entirely equal, have so many more opportunities. We are in all spheres once considered the realm of men. There are women in government, in industry, in the military, everywhere. We even go to university like men," Grace whispered.

"Truly?"

"Indeed. I went to Oxford myself."

"You!"

"Me."

"Outstanding," Elizabeth said, laughing. "What of Euan? Did he go, too?"

"No," Grace replied. "He was unable. Euan is. . .well, he is a different story for another time, and I promise to tell it to you before we leave you."

"I very much look forward to it."

The sound of the door opening caused both women to stand, as not only Walsingham entered the room, but also Burghley. "Lady Cameron, what is it?" Walsingham asked, his face a mask of concern. "I know you would not have called for such a meeting if it were not of the utmost importance."

"Sir Francis," Grace said, not bothering with courtesies now as she pulled the letters from her pocket and laid them out on the table. "There is a plot on the queen's life entirely aside from the one we have been monitoring."

"What!"

"Look. The ciphers changed, you see, but I figured them out. The intent of the main plan is to have Sir Euan be the assassin, but for some reason, they have decided to make an attempt ahead of him. If this plan is successful, they intend to make use of the chaos engendered by it to free Mary and get her to London, but if they fail, they still have their original plan to fall back upon."

Walsingham snatched the letter from the table, his eyes darting across the page. "It is intended to be done tomorrow."

"At chapel," Grace confirmed.

"They would try to take my life in such a holy place!" Elizabeth exclaimed, aghast at such blasphemy.

"Then clearly she cannot go," Walsingham said.

"No, she cannot, but *I* can," Grace said, bringing everyone to silence as they stared at her in shock. "We can draw the killer out. If your men are hiding there, waiting, you will catch him before anything happens to me."

"You are suggesting disguising yourself as Her Majesty to draw an assassin out?" Walsingham asked, incredulous.

"That is *exactly* what I am suggesting. If I come into the chapel a different way, dressing and moving strategically, you will not see my face well enough to know it is not her."

"And if we cannot stop him?"

"Then it is better me than Her Majesty."

"Grace!" Elizabeth cried out. "No, I absolutely forbid it!"

Grace looked back at her. "Please, this is my job, Your Majesty. *This* is why I am here."

"What will your husband say?" Burghley asked.

"He would say exactly what I have."

"Francis, what do you think?"

Walsingham was silent for a long moment before he spoke. "As much as I dislike it, she is right. There is no time for us to do anything else that would not put Her Majesty in the gravest of danger."

"Your Majesty?" Burghley asked, turning to Elizabeth now.

Elizabeth shifted on her feet; her expression full of the conflict she was feeling. "If this is what must happen, then so be it. Grace, you shall come here early to attend me, or at least that is what you will say if you are asked. Sir Francis, Lord Burghley, I expect you to have your side in place. If something happens to her, it will be *your* heads on the block along with the assassin's."

The two men bowed, and Elizabeth retreated to her privy chamber, leaving them alone with Grace. They looked at each other in silence before Walsingham spoke. "How came you by this letter, Lady Cameron?"

"The network helping me brought it to me. I will find out from them who it came from."

Walsingham smiled wryly. "Well done, Lady Cameron. I appreciate your hard work and Sir Euan's as well. I know it is weighing heavily upon you both, but it seems we are nearing the end of the game."

"We are. I am sure of it."

"I am not sure if you are brave or foolish for this plan."

"Neither. As I said, this is why I am here. I must, however, retire. Please excuse me." She curtsied, then rose and walked to the door before she stopped to glance back at them over her shoulder with a small smile. "You should probably wait here a while."

Grace moved through the darkness of the palace halls back to her own rooms, encountering no one and slipping back inside just as quietly as she'd left. At the sound of the door shutting, Euan emerged from the bedchamber, looking relieved. "There ye are! Where have ye been?"

Grace said nothing, crossing the room and taking his hand, pulling him back into the room before shutting the door. Sitting down on the floor, she gestured for him to do the same, and when he joined her, she moved close to him to whisper in his ear, switching her language for added security. "I uncovered a plot tonight. They tried to change the cipher, but I figured it out. They mean to kill the queen at chapel tomorrow and use the chaos to free Mary and put her on the throne. If they do not succeed, they will move forward with the original plan."

"What? I have heard nothing of this!" Euan said, looking at her in shock.

"I have a feeling this is being done outside of the duke's knowledge, too."

"I would hate to be those fools when he finds out."

Grace laughed and kissed his cheek. "They will be stopped."

"How?"

"Well, clearly, Elizabeth cannot go to chapel tomorrow. . .but I can."

"Grace . . ."

"I will draw the assassin out, and they will catch him before he gets to me. Even if he does, you and I both know it will not matter."

"It does matter; it will give us away. How would ye explain the lack of an injury?"

"We would need to fake one on the queen, but it will not come to that."

Euan sighed but smiled. "Excellent job on the discovery, love."

"Thank you," she replied with a smile of her own before she nuzzled his cheek. "I have missed you."

"And I ye," he whispered, reaching up to stroke her cheek. "So much."

"What happened tonight?"

"Naught new. The date has been set for a money transfer to her supporters. When that happens, it will be the beginning of the end."

"Thank Christ," Grace muttered, which brought a laugh from Euan.

"I agree with ye, love."

"Well, at least we have our time now. Unless someone chooses to interrupt it."

"He will nae; he has company."

Grace rolled her eyes. "Well, good for him," she whispered before her expression changed.

Euan looked at her curiously but remained silent when she reached up and drew a fingertip along his jawline before placing the barest of kisses behind his ear. She felt him tense and then sigh with pleasure. The reaction brought a smile from her, and she kissed her way down his neck, wrapping her fingers in his hair and giving a gentle tug to expose more of it to her lips. A small groan from Euan followed as she gently bit the skin where his neck met his shoulder. There had been too much constant chaos for anything to happen between them, and it had been too long, far too long. She, however, intended to change that now. She needed him, and Euan was more than happy to submit.

***

As morning dawned, Grace reported to the queen's rooms as directed to help her ready herself for chapel, and the woman who later emerged with ladies flanking her seemed to be blissfully unaware that there was a murderous plot in motion. Chapel was a private affair on all days but Sundays, so the ladies remained outside as she entered, knelt before the altar, and lowered her head. There was such silence here, and Grace was certain she could hear the flames of the candles themselves. The scent of the beeswax at the altar rail swirled around her, and she closed her eyes. On high alert, every sense seemed enhanced as she waited to see if the plan would move forward, and if she'd been right.

After what seemed an eternity, the sound of unfamiliar footsteps caused her to open her eyes, but she didn't move. In the next moment, the click of a pistol hammer raised her head, but before anything else could happen, the man was seized and turned away from her. He howled in rage as they dragged him out, even as her back remained to him, shouting that she was a devil, evil, a usurper who must die. The chapel fell silent as the doors shut and his screams died off, leaving her alone once more, and Grace smiled in satisfaction. It had all gone to plan, this potential disaster averted, and now the rest of their mission could continue.

***

"Yer Majesty."

Grace stood slowly, turning to face Euan, and his eyes widened as his jaw dropped. Unable to take his eyes from her, he did the only thing he could think of and knelt before her. He hadn't expected this, hadn't expected the way she'd look in the guise of a queen. The very sight took his breath away, rendering him speechless. He'd imagined she'd look beautiful, but nothing like this. In truth, it was more than beauty. She seemed to glitter in the sunlight streaming in from the chapel windows, the rays dancing off the gems on her dress, her fingers, her neck, and the diadem nestled in her hair. A veil sat underneath the diadem, hiding her golden hair so that there was no indication it wasn't red and thus not Elizabeth. *This* was the image all royals wished to convey, the image of the divine, of something larger than the common man, something to defend. It was what Charles Stuart would want to inspire in two-hundred years, but he had *nothing* on what stood before Euan now. Had the prince somehow been able to show this, perhaps no one would ever have questioned the claim that the English throne was his right, ordained by God. In this moment, Grace looked like what one assumed an anointed queen would, someone touched by the Almighty and tasked to lead a country through whatever might come.

As Grace stepped down from the altar and made her way

158

down the aisle to him, he held out his hand to her. Once she placed her hand in his, he kissed it reverently before touching the back of her hand to his forehead. "You got your wish. Now you have seen me dressed like a queen."

"Ye are beyond anything I could have *ever* imagined ye to be," he replied as he looked up at her, still holding her hand. "I could nae hope to conjure adequate words to describe it."

"As sweet as that is for you to say, you should stand."

"I cannae. I just want to look at ye, to remember ye this way forever. God help me, but if ye asked me to overthrow every kingdom in the world for ye, I would do it. I would find a way. Ye look like a divine being, my love, and I am nae sure I know a man who would nae give his all for ye if ye were his sovereign."

"But I am not."

"Ye are. Ye are mine, my own queen. The others are all imposters who cannae touch ye and are nae fit to be anywhere near ye."

"Shhh, do not let anyone hear you say that!"

"Let them. I dinnae care if the whole of England hears me."

Grace reached out and ran a hand over his hair before she caressed his cheek. "If I am a queen, what does that make you?"

"Nae a king, for I would nae place myself where I might take anything from ye, nae that I would be worthy to be there anyway. Yer humble servant, perhaps, or the warrior who protects ye with all that he is."

"How about just my husband?"

Euan smiled. "That too. Ach, I wish I could take a picture of ye."

"Yes, yes, but you cannot," Grace said, chuckling. "Please rise, Sir Euan."

Euan stood, sliding a hand onto her cheek and cupping it. "As my queen commands it. May I have permission to kiss Yer Majesty?"

"You may."

Euan used the hand on her cheek to draw her close and press his lips to hers in a gentle kiss, placing his other hand on her lower back to pull her against him, holding that kiss until he heard someone clear their throat. Pulling back from her, he looked in the direction it had come from to find Walsingham, who actually looked exceedingly amused for once.

"I am quite sorry to interrupt, but Her Majesty is ready to go about her day and needs the clothing you are currently wearing in order to keep up the ruse that she was here."

Grace stepped back from Euan and walked back down the aisle toward Walsingham, who turned and walked out ahead of her. Before she stepped out of the chapel, she looked back at Euan over her shoulder, smiled, and winked, causing Euan to grin and shake his head as she disappeared from sight.

CHAPTER 17

<u>AUGUST/SEPTEMBER 1571</u>

"Six hundred pounds in gold meant for her supporters from the French ambassador. Ciphered letters. We cannot wait any longer, Francis. We *must* act before this plan gets any further."

Walsingham regarded Burghley coolly. He didn't know the man to be rash or to act emotionally, quite the opposite, so he knew he wouldn't say such a thing unless he felt he must. They'd worked together far too long for such pretense. "We have heard nothing about any escalation from Sir Euan."

"While that is all well and good, what if there is another plot he is not aware of, like the one Lady Cameron caught?"

"That is certainly a consideration," Walsingham conceded, running a hand over his beard in contemplation. "We should search Howard House. It is time to close the door on our trap."

"And if we find nothing there?"

"We will," Walsingham replied. "He is foolish and believes himself to be smarter than everyone else; it is that hubris that will be his downfall. But," he said as he picked up a stack of letters from his desk, "due to Lady Cameron's excellent work, we have copies of all correspondence between him and several others, as well as with Mary. If he has burnt them to avoid us, well, he will just have to believe his servants were careless."

Burghley smiled wryly. "I should have known you had a plan."

"I *always* have a plan, William. However, this would not

have come as far as it has without the help of Sir Euan and Lady Cameron. Their skills have been essential in this."

"You should see if they will stay on to work for you."

"Her Majesty has informed me that when all is said and done, they have a home and family they would like to return to, and I will not begrudge them that. They have lived a very difficult existence these last many months."

"As we all do."

"No, this is more than that. This is living on the edge of a knife, knowing one slip will kill you. One moment out of place, one word, even a wrongly interpreted facial expression, and all you have done will be for nothing. You will expose it all and ruin it, not to mention ensuring that you will be dead soon enough. It is something few are familiar with, but they have managed it admirably."

"I suppose that is true. I forgot to ask: What have Norfolk's secretaries, Barker and Higford, answered?"

"That the money was meant for the plot, and that there *is* a plot, but they were merely pawns in it. The same thing anyone would say when they are facing death for high treason. They have named their co-conspirators, but we need more. You know Her Majesty will not act on just their word."

"Indeed, she will not. Norfolk is here at court?"

"Yes, he is even now with Her Majesty and others on a hunt."

"I will send the guard."

***

As Walsingham predicted, a search of Howard House turned up other letters, a cipher key, and a recent letter from Mary found under a doormat. Norfolk's servants were arrested and removed to the Tower before he'd even returned from the hunt with the queen. When he discovered it, he was outraged and made it known, but there was nothing he could do. Sitting secure in his belief that all had been hidden and nothing linked him to the plot, his surprise when two men were sent to confront him about the money was genuine, though Norfolk denied all of it and told them the money was for his own private purpose.

On the seventh of September, Euan was there when the guard arrived at Norfolk's door with the warrant for the man's arrest. Any others there were also arrested, including Euan, though he'd known it was coming. All the same, it still unsettled him to feel the heavy weight of the shackles on his wrists and hear the clanking of the thick chains as they walked and tried to avoid the stares of the other courtiers. As they were led down to the river steps, there was silence as the group of men stepped into the barge for the trip upriver to the Tower, and abject fear spread across the faces of many. Norfolk, however, seemed entirely unperturbed. Euan thought it stupid of him to truly believe he would come out of this unscathed, but it didn't surprise him either. Men like Norfolk believed they were smarter, better, and above the law by virtue of their station alone, and this man's surety of his own mental prowess doubled it.

Euan felt sick as the barge rowed nearer the foreboding structure before turning into the infamous water gate, later to be known as traitor's gate. Stepping out onto the stone stairs, Euan looked up at the gray buildings looming over him, and he swore he could hear the moans of prisoners. From the cells that had windows, wan faces peered down to see who now joined them in this hellscape of torture and confinement. Behind him, someone shoved his shoulder to move him along, and the sound of his boots on the steps seemed to reverberate through his mind like some warning from a dark fairytale. Heart hammering in his chest as they were marched into the White Tower, Euan could only think about how this was a prison now, as it still had been in his own time, and the thought of being locked up here horrified him. He'd been meant to come here once, to suffer here, and now he would experience at least part of it.

Once inside, Norfolk and Euan were separated from the rest

and taken together to a room that was empty but for a table, two empty chairs before it, and Burghley and Walsingham waiting for them. Euan knew this was the last sight he would *ever* want to see after being arrested in this period, and he was thankful his part in this wasn't real.

"What is the meaning of this!" Norfolk shouted indignantly, not even bothering to wait to be addressed before launching into the outrage that usually got him his way.

"The meaning of this is that you have been arrested for treason, Your Grace. *Again*," Walsingham replied. "Though you will not be so lucky this time."

"I have done nothing of the sort, and you *will* release me!"

"By the queen's orders, we will *not*."

"I have already told you I had nothing to do with this plot with the former Scottish queen, so I do not care what your orders are!"

"You are also lying."

Norfolk sighed in irritation. "You do not understand, Walsingham. I have been trying to talk someone *out* of this course of action, not *participating* in it."

"Indeed? Who would that be?"

"I will not condemn another."

"Not even to save your queen?"

Norfolk was silent for a moment, as though he needed to actually contemplate the idea of sacrificing someone else to save himself. "I have been trying to stop Sir Euan, trying to sway him from his plan. He desired to strike a blow for his country by putting his former queen in place and murdering our own. He even had designs on becoming king by having his wife murdered and wedding Mary himself. All of this after the queen was so gracious to him."

Euan turned his head, and Norfolk looked at him with not only defiance, but malice. He remembered what the man had said about tying him so tightly in this plan that it would be he taken down instead of Norfolk, and Euan knew that in his head Norfolk was congratulating himself on his success. Euan, however, knew better. He put an expression of fear on his face to allow Norfolk to believe it for a moment, but it was soon overtaken by a sort of twisted amusement as a dark smile spread slowly across his lips and he laughed, bringing a curious look from Norfolk.

"Me? No, I dinnae think so."

Walsingham stepped forward with a smile that mirrored Euan's and produced a key, unlocking and removing the shackles that bound the younger man. "Well played, Sir Euan. Your excellent work has been much appreciated."

Euan rubbed his wrists, thankful to be free of the shackles, as he walked forward to stand next to Burghley. Turning to face Norfolk, he folded his arms and Norfolk finally had a hint of panic in his expression.

"*You. . .*you have betrayed me?"

"It was the entire reason he came here, Your Grace," Walsingham replied. "Though, I am not surprised you sought to blame someone else for this to save yourself."

"I do not know what he has told you but —"

"He has told us a great many things, so I would take care, Your Grace, with what you say."

"I only sent money and correspondence. I was a go between, and that is all I did."

"Come, come now, you were *far* more involved than that."

"I was *not*, and you have no proof otherwise but the word of this *traitor*," Norfolk spat, gesturing to Euan. "He must have been working both sides because I know he was for having Mary upon the throne. He went to see her!"

"Everything Sir Euan did and said was to draw the trap quite tightly around you, a job he performed admirably, I must say. We were aware of every step you and your fellow conspirators took."

"The man ye think ye knew? He did nae exist. The true Euan Cameron is entirely behind Her Majesty, Queen Elizabeth, and serves her faithfully. I let ye believe I was like ye, but that could nae be farther from the truth. I am *naught* like ye," Euan said, nearly spitting the last words at him.

Norfolk's face darkened with rage. "You have proof of nothing."

"Oh, but we *do*," Walsingham replied as he lifted his hand and made a beckoning gesture.

Grace emerged from the darkness at the back of the room like a phantom. Gone was the terrified wife Norfolk had known, and in her place was Watcher Cameron, her bearing fearless and confident. Those in the room could feel the power radiating from her, and on her face was a sort of dark enjoyment at watching this man who'd so terrorized her brought low.

Norfolk shrank at the energy Grace gave off before he shook his head and his rage returned even deeper than before. "*This*? This is your proof? This stupid little whore? She knows nothing!"

Euan bristled at the man even daring to think of calling Grace a whore, much less saying it out loud. "A whore?" he said as his arms dropped from his chest and his hands curled into fists. "How dare ye even th —"

His words ceased in an instant as Grace held up her hand to stay him and indicate she needed none of his help in dealing with this. "I knew enough to decipher all your letters. I knew enough to have them brought to me as well as the letters of your associates." She moved toward him with slow, measured steps. "I knew enough to give copies of them to Sir Francis so that even if you destroyed the originals, we had proof of your treason."

They all watched the color drain from Norfolk's face as Grace produced the stack of letters she'd been holding behind her back with one hand, proof that his attempt to destroy his trail had failed and he'd been outsmarted by a woman. Grace smiled as he squirmed in front of her.

"No. . .no. . .I . . ." he stammered, searching for an excuse.

"Yes, oh yes," Grace replied, whispering near his ear in a sultry voice to mock him. "Words you wanted to hear just this way in another situation, hmm?" Stepping back from him, she put on a fake pout. "Do you still want me for a bride after you are king and dispose of your newest prize?"

Norfolk looked sick even as Grace's demeanor turned dark and angry. "You are lucky I did not kill you that night and that the need to bring you to justice was more important, but know I *wanted* to do it. I would not have been sorry when I shoved that knife into your heart. I would have enjoyed the look on your face, the sound of your strangled wheezing, and watching you die on the floor in front of me knowing I was the *last* thing you ever saw."

Walsingham and Burghley looked shocked, but they knew nothing about what he'd tried to do to Grace. Euan, however, grinned. He knew and loved this side of his wife. "And ye would have been right to do so."

"Oh, I know," Grace replied. "But I had a job to do and killing this piece of spineless filth was not a part of it. Or at least not killing him with my own hands directly."

"What are you insinuating, Lady Cameron?" Burghley asked.

"His Grace planned to rid himself of England's new queen and his new bride by murder once she had served her purpose and made him king. This was *always* about putting him where he felt he belonged."

"It was his desire to make Grace his own, an English bride for an English king. I will have ye know," Euan said, glaring at Norfolk with utter hatred. "I never meant a word I said to ye about my wife. I never planned on harming her in any way, for she is everything to me, a feeling ye cannae understand. Ye are lucky ye survived yer demand of me to strike her, though ye should know she knew it was coming and accepted it to bring ye down and protect her queen. Striking a woman solves naught."

The two men looked at Norfolk in disgust. "I think we have all we need from you both," Walsingham said. "You are free to return to the palace and are at liberty to return to your normal lives whenever the queen sees fit to dismiss you."

Euan and Grace lowered themselves in respect, and when they rose, Walsingham walked them to the door. When he knocked on it, the door was opened, and the two of them stepped out into the hallway. "Send one of your men with Sir Euan and Lady Cameron to the carriage that is waiting for them, then have it return to wait for Lord Burghley and me," he said to one of the posted guards.

"As you wish, Sir Francis," the guard said, bowing to acknowledge the order.

As the man departed and the door shut, the last words they would hear from Walsingham drifted out to them. "Now, Your Grace, we have *much* to discuss. Let us start from the beginning, shall we?"

Grace looked up at Euan, and he shook his head. He would never in a million years want to hear those words when shackled in a room with the man because it would tell him that he was already meant for the block. Taking her hand, he went down the same stairs he'd just been led up as a prisoner, this time a free man, and he could feel the weight leaving him with each step he took away from that room. When they stepped out into the sunlight, Euan relaxed fully and let out a relieved sigh. As fraught as this place was for him, he was once again walking out of it unscathed with no one the wiser as to who they'd let in and back out. The door to the waiting carriage opened, and they climbed inside, the door shutting behind them. They looked at each other in silence for a moment before they started laughing and embraced each other. It was done, and they were one step closer to going home.

<h1 style="text-align:center">Chapter 18</h1>

A short time later, Euan and Grace stood before Elizabeth, who looked at them with a sad expression. "While I understand your desire to go home, I do wish the two of you could stay a bit longer so that we might spend time together where I am not under the threat of death."

"Is there ever a point where that is nae so?"

"Euan," Grace said in a chastising way, elbowing him.

Elizabeth laughed, however. "Far truer than I would like to admit, I am afraid."

"Aye, but we have been gone overly long from our home as it is, and we are weary."

"Of course you are, and you have every right to be."

"We could spend the rest of the day and evening with you if that would help. There are many things I promised to tell you, after all," Grace said with a smile.

"I would like that very much," Elizabeth replied. "Blanche, please inform any and all of the relevant parties that I am indisposed and shall meet with them tomorrow."

"Yes, Your Majesty," Blanche said, lowering herself and then departing to do as her sovereign commanded her.

"Please sit, make yourselves at ease now that you may truly be who you are. At least to me." As they joined her in the seating near her, she seemed to be studying Euan. "It is good to see you back, Euan."

Euan looked at her curiously. "Yer Majesty?"

"You are back to the man I knew before, back to being the

man Grace knows. It is good to see. I was worried for you; worried you might never recover from the disease you were forced to expose yourself to."

"I am far stronger than that," Euan replied, smiling.

"Grace told me you come from quite far ahead. I wish I could see the advancements made."

"Aye, we do, and I can say from experience that the modern world offers a great many conveniences."

"Experience?"

"Remember I told you that Euan was a different story?" Grace asked.

"Yes."

"I am different because I, too, am from the past, though in yer future. I left my former life in the year 1746."

"What a strange thing that must be. To leave all you know to go to a place so foreign it could be an entirely different world."

"It was, at first, but I got used to it quite quickly. Hard nae to, honestly."

"What sort of conveniences do you speak of?"

"Well," Euan began, thinking for a moment. "We can harness the power of lightning and the sun so that we no longer need candles. We have light all the time, turned on and off at will by the press of a button on the wall. The insides of homes are as bright as the outside in the day even if it is the middle of the night."

"Really! What a miracle that must be!"

"It truly is, though it took me a bit of time to adjust to how bright it could be. We can travel long distances in a matter of hours instead of days or weeks. For instance, when I went to meet with Mary, it took me five days to get there, but where we come from, such a journey would have taken me less than two hours."

"How is such a thing possible?" Elizabeth asked, incredulous.

"There are things called cars," Euan said. "Like carriages but much faster and without horses. There is nae time enough to explain how it works but believe me when I say it does."

She laughed and shook her head. "This is wonderful! Please tell me more."

"There is hot and cold running water in an instant. Ye turn a handle, and it just comes out to ye, clean enough to drink."

"Water clean enough to drink! And no one needs fetch it!"

"Aye," Euan said, chuckling. Of anyone, he entirely understood Elizabeth's reactions. "There is more, but there are only so many things we are allowed to say."

"What happens to me?" Elizabeth asked. The question caught the pair off guard, and Euan looked to Grace for an answer as to what could be said.

"Nothing," Grace replied in a soft voice. "You will remain as you are, a beloved queen, for decades to come."

"Will I marry?"

Grace bit her lip and shook her head.

"Just as well then if I cannot have Robin."

"I am sorry. I know that —"

"You know my heart, Grace, and I am glad someone does. I am glad someone understands it. I think you would want no one if you could not have Euan."

"That is true, I would not. Then again, I died to have him with me."

"You died? How do you mean?"

"It is a very long story, but a Watcher will gain a Companion only if she chooses him. She must make the choice to choose him over herself, and I did that. I did it because I loved him so much I could not allow him to die in battle, as I knew he was meant to. My death to save him is what brought him forward. All is well now, but I understand the totality, the feeling of your heart only ever being able to belong to one."

"Good Lord, Grace. That sounds awful."

"It was, but it was worth it, and I would make that choice again a million times if I had to."

Elizabeth smiled a bit, then frowned. "If I do not marry, I do not have an heir."

"No, you do not. A solution will present itself, but that is as much as I can tell you about it."

She nodded and then stood, waving at them to remain seated as they started to rise with her. She crossed the room to her privy chamber and returned with a small casket, which she held out to Euan. "This is for you, and I hope you may take it with you."

Euan took the casket and opened it, hearing Grace gasp loudly beside him. He looked at Elizabeth in confusion. "What are they?"

"She is giving you a very great honor," Grace interceded. "It was not something anyone you knew or even any Scot would have encountered."

"I cannot truly make you a member of the Order of the Garter, but know that, to me, you are and always shall be. It is the highest honor I can give you as a knight. There are only 24 living members at a time, which is why I cannot formally invest you. I did, however, wish you to have the insignia to which I believe you are very much entitled."

Grace reached in and pulled out the Greater George, the heavy golden collar made up of heraldic knots and enameled Tudor roses. From the bottom hung the St. George pendant. Elizabeth took it from Grace and lifted it over Euan's head, placing it around Euan's shoulders before arranging it so that it sat properly. Inside remained the Lesser George, the pendant on a sash that could be worn instead of the collar and often was. Beneath all of it was the garter itself, the same blue as the sash with gold embroidery spelling out the motto: "Honi soit qui mal y pense." *Shame on him who thinks ill of it.*

"Perfection," Elizabeth said as she smiled.

"Yer Majesty, I . . ." Euan found himself at a loss for words for a moment. This was never something he would have expected in any life, not to mention this one. A knighthood had been beyond imagination, but this? "I. . .I cannae accept such an honor, for I have nae done anything to deserve it."

"Foolishness." Elizabeth scoffed. "You have done *everything* to deserve it. You have saved my life more than once at great personal cost, and that more than entitles you to it. It is *my* decision whom I give it to, and if you were to remain here, I would raise you in title and grant you other favors, but as you are not, I cannot. Your humility at being offered this honor only proves I have made the correct choice."

"Thank ye," Euan replied quietly, trying to hide the emotion that made his voice thick.

Grace smiled, placing her hand on his. "You *do* deserve it, my love. All of it."

"Oh, but I have not forgotten about *you*, Grace," Elizabeth said.

"What?" Grace said in shock while looking back up at Elizabeth, who'd gone to pick up another casket from a table.

"This one is for you. You have done *just* as much work as our dear Euan has and are thus just as deserving of tokens of my appreciation."

Grace took it and opened it, peering inside before she gasped and quickly shut it again. "Oh no, Your Majesty, I cannot . . ."

"You can and you shall. You would not think of defying your queen, now would you? Besides, that looked far better on you than it ever did on me. In fact, I intend to send that whole outfit with you, even if you would not have any need for such a thing where you live. It is waiting in your rooms."

Grace laughed. "That *is* true. I would be quite out of place, but Council Wardrobe will be ecstatic."

"What is it, love?" Euan asked, curious what had garnered such a reaction from Grace.

Opening the box once more, she pulled out the diadem she'd worn that day in the chapel, followed by the diamond, pearl, and emerald necklace that matched it. Euan's eyes widened, knowing full well that Grace held a fortune in her hands. After lifting the diadem out, she noticed something else nestled in the velvet at the bottom. Arching an eyebrow, she reached inside only to pull out a Lesser George. Grace looked up at Elizabeth with a questioning gaze.

"Oh yes, one for you, too. I cannot, for obvious reasons, give you the full set, but I would if I could. Your secret membership is between us," Elizabeth said with a sly smile.

Grace laughed even though her eyes welled with tears. "This is amazing. Thank you."

"It is the very least I could do for the both of you. I do not think you realize how very much you have done for me or how much it means to me. You are true friends and have always been, some of the very few I have. I can always trust you, and you will always keep me safe."

"We will," Euan replied. "If ye need us again, they will send us, but dinnae do something that will require it with the hope of getting a social call."

Elizabeth laughed. "I promise I will not, and as desperately as I might want to see you again, I will consider it a good omen if I do not."

"Aye, ye should, for if ye do see us, something has gone *very* wrong," Euan said, laughing with her.

Grace and Euan spent the rest of the day and night with Elizabeth in laughter and discussion, with Elizabeth telling them all about some of the true events in her life that conflicted with what Grace might know, much to Grace's delight and sworn secrecy. It fascinated Euan to watch Elizabeth become a different person then, someone lighter and freer with her smiles, laughter, wit, and humor. It was as if sharing those things with others without varnishing them or needing to omit details was what she needed, along with the knowledge that somewhere out there were two people who knew the full truth even when the past had been made rosy by time. In turn, Euan and Grace spoke candidly of themselves and their lives, what had been and what they hoped for, what could be and what never would, four centuries of life coming together for the briefest of moments.

When it finally came time for them to leave her, she walked them to the door, but Euan stopped her from opening it. "I have a favor to ask of ye, Yer Majesty."

"Oh? What is that?"

"I have a *great* desire to see Norfolk's end. I know ye will nae want to do so, but ye also know ye must order it."

"Yes, I know I must," she said with a sigh. "If I do not, he will just continue, and who knows if one of these times he would succeed. If you wish to be there, I shall make sure you are allowed in."

"I thank ye for it. He has done me more than a few wrongs, as well as Grace, and I would like to see him pay for them even if indirectly."

"I cannot say I blame you for it," Elizabeth said before she smiled and hugged them both. "Oh, my dear friends, keep safe wherever you go and wherever you are, and know you will always be in my prayers. When it is your turn to leave the world one day, I shall be there to meet you, though I expect there shall be a great crowd."

"And you," Grace said, hugging her tightly. "Stand strong, Your Majesty. Always."

"Go. Go home to your family," she said with a sad smile. "I know they must miss you as much as I shall, though I think Francis may miss you far more and is like to weep when he knows you are gone and no longer available to press into his service."

The comment made both Euan and Grace laugh through tears, as did Elizabeth, before she opened the door and shooed them off. Returning to their rooms in silence, both thought about all that had happened here. After such a long mission away, the readjustment would be difficult. Routines established over months would now end, faces that had become familiar would fade back into the mists of history, and the sounds of palace life, the constant hum of human activity, now moving to silence. Moving about the rooms to ensure anything that needed to go with them or be removed was placed in an easily accessible location, Grace and Euan took all of it in for a final time to etch it into permanent memory.

Once they completed these final tasks, Grace reached out to

The Council. *"Watcher Cameron for The Council."*

"Go, Watcher Cameron."

"Watcher and Companion Cameron reporting mission completion."

"Are you requesting mission extraction, Watcher Cameron?" the team member asked, picking up on the omission of the usual phrase.

"Nae yet. I need to speak to Councilwoman Rochford, please."

"Copy, Companion Cameron. Stand by."

"Companion Cameron," sounded the familiar voice a moment later. *"Is everything all right?"*

"Aye, Councilwoman, however, I am desirous of an extraction delay and a shift forward."

"For what reason?" Rochford asked in a tone that told them both she suspected his motives.

"I would like to be present for the execution of His Grace so that I will be sure the threat is eliminated."

"It is. We can see it."

"But I cannae."

There was silence for a long moment, and Grace covered her mouth to smother a laugh while Euan looked like a small child trying to appear innocent in the hopes of earning a sought-after prize.

"All right, I will allow it because we all know full well what he put you both through. There is no need to lie to me about why you really wanted to see it, Euan, and terribly at that."

Euan and Grace laughed outright at her dropping of titles to playfully chastise him, and they could hear the laughter of their team in the background as well.

"I want to go, too," a familiar voice called out.

"Andy, no," Rochford said, which only led to more laughing from Euan and Grace, who were by now crying from laughing so hard. *"Anyway, before you ask, yes, you may take your hard-earned honors with you. It is a bit of a rare case, and we will make an exception for it. However, Grace, you need to know that*

"I will be," Grace said, trying to stop laughing.

"A Guardian will be there momentarily to collect them. See you in debrief."

"Thank you, Councilwoman."

"Are ye ready for an execution?" Euan asked, smiling.

"Oh, I am most *definitely* ready. The readiest I have ever been."

Euan laughed and closed his eyes, the transport happening the moment Grace closed hers, putting them in a currently empty area inside of the Tower. It was now the 2nd of June 1572. The former duke was to be executed within the walls instead of outside in front of a jeering, bloodthirsty crowd, a privilege his royal position entitled him to, but Euan would never be convinced he deserved. He would thereafter be interred in the chapel of St. Peter ad Vincula, and the chapel being within the walls meant Norfolk would never leave this place, his bones mingling with those of others considered traitors over the years.

Norfolk was being led to the scaffold as they joined the crowd, most of them there by the queen's orders to witness the execution, Walsingham and Burghley among them. The two men nodded to Euan and Grace, who returned the gesture. The gathering was a mixture of those who felt this was the proper course of action and that the man had earned this fate, and others that supported him and thus stood in silent and somber protest because they could do nothing to stop it. It was so quiet within that the shouts of mongers could be heard from outside, along with those members of the public who knew what was happening beyond the walls and gathered to jeer loudly anyway.

As the clergy prayed for him and offered him last rites, he looked resigned to his fate, but he still held an attitude of defiance as he declared his innocence in his last opportunity to speak. The executioner instructed him to kneel, and as he did, his eyes fell on Euan and Grace, two of the people who'd put him here. A mixture of anger and fear leapt into his eyes, only to be met by a smile from Euan, making it plain to Norfolk that Euan was going to get a *great* deal of satisfaction from what was about to happen.

The executioner directed Norfolk to put his head on the block, and he did so, although reluctantly. Euan couldn't blame him for that, really. This was a manner of execution that could go wrong *very* easily and *very* quickly, and often did. Most people truly didn't wish to die, so to be asked to willingly place themselves in the position where they would end their lives was asking a great deal, and it was something that required the prisoner to have courage. Luckily for Norfolk, no one had paid the executioner extra to make it painful or gotten the man so drunk the night before that he could hardly stand by morning, much less swing an axe, and the deed was done with efficiency. To Euan's surprise, Grace didn't even flinch beside him, where she might've done so for anyone else. After her treatment at his hands these last many months, he knew she was more than happy to see him gone and unable to transgress against anyone else.

As the crowd moved forward to examine the scene, Euan stepped backward, bringing Grace with him. As they turned to go, they almost ran into Walsingham, who, in his usual fashion, had manifested in silence behind them. A sharp intake of breath and a small stumble back from them both brought a smile to his face.

"I see you are afraid of me at last, Lady Cameron."

"Not at all, Sir Francis. You just surprised us by appearing out of nowhere like a wraith, an ability I am quite envious of, to be honest."

Walsingham smiled, but there was no malice in it, and for once he actually laughed in their presence. "If there were more time for me to teach you the black magic so many claim I possess, I would be happy to do so. However, I do not think you need any other tools at your disposal to terrify your enemy. Your mind will do that well enough."

"Ye have no idea how true that is," Euan said before Grace elbowed him in the ribs.

"It truly is a shame you must go. I have never worked with anyone at all like either of you, and I know that together we could ferret out a good many dark deeds."

"Aye, perhaps," Euan admitted. "But we have lives of our own to return to."

"Indeed. Her Majesty hinted to me at what those might be, and I am saddened there is not more time to truly get to know you both now that the threat of danger has passed."

"The threat of danger is never passed," Grace countered.

"Too true, Lady Cameron, too true, but it is not always so drastic."

Grace raised an eyebrow.

"Some of the time it is not always so drastic," he said, but met with Grace's continued gaze, he twisted his lips into a wry smile. "All right, I will admit it is almost always this drastic, but life is never boring on account of it and my continued employment is secured."

"I know, but I am glad you are at least willing to admit it to someone."

"Consider yourself lucky, then, that I admitted anything at all."

"I shall treasure it always, I assure you," Grace dead-panned, which caused Walsingham to laugh again despite his most valiant efforts.

"Now I really *am* sorry that we do not have more time, for had you shown this much wit and humor prior, I would have appeared in your rooms far more often."

"Tell me, Sir Frances, did he ever admit to it?" Euan asked.

"Norfolk? No, of course not, but his co-conspirators all did, and we had plenty of evidence of his involvement, so we did not really need him to. Not as though we were not expecting that anyway."

"What comes next?"

"More of these events are to follow for those who participated, and then we must deal with Mary."

"Deal with her?"

"You cannot tell me you are surprised by the suggestion, Sir Euan."

"No, I am nae. She is a danger, to be sure." Euan reached into a pocket and pulled out the vial she'd given him, holding it out to Walsingham. "Ye will be wanting this."

"What is it?" he asked even as he took it from Euan's extended hand, studying it as he turned it different ways.

"Poison."

Walsingham's eyes snapped up. "Meant for the queen?"

"No, meant for my wife."

Grace turned her eyes up to him from her place at his side, her expression angry but not shocked.

"For Lady Cameron! Whatever for?"

"Part of the ruse was telling her, as well as Norfolk, that I wished to dispose of Lady Cameron once she had served her purpose in getting me access to the court. She posited that I might find my new wife amongst her own ladies, a proper Scottish wife, and gave me that. It would 'accomplish what I wish with very little inconvenience to myself,' she said."

Shaking his head, Walsingham closed his fist around the vial with a dark expression. "She is a merry murderess is she not? I thank you for giving this to me and telling me what it was intended for. I will have Dee analyze it to discover what it is made of. Assisting a murder is another step closer between her and the axe, whether it came to pass or not. I assure you that there will be a charge laid for her plot against Lady Cameron."

"A merry murderess she may be, but I am certain she feels wronged by everyone and everything. Her captivity, the regency, all of it."

"As wronged as she may feel, it does not make her conduct excusable, nor does it mean she has actually *been* wronged."

"I dinnae disagree. She lives far better in captivity than

most of her subjects will ever live in the whole of their lives. Most of them would gladly trade total freedom for the benefits her limited captivity offers."

"And how sad that is; do you not agree?"

"I do, but it is the same here, and ye know that as well as I do. England's poorest people are nae any better off than Scotland's."

"A sad truth that is within neither my power nor yours to correct."

"Sir Frances!" Burghley called out from a short distance away. "Come, we have business to attend to!"

"When do we not," Walsingham muttered. "Farewell to the both of you and safe travels."

"Thank you, Sir Francis," they said in unison, with Grace curtsying.

Walsingham held out his hand to Grace, and when she took it, he brought it to his lips and kissed it. "Watch yourself, Lady Cameron, and please do try not to place yourself in positions where you desire to murder a man and gleefully watch him die before you on the floor, hmm?"

"I promise nothing."

"Of course you do not," he replied, winking and releasing her hand before he turned away to rejoin Burghley.

Grace took Euan's arm, and they walked back to where they'd come in. "Let us go," he said to her in a whisper, smiling as he stroked her cheek. They both closed their eyes, and Euan reached out to The Council. *Bring us home.*

CHAPTER 19

When they arrived back to debrief the mission, they were back in uniform, the lightness of the clothing a shock after so long in the heavy silks, velvets, leather, and brocade of the period. Still in mission body to keep them from being overly exhausted and unable to adequately report, they weren't yet facing the full impact of their return. So many months away meant an exceptionally long debrief that neither was looking forward to. They weren't kept waiting long, but this time they were taken to a larger conference room behind Council Chambers to accommodate all of those who wanted to be or needed to be involved. The heads of Wardrobe, Medical, Archives, Artifacts, and varying departments were always required to be present, The Councilwoman and at least one other Councilmember were always required as well, but this time it seemed all of them were there.

Applause erupted when Grace and Euan entered and took their seats, turning their focus to giving a complete and thorough reporting and answering questions from Councilmembers and department heads to better aid their next mission or the mission of another team. They were both glad when it was over, and Euan expressed a wish to somehow get a picture of Grace dressed up as a queen. The Councilwoman, with a small smile, promised to see what she could do, that smile indicating the picture would probably be coming his way soon.

When it was finally time to go home, they were granted an extended break of six months; after having worked so long on this mission it would give them time to process, rest, and read-just. When the pair opened their eyes at home, their bodies felt stiff and heavy. A wave of exhaustion swept them both but not enough to take them down just yet.

"Welcome back!" Caia said, smiling as she opened the curtains. "Success?"

"Aye," Euan replied as he sat up, rubbing his eyes.

"That was a really, really long one, wasn't it? Three weeks here, but six months there? You must be so out of sorts. Here, let me help you," she said as she reached out and started pulling the patches off them that kept their bodies sustained and hydrated on such a long mission.

"I hope they didn't make you sit here the whole time," Grace said.

"No, I switched out with others for a day or two and then would come back. Not that I wanted to switch, but they made me all the same."

"I am sure they did it for yer own good, Caia," Euan said with a smile. "But thank ye for yer dedication to us."

Caia smiled in return. "My pleasure and honor, as always. Everything here seems to be fine. There was a great deal of commotion for a while, but that was Dr. Fraser moving in. At least that is what Vanessa said."

Euan and Grace paused and looked at each other, having entirely forgotten about Drew's move. "Well, that will make things more interesting in a few moments," Euan said.

"The question is: Do we proceed as normal and make a show of coming in like before, or do we just tell him?" Grace replied.

"They have already approved it," Caia continued. "It was not as if they did not know this was coming, and I alerted them when I found out from Vanessa he was here full-time."

"If I am being honest, I am too bloody tired to make a show of it," Euan said. "I know ye feel worse than ye normally do, love; I can feel it no matter what sort of front ye are putting up. Ye have nae the energy for it either."

"You're right, I don't," she said, dropping her guard to show how tired she really was.

"Then let us go down as we are and be done with the pretense. Caia, ye should come along, as ye will be needed."

"Of course," Caia said.

Once they washed up, Euan took Grace's hand, opened the door, and walked out into the hallway with her. The light from the window at the top of the stairs was harsh in its brightness, and both shrank away from it for the first few moments. Once they adjusted, they made their way down the stairs and could hear everyone in the kitchen, knowing that Vanessa was waiting for them to come in through the back as normal.

"Afternoon to ye," Euan said as he walked in with Grace, barefoot and still in his mission clothing, followed by Caia. Vanessa's jaw dropped, and Mal stared at them wide-eyed. There'd been no warning they'd intended to do this, and Vanessa was clearly wondering if she'd missed something.

"Hi, Eu —" Drew began as he turned around, but his words stopped at the sight of them, and he examined them in confusion. They certainly didn't look as though they'd just walked in from outside or off a plane the way they were dressed.

"Um. . .guys . . ." Vanessa stammered. "You. . .um. . .you forgot something?"

"We know, Van. We didn't really have the energy to deal with hiding it, and he'd find out eventually anyway," Grace said.

"Find out what?" Drew asked.

"What we really do," Grace replied. "This is Caia. She'll help us explain."

"Explain *what*."

"But before she does, we really need to eat and get something to drink," Euan said, ignoring Drew's question for the moment.

Vanessa pushed the tea toward them, and they both picked up a cup without even hesitating. Grace closed her eyes and sighed in happiness. "This was a long one," Vanessa said.

"Aye," Euan said. "Long and complicated."

"Can ye say what ye did or . . ." Mal said, his eyes shifting to Drew and then back.

"We had to stop the Ridolfi plot from being successful this time," Grace replied.

Vanessa's eyes went wide. "Jesus, really?"

"Yep."

Drew laughed, then stopped when he realized no one else was doing the same. "Wait, ye are saying this seriously?"

"Aye," Euan said. "It is what we do."

"They are part of a group who goes back to the past and makes sure history doesn't change," Vanessa offered.

"What? That is nae even possible. History is history, and ye cannae go back to it."

"*We* can," Grace said, her voice soft and beginning to betray her exhaustion. "*You* can't."

"What they are saying is the truth, Dr. Fraser," Caia added. "It is a complicated thing, and I know they are intending to explain it to you in the same way they did for both Vanessa and Mal: by showing you."

Drew appeared skeptical and concerned that his friends and new roommates seemed to be part of some strange delusion that anyone could do anything like this. Euan smiled a bit and shook his head.

"I understand ye, Drew. It is a hard thing to comprehend, and it will only get stranger, but by the end ye will understand everything and discover that the world ye think ye know is only a fraction of it."

"Vanessa will come with us, but you will have to trust us," Grace said.

Finishing their tea, each one grabbed a biscuit and stood up. Caia held out her hands, Grace and Euan taking one, then holding out theirs to Vanessa and Drew. Vanessa stepped past Drew and took Grace's hand, then looked at Drew and held out her hand to him. He eyed her warily but stood and walked over to her all the same.

"When you take Euan's hand, Caia will transport all of us once you close your eyes. You'll feel something weird, though it isn't the same for everyone. Mine feels like someone pulls me forward quickly. When we stop, you'll be dizzy, but it will pass in a moment," Grace explained.

"Don't open your eyes right away," Vanessa added. "I usually wait for it to pass before I do."

"I'll keep watch here," Mal said before he smiled at Drew. "Enjoy this. Ye are never going to be the same again after this moment."

"What?"

"You'll see."

"Close your eyes, Dr. Fraser, and let us be on our way," Caia said.

***

Drew watched as everyone else closed their eyes, unsure whether he wanted to do the same. Perhaps they were playing him for a fool, but they wouldn't do that to him, he knew that. Shaking his head, he took a deep breath and closed his eyes. As soon as he did, however, he understood immediately what Grace had warned him about. It felt as though the ground beneath his feet disappeared for a moment, but then as soon as it had gone, it was back.

"And here we are," he heard Caia say.

Drew felt Euan's hand drop away from his but could still feel Vanessa's. He *did* feel dizzy, but it passed quickly, as Grace had said it would. Opening his eyes, he expected to see the same kitchen they'd been in because what they'd said was impossible, but that wasn't at all what he saw. He gasped as he observed his new surroundings, open-mouthed. They *were* in an entirely different place. "No, this is. . .ye cannae . . ."

Caia laughed. "We can. Welcome to the future, Dr. Fraser."

"Wait. . .what?"

"A few centuries in the future, to be exact," Grace said with a small smile.

"The Council is waiting," Caia said.

Euan looked at her with concern. "The Council? Why?"

Caia shrugged. "It is what I was told."

Grace frowned, as did Vanessa. Caia turned and started walking in that direction, the rest following her, though Drew stopped every few steps to simply look around him in amazement. When they stopped before the doors, they opened immediately, and the group walked inside without Caia. Grace, Euan, and Vanessa all bowed to the women sitting at the long table before them.

"Councilwomen," Grace said.

"Ah! Dr. Fraser, here you are at last," Rochford said.

"Sorry?"

"You *are* Dr. Andrew Fraser, are you not?"

"Aye, but how —"

Rochford laughed and shook her head. "We are the future, Doctor. We know a great many things you have yet to even conceive of, and this is only one of them. We knew you would come eventually, and here you are. It is my great pleasure to meet you and welcome you, though you already have so many questions."

"Aye, I do."

"And we will answer all of them for you, within reason."

"What does that mean?"

"It means there are things we cannot tell you because you cannot know them so far back as you are. It is not personal."

"Far back?"

"You are the past to us, Dr. Fraser. I am Councilwoman Rochford, and I am the head of The Council. Grace, Euan, and Vanessa work for us."

Drew looked at Vanessa quickly, and she smiled at him.

"Yes, they are actually human beings," Rochford said. "They just have extraordinary jobs. Come," she said, gesturing him forward.

Vanessa nodded to him, and he walked forward to where

Rochford was as she stepped down. "Here in the future, we have eliminated war. Eliminated suffering. We are a society where all are equal, and The Council ensures that does not change."

She pointed at something Drew had yet to notice, a giant tapestry of sorts. "This? This shows the whole of human history. As you can see, there are many lines and not just one, and that is because there are multiple timelines running at once. All the same people but different in their own small ways. All the major history points, however, are the same. After a time, history will repeat itself by simply starting over again. Every time it repeats, it can be changed in ways large and small."

Drew shook his head as he stared at the tapestry. "But how? How does it do that and we nae notice?"

"That is far more complicated and not something we can explain to you now. Just know that it does. Each repeat threatens what came after it because it can change and alter what is to come. When that happens, we see it here. Now, some changes are small and do not matter, so we leave them be. Those that would destroy what we have now must be prevented, and that is where Grace, Euan, and the others like them come in."

"What do ye mean come in?"

"Their job is to go to the past and prevent those changes from happening by whatever means they must. The only thing they cannot do is kill unless their target is threatened. On every mission they have a person or persons they must keep safe or interact with, for they are the key."

Drew looked over at them in sudden understanding. "Ye travel to all these places in the past? That is what ye do?"

"Aye," Euan said with a small nod. "It happens often, and that is why we are gone regularly."

"Euan and Grace happen to be our best team, and before she met Euan, Grace was our best Watcher."

Drew's face went pale. "Watcher . . ."

"Ah, you have heard the stories, I see."

Drew looked at Grace once more, and it felt as though he'd

never met her. "My nan told me those stories. She said they were angels who came to do God's work."

"In a sense they are, I suppose," Rochford said with a small shrug. "If they did not do their jobs, then the world as you know it now would not exist."

"Christ," Drew whispered, trying to grapple with all of it. "But time travel is nae possible."

"It is, just not for you. Not yet. Well, not for everyone *else*, I should say. Now that you know, it is quite possible for *you*."

"How long have ye been doing this, Grace?"

"About four and a half years, but Euan has only been working with me for a year and a half. Before that, it was my grandmother, and her grandmother before that, and so on."

"It's a family thing," he said quietly, almost to himself, and then he looked at Vanessa. "That is what ye meant when ye mentioned marrying into a family. Ye meant *this*."

"Yes," Vanessa said. "I told you it wasn't the mob." He laughed a little while the others look confused. "The Cameron Watchers, which is what Grace and Euan are, well, they still exist," she said with a nod to Rochford, who smiled at him. "I work for them, and someday one of my grandchildren will work for the next Cameron Watcher after Grace is gone, and it continues."

Rochford nodded. "As I told Vanessa when she began with us, one of her line is *still* my Keeper, and that will continue for as long as I am currently aware. Her job is vital to the team, and it is crucial that she remains focused on it. She makes sure Grace and Euan's lives run smoothly so that they can turn their minds solely to their tasks instead of worrying about whether the electric bill has been paid or when a child's next appointment with the doctor is. If they miss something in a mission because they are thinking about such things it could be a disaster."

"This is incredible," Drew said. "I had no idea."

"And you should not because that means we are all doing our jobs correctly. And by tying yourself to Vanessa, you will become part of all of it."

Vanessa looked at him, her expression nervous. "Though I'll understand if you don't want to now. This is a lot, I know that."

Drew frowned. "Why would ye think such a thing?"

"Because this is a huge secret to keep, because it's a lot to take in, because it's all so strange. I understand if you want nothing to do with any of it."

"It may be all those things, but none of it changes who ye are, Vanessa. I fell in love with *ye*, nae yer job. I am surprisingly flexible."

Grace chuckled. "I would think you'd have to be in emergency medicine with the way things change from moment to moment."

"Exactly," Drew said, pointing at Grace. "I have seen my share of strange things, and while this is, by far, the strangest, it will nae scare me off."

Vanessa relaxed and smiled. "I'm glad. I didn't want to lose you."

"And ye will nae," he replied.

"Your descendants will be responsible for a great deal of our medical practices, just so you know," Rochford added. "Not all of them are Keepers."

Drew glanced at her. "Medical? May I —"

"See it? Yes," she said with a knowing smile. "But before you do, there is more you need to know."

"More?"

"Yes. Grace and Euan are. . .well, they are not what they seem."

"What does that mean?"

"Euan?" Rochford queried. "Did you want to go ahead, or shall we?"

"Drew, do ye remember the talk I gave at the gathering? About military tactics and strategy?"

"Aye," Drew said, smiling. "It was brilliant."

"Did ye nae wonder how I knew any of it?"

Drew paused. "Actually, no, I had nae thought about it. I just assumed ye had done yer research. Now that ye mention it, though . . ."

"I knew because I was there. Because I did it. I fought in that rising. The Euan Cameron we spoke of as my ancestor? That is *me*."

"Ye? Ye are. . .ye are telling me ye are from the past?"

"Aye," Euan said. "I am. So is my mam, and we are here because of Grace."

Drew shook his head in disbelief. "How is. . .this is . . ." he stammered, unable to think of what he wanted to say.

"Impossible, aye. It should be, but it is nae. It is the truth. I can even show it to ye."

"What, did ye just see Grace about her business in yer time and decide to come with her?"

"No, it does nae work that way. She had to choose to do it, and she died to bring me here."

"But she is right here."

"Aye, through the miracle of science, she is here, and so am I."

"I dinnae understand."

"Grace was always meant to have Euan as her Companion," Rochford explained. "All Watchers must choose to sacrifice themselves to save their Companion, and that is how it works. She saved his life, and it killed her. Her mission had been to go back and make that choice, though she did not know that."

"Save him from what, though?"

"Culloden. Dying at Culloden," Euan said.

"No . . ."

"Oh, aye, I was there. I was there and I fought and I died. Over, and over, and over again until she came for me. As the Councilwoman said, history repeats. My history, those battles, all those deaths, my own death — all of them repeated goodness knows how many times before Grace pulled me away. They are still happening and will continue to do so."

Drew ran his hands through his hair, struggling to make sense of what he'd just been told about the young man he'd befriended. A young man who should, by all rights, be long dead. "I cannae believe it," he said. "Grace, are ye from the past, too?"

"No," she said, smiling. "I am just as modern as you are."

"Euan, as I understand it, has just offered to take you back to the past to see it for yourself. It is through a process we call Observation, and it is how we train new Watchers and Companions."

"See it?"

"Aye, as if ye were right there, though ye cannae be hurt and no one can see ye. Anywhere in my past ye want to go, I will show ye."

"But, Euan, the —" Grace began.

"I know, love, but I mean it. Anywhere. I can do it now. Well, anywhere but the last."

Grace nodded, and Drew looked at him with a raised eyebrow. "Did ye ever go to see our clan?"

"Aye, many times. I would be happy to show it to ye."

"Oh, ye best believe I want to see it."

Euan laughed. "Perhaps nae today, though. I am a bit tired."

"That makes me think of a question," Drew said, turning back to Rochford. "How does it work? If something will take weeks, are they just gone for weeks?"

"No," she said. "When they depart on a mission, their actual bodies remain behind and they are placed at their mission location in bodies that cannot be harmed and will withstand anything as they need to. Back in their time, Caia sits with them and guards their bodies. She makes sure no harm comes to them and that they remain properly hydrated and nourished if the mission takes them more than a day. Oftentimes, it is only a day or two, though a few weeks may pass wherever they are."

"That is amazing. How does she do that? An IV?"

"Oh no, we no longer use those. No, there are patches that are far less invasive. We need not use them often for Watchers, as they are not gone long enough. This last mission, however, we had to make extensive use of them."

"That is why ye have a headache," Drew said to Grace as it clicked. "Because ye wake up dehydrated after a day or two."

"Yep," Grace said. "Exactly why we want tea."

"It is nae particularly hydrating," he countered.

"It is a good start," Euan said with a chuckle.

"The caffeine helps," Grace added.

"Ye said they are in different bodies that cannae be harmed. Can ye explain that?"

Rochford smiled. "You are clever and inquisitive, just like the others."

"Others?"

"Never mind that now. To answer your question in short, we have the ability to insert our Watchers into different timelines, in the exact places where they need to be. When they materialize there, they do so in bodies that are engineered in a certain way. They are there, but not there. Solid, but more energy than anything, as you would imagine a very advanced hologram to be. To anyone who sees them, there is no way of telling the difference. These bodies protect them from anyone who may mean to do them harm. If they are injured, it heals immediately. They cannot die, do not need sleep, do not need food or drink. The latter two are also for safety. If they do not sleep, they cannot be attacked, and neither can their targets. If they do not eat or drink, they cannot be poisoned or be harmed by any illness they might contract from the food and drink."

"Brilliant, and it makes so much sense. If they fell victim to any of that, it would end their work."

"Precisely. He should go to Medical," Rochford said. "Caia will take him while the rest of you stay here."

"May I go with him?" Vanessa asked.

"Yes, if you wish."

Vanessa nodded, and the doors opened, where they found Caia waiting outside. "Next stop, Medical," Caia said, grinning. "Welcome aboard, Dr. Fraser."

Drew grinned despite himself. "Thank ye, though I dinnae know if I really understand what I am getting into."

"None of us really do at first," Vanessa said. "None of us really do."

CHAPTER 20

When they reached Medical, the doors opened for them, and Caia gestured them inside. "I will be here waiting for you when you are done."

Vanessa entered next to Drew, who was looking around in awe. "Christ, would ye look at this! This is a thing of beauty! Ye would nae even think this was any sort of medical unit. It looks more like a museum!"

Vanessa laughed and shook her head as some of the Medical personnel stopped and looked at them. One of them came forward, pulling a mask down from over his nose and mouth. He was tall and slender, his shoulders broad but not like Euan's. His dark brown hair was cut in a fairly traditional shorter style, and his blue eyes stood out against not only that color, but also the white of his coat.

"It is ye!" he said as he reached them.

"Me?"

"Aye! Well, both of ye anyway." When they stared at him blankly, he laughed and shook his head. "I apologize. My name is Andrew. Well, same as yers, but I was named after ye anyway. Ye can call me Andy, as most everyone else does."

"Wait. . .ye are . . ."

"A Fraser? Aye, that I am. Ye are my . . ." He paused to count it in his head. "Triple-great-grandparents. I think that is right. Eh, does nae matter," he said with a shrug.

"Wow," Vanessa said. "That's. . .weird. Now I know how Grace feels."

The young doctor laughed. "Aye, I imagine it would be, though I always knew this would happen eventually. Ye do get used to it after a time, though."

Drew shook his head in disbelief. "What is it ye do here?"

"I am the head of Medical," he replied with a proud smile. "I assume ye are here because ye wish to see everything?"

"Oh, aye."

"Happy to. Follow me."

They walked with him to what looked to be a conference room, where he shut the door behind them. "I thought you were going to show us everything?" Vanessa said.

"I am, but I can do it from here. It is safer that way so that ye dinnae need to risk exposure to anything ye have nae yet encountered, as well as to keep things sterile."

"Aye, makes sense," Drew said. "I am sure there are illnesses we have nae even seen yet and illnesses ye no longer have."

"That is exactly it. Would nae want to have to treat ye right away, though ye will both be getting vaccinated against anything and everything before ye leave today anyway," he replied as he walked over to what looked like a clear, flat piece of glass. He touched it and it came to life with a diagram of the Medical unit. He tapped on it, and it popped out into a 3D model in front of them.

"Ohhh, I want one of these," Drew said.

"They *are* fantastic," Andy replied. "Ye can really get into a body and look at it with one of these."

"Really?"

"Oh aye, and I will show ye that in a few moments. Here is where ye are," he said, pointing to the room they were in. "Over here is where we do basic care for the Watchers, Companions, The Council, Guardians, and anyone else who works here and needs it. Vaccinations, typical illnesses, small injuries, things like that. Over here, we treat any emergencies, and here is surgical."

"Do ye see many emergencies?"

"All the time, though nae usually with the Watchers or Companions except the once. Mainly it is The Council, Guardians, staff, and the like. We are all normal human beings here, our bodies just as fragile, but we are better at fixing them now."

"Incredible. Have ye eradicated things?"

"Aye, a good many diseases. We can cure cancer, but the treatment still takes time. It is nae the way ye do it though and is far easier on the patient. We can cure heart ailments, some brain ailments, most anything that affects the body. There are still some things we have nae been able to stop."

"Such as?"

"Old age," he said, smiling. "We can none of us stop that. We still die eventually. All the same, there are new diseases we are working on. As ye well know, sometimes when ye figure out how to stop one thing, it causes another."

"Aye," Drew said, rolling his eyes. "The bane of medical advancement."

"Indeed. I wish I could show ye how we do some of it, but I cannae. Ye should know, though, that the Fraser doctors have developed a great deal of it through time. If anything, ye can be proud of that. Just know that yer children, their children, and so on continue in the medical field, and the result is much of what ye see here now."

Vanessa gasped softly, staring at the model in front of them with a different perspective, even as a wide grin appeared on Drew's face. "I will definitely take pride in that. Well done to the lot of ye."

"We are still working on it," Andy said. "Always learning and improving. It is because of us that Watcher and Companion Cameron are even here at all."

Vanessa's head snapped up. "What?"

Andy swiped his hand across the model and cleared it from their view. "Let me show ye, though I will warn ye that the images may be difficult for ye to see."

"Go ahead," Drew said, his curiosity winning out over any squeamishness at seeing injuries to his friends.

The first picture he pulled up was of Euan. He was on a table, his skin pale and his lips purple, and it was clear even to Vanessa that he was dead. "Here is Companion Cameron, dead from a gunshot wound to the back. The lead ball struck his heart and killed him."

Drew turned his head toward Andy. "If he's dead, then how —"

"Ah, we have our ways." Andy flashed a secretive smile, manipulating the image so that it changed to a 3D anatomy view of Euan. "See, here is the point of entry," he said as he zoomed into it, "and the wound to the heart. The ball hit the sternum and flattened out, but it stopped any exit wound."

Drew studied it and nodded. "That would have been instant or nearly so, but he is still dead."

"Aye, he is, but he was brought here quickly enough that we could keep his brain from dying while we repaired his heart. I cannae tell ye *how* we do that or how we keep the body from decaying in the process, but we *can* do it unless it takes too long to get to them. When he was ready, we brought him back none the wiser."

Drew shook his head, incredulous. "I cannae fathom being able to do such a thing, but I wish I could."

"Aye, I am sure ye do. I would, too, if I were ye, but that is also why we cannae tell ye how any of it is done. Even here that technology is used sparingly and usually only for Watchers and Companions."

"I understand," Drew said. "I also wish I had one of these screens to look at patients. It must be so much easier to find problems."

"I cannae imagine working without it, so I have to hand it to ye for doing so and still managing many of the outcomes ye obtain. Ye are an amazing doctor, and I would love for ye to come back sometime and show me how ye do it with yer technology."

"Thank ye," Drew said. "I try, and sure, I would be happy to. Fair trade."

"Thank ye, and credit where credit is due," Andy replied,

pushing that image away. "This one, this is where it gets complicated." The next image he pulled up was of Grace. She lay on a table as Euan had first seen her, covered in blood. Vanessa gasped, covering her eyes and turning away.

"Jesus Christ!" Drew cried out. "How. . .ye cannae come back from something like this!"

"Ye would think so, but we managed. . .barely. I dinnae think they ever anticipated what would happen to her there, none of us did, or we would have been more prepared." He changed the image to the anatomy again. "Watcher Cameron, well, she was Watcher Evans then, suffered four gunshot wounds to the torso and a bayonet wound to the chest."

Drew winced. "Ach, Grace. I cannae imagine the pain she must have been in."

"Aye, precisely. I shudder to think of it. As ye can clearly see, the wounds destroyed her heart and her lungs, along with several other organs. We were able to do as we did with Companion Cameron but in a different way because of the extensive damage. We had to use a few tricks, including essentially re-growing the damaged organs and replacing them."

"Re-growing them. Ye have come that far?"

"Aye. Obviously it is a bit more complicated than that, but that is the idea. However, because of it, she is more us than ye now."

"What do ye mean?"

"There is very little left inside of her now that she was born with after we treated those injuries, and there is a reason they create a protocol for Watchers to step down instead of it being the normal way where it ends with their deaths. It is because of *her*. Even if she is injured in her time, she is far less likely to die. She *can* die, she is nae immortal, but it would be harder to accomplish. By the time ye saw her, the injury would be far less severe than it was originally. Nae entirely gone but at least nae fatal. It is a bit like when she is on a mission. Those bodies? Ye cannae do a damned thing to them. Try to hurt them, and it will heal right before yer eyes while they just laugh at ye. Same goes for Companion Cameron with his heart, really, though the two of them dinnae know that."

"Wow. I think I would like to see that, honestly. If ye cannae kill them, then how did she die?"

"Ah, excellent question," Andy replied with a knowing smile. "Something happens when the Watcher makes the choice to sacrifice themselves for their Companion and it happens only once. There is a sort of energy burst that changes the makeup of the mission body to the point where they are as real there as they are here, and that is what kills them. Now, the thing is, it changes it, but it does nae eradicate it. There is still a good amount of the mission body lingering in them even after the choice is made, and that is the only thing that saved her. It is what allowed her to get up after they shot her so that she could try to drag his body away from the field before they bayoneted her to finish the job. Those gunshot wounds would have killed ye or me or anyone else immediately. It is the only thing that saves any of them in the end and allows us to get them here quickly enough to fix them."

"That's absolutely mind boggling," Drew said. "Do they have scars from any of these procedures?"

"No, none. The only scars Companion Cameron has are the ones he came to us with. We could have repaired those but decided nae to do so unless he consented, and when we asked him, he declined. We were able to fix any other problems we found with him as well: dental, eyes, hearing, and all that. Nae that he needed much because he was surprisingly healthy for the period."

"I wish I had access to this technology."

"Ye do. Any treatment ye need will come through us from now on. Unfortunately, yer patients dinnae. I know that is how ye wish ye had it, nae thinking of yerself. At least ye can know that ye will be free from many of those things that would ail those ye know. Ye and yer wife, yer children, everyone after them. Same with Mal and any of his family. All of those connected in such a way with the Watchers are cared for by us and taken care of by The Council."

Drew nodded, reaching out to touch the images before him, manipulating them as he'd seen Andy do. He studied the wounds to Grace and what the weapons had done to her body. These were weapons they no longer saw wounds from even in his own time, though there were others that did similar damage. He could see where her lungs had filled with blood, the way the bayonet had shredded her heart and damaged her spine, able to examine the damage caused by the musket balls flattening out and bouncing off bones, burning their way through tissue, muscle, and organs. Of anyone besides Grace and Andy, he was well aware of the agony those wounds would've caused her or anyone who experienced them. That her death was not immediate meant she most certainly felt it when anyone else wouldn't have. Drew sighed heavily and shook his head; the things humans could do to one another still managed to horrify him even after all he'd seen.

"I am glad ye can save people from this now. No one deserves to die this way."

"I agree. Nae that we really see these sorts of injuries now. War is nae something we deal with."

"Lucky ye."

"I should nae keep ye longer. I am sure The Council has more for ye, including showing ye how to contact us if ye need assistance. It was my honor to meet ye and will be my honor to treat ye when ye need it."

"Thank ye," Drew replied, reaching out to shake Andy's hand. "I look forward to speaking with ye more."

They were shown out, and Caia waited for them as promised. Drew was silent as they walked back, fighting to get the images of his injured friends out of his mind, along with ideas of how he might treat those injuries in the present with what they had access to. When they arrived back in Council Chambers, Euan and Grace were in the middle of what seemed to be a friendly conversation with Rochford, though it stopped as soon as Drew and Vanessa came inside. Drew looked at Grace, standing there whole and alive, nothing like how he'd seen her just moments ago. He realized he knew something they didn't, and that it was something those in charge didn't seem to want them to know. He understood why, of course. It might lead to them being reckless, and as Andy had said, they weren't immortal. What he couldn't help doing was going to where she stood and pulling her into an embrace. No matter what had happened, no matter that they were at war, she hadn't deserved such a fate. In his head he could see it, hear her screaming, watch her struggle, see the pain in every bit of her. He didn't know how he could, but he knew those images weren't his own. They were too real.

"I'm so sorry, sweet friend," he whispered in her ear.

"I'm all right," she whispered in return.

"Now ye are, but ye weren't. I saw it. I cannae —"

"I know. All that's important is that I survived it and I'm here."

"Aye," he said, giving her a small squeeze and releasing her. "Thank ye for letting me see that," he said to Rochford. "It's quite an incredible setup ye have, and though I wish I could see the developments in procedures, I know why I cannae."

"Yes, I *am* sorry about that," she replied. "I absolutely understand why you would."

"They mentioned I will get care through ye now?"

"Yes, you will. A perk of the job, so to speak. All your healthcare will come from us, as will the care of those who come after you. Your children will be born here to ensure the best outcome, just as Grace and Euan's children will be. Grace has been coming here for care since her childhood."

Grace nodded. "Anytime I was sick as a kid, anytime I got hurt, my grandmother brought me here, though I didn't really understand it was different at first."

"You will, of course, have the option of bringing your grandmother here for care as well, Dr. Fraser, and assisting in that care in the ways you can."

"What? Really?"

"Of course. She is your family, and if you choose to tell her what your future wife's employers really do for a living, she will fall under your care. We all of us understand how important those loved ones can be."

"It amazes me what ye can fix here."

"We have come incredibly far. Unfortunately, there are some instances where we will not treat even though we could. This is simply because, eventually, we must all pass on. It is a choice we all must make at some point."

"It is a choice I will have to make for my grandmother eventually," Drew replied, realizing what such advanced care might mean for both of them.

"Yes, that is true, or she will make it for you by telling you she does not wish for it. But you need not worry about that for quite some time."

Drew smiled in relief. "What else do I need to know?"

"You now have a choice to make: You can either remain as you are and simply be the husband of the Keeper, or you can choose to officially work with us as she does. You would keep your current job, of course, but you would also work for us if we needed you."

"Doing what?"

"Consultation on things that come up that we may not have seen before but you have, for a start."

"Oh. What is the difference?"

"The difference is coming further under our protection as well as earning a stipend from us. Doing so would bind you to the Cameron Watcher, however, and would earn you the same mark Vanessa has."

"Mark?" He looked over at Vanessa. "Yer tattoo . . ."

"That one, yep. Grace and Euan have them, too, but theirs are different," Vanessa explained as the pair held up their wrists to show him the marks.

Drew was quiet for a long moment. "I cannae and will nae

let Vanessa do this alone. I will come as far in as I have to in order to help her as much as I can." He looked over at Euan and Grace. "And ye two as well. I owe both of ye so much I cannae begin to say, so the least I can do for ye is promise I will always do my best to care for and protect ye so that ye can do as ye must for the rest of us."

Rochford smiled and then nodded. "Then so be it. Grace and Euan, you should go home and get some rest; you have certainly earned it. Vanessa and Dr. Fraser can remain while we teach him what he will need to know as far as contacting us and the rest."

Grace and Euan both bowed and departed and Drew gave her a small nod. "I am ready for whatever ye need me to do."

"Of course you are. There is a reason you are where you are, Dr. Fraser. You have as big a sense of duty as the rest in the Cameron Watcher's group do, and it is what drew you to them in the first place. You felt it, understood it, even if you did not realize it."

"I suppose I did, but I've always wanted to help others. It's why I'm a doctor."

"It is, and it is why you are a good one. It is why those who come after you share the same desire for service to their fellows. Now, we have some things to discuss. As I mentioned to you, you will receive a stipend from us. As it happened with Vanessa and all the rest, the money will just be there. You will not need to think about it or ask. We also will give you a few bonuses," she said with a sly smile. "Just as we did with Vanessa."

"Bonuses? At the end of the year if I help ye?"

"Oh no, much sooner than that. You have educational bills you are paying, correct?"

"Aye, dinnae remind me," he grumbled.

"You no longer will."

"Sorry?"

"They will be paid. The payoff notices will arrive for you at the lodge, as that is where you are living."

"I. . .that is too much. Really."

Rochford laughed. "It truly is not. The cost that, to you, is prohibitive, is nothing to us. A bit like how you look at the past and marvel that something only cost a penny. We paid Vanessa's, too. The whole of Grace's education from kindergarten through university was entirely paid for by us, as will be the educations of her children. It is important to us they all receive the best education they can get because it benefits *us* in the end. Your children and those who come after will receive the same benefit. Money is not something any of you will need to worry about."

Drew didn't know what to say. It was such a foreign concept to him, the idea of not needing to think about money. Now he was being told he never would have to again, but it also made sense to him now why Grace, Euan, and the rest lived so comfortably, though not ostentatiously. If they had to be concerned about money, they wouldn't focus on the task at hand. The lines drawn between all these actions were becoming clear as crystal to him.

"Thank ye so much for yer generosity. I dinnae mean to sound ungrateful, but does no one ever wonder if ye will use such gifts to manipulate them?"

"It is a question often asked. We have no desire to do any such thing. Our assistance to you is freely given, as we want your assistance to us to be. We will never force you or ask you to do anything that compromises you."

Drew nodded. "And if ye do, then what?"

"Then you can say no. It is as simple as that."

Drew smiled. "Then I suppose we should get on with it."

CHAPTER 21

By the time Drew and Vanessa returned, Grace and Euan had gone to bed. Even though their bodies had been at rest, the rest of them hadn't been, and as always it manifested in exhaustion. Drew, likewise, found himself feeling run down and excused himself to go to sleep after promising Mal they'd talk the next day about his experience.

When he woke in the morning and shuffled out of their room, everyone was gathered around the table, and Grace was making breakfast. *This* was the way he'd always known them, and if he didn't know better now, he'd never think anything differed about any of the people gathered there. He was welcomed warmly, had a cup of hot coffee handed to him, and dropped into a chair with a yawn.

"I was thinking that perhaps today I would take ye out as I promised," Euan said. "Mal wants to come along."

"Are ye sure ye are up to it?" Drew asked.

"Aye, a good night's rest usually sets me to rights, and if I am still tired when we return, I can always go back to sleep. So, other than yer own lands, what would ye like to see?"

Drew took a moment to consider it. "What are the limitations on that?"

"I had to have been there unless Grace has been and allows us to access that mission. That gives ye a rather enormous range at this point."

"I think, maybe, what ye last did? At least a piece of it. If ye have instances where ye were hurt on a mission, I want to see one of those. I want to see what they told me about ye with my own eyes."

"Easily done," Euan said with a nod. "Anything else?"

"I'd like to see a battle."

Mal's eyes darted to Euan. "I dinnae think we can, Drew. Euan does nae want to remember those."

"It is fine, Mal, I offered it to him. Anything but the last one, and ye know why."

"Christ, are ye sure?"

Euan nodded. "I may keep my distance, but I can take ye there and ye can go where ye will."

"If ye are sure. There are a couple I would like to see, certainly."

"Which ones?" Drew asked.

"Prestonpans and Falkirk, two major victories. I want to see for myself how it was done."

"I am fine with those," Drew said. "Nae sure I'd want to see us defeated."

Euan chuckled. "There are nae many of those, really, at least nae that I was involved in."

"I will be interested to see what Drew has to say about what happened to ye at both of those places, Euan," Mal said.

"Aye, that could be interesting, though I suspect he will say what Archibald said."

"The lord was on yer side?" Mal offered, having heard the story.

"Aye," Euan said, laughing before taking a drink of his coffee.

"That sounds ominous," Drew said.

"It is," both men replied in unison as Grace laughed.

"Did ye want to come, Vanessa, love?" Drew asked.

"No, I'll stay here with Grace. I think I've had enough of Observation for a little while."

Grace looked at her sadly and Drew frowned. "Why? What happened?"

"I got to see . . ." she trailed off, looking over at Grace.

"We went to Culloden," Mal finished. "Vanessa asked to do it when she was brought in. We saw what happened."

"Ach, sweetheart, ye should nae have."

"I'm glad I did, though," Vanessa said. "I understand a lot about them now without being told. But everything you saw in those images yesterday, I watched it happen in real time, and it was horrifying."

Euan reached out and gave Vanessa's hand a gentle squeeze. "Trust me, I understand. Let us see what mark they gave ye, Drew," Euan said, changing the subject. "I am sure yers is different."

"Ye got one? I didn't," Mal said.

"I am sure ye will eventually," Euan countered.

Drew lifted his arm to show them the mark on the inside of his bicep. "They put it here so that I dinnae have to explain it to patients who might see it."

"Makes sense," Euan said. "It is a different design, wait. . .is that the same as yers, Vanessa?"

"Yeah," she replied. "Because he's going to marry me and stuff."

"Ye sure about that one? I am sure we could find ye a nice Fraser lass from the past," Euan joked. "Ow!" he exclaimed as Vanessa kicked him under the table.

"Serves ye right for saying that," Drew said with a small, amused smile.

"I was kidding! Anyway, as soon as we eat and ye get dressed, we can go."

Quick work was made of breakfast by the three men, two of whom were extremely excited to go and one who was simply hungry for actual food. Vanessa and Grace took their time and were only partway into their meals when the three stood up, and Euan leaned down and gave Grace a kiss.

"Back in a while, love."

"Bye, bye, boys. Have fun storming the castle!" Vanessa said, quoting a movie they all knew and bringing laughter from all three men.

"Literally. There *are* castles involved, after all," Grace said, smiling wryly at Euan as Drew kissed Vanessa goodbye.

"Hush ye," he said, matching her smile. "We will leave from the mission room. Is Caia already there?"

"She will be."

"Excellent. Let us be off then, lads," Euan said as he left the kitchen and started up the stairs to the second floor. When he opened the door to the mission room, Drew looked at it curiously. "I will explain soon. Come back here once ye are dressed."

Drew nodded and returned to their bedroom to take a quick shower, dress, and otherwise ready himself like any other day, and when he returned, Caia had arrived. "Oh. Hello."

"Hello, Dr. Fraser! Good to see you again."

"Likewise," he replied as Euan shut the door behind him.

"This," Euan began, "is the mission room. This is where Grace and I go when we must leave. We lie on this bed, Caia pulls the curtains so that we are in darkness, and we remain here. Once we close our eyes, we are transported to wherever we must go."

"Which is why this room is always closed," Drew finished.

"Aye. For today, though, we will leave from here. Are ye ready, Caia?"

"As always," she said, flashing her customarily bright smile.

The three men joined hands with Caia and were transported straight to Observation. Euan went to speak to the Archivist to let her know what she needed to pull up while Drew tried to soak in everything he saw. All of it was technology that didn't currently exist, and he found it fascinating even though he had no real way of knowing what any of it was or what it did.

"I'll help ye get set up," Mal offered, having moved to one of the tables.

"All right, what do I do?"

"Ye get up here on the table and lie down, then ye put this headpiece on and they do the rest."

"Right," Drew said as he got onto the table. Mal placed the headset on him and helped him adjust it.

Euan returned as Mal was hooking himself in and looked at Drew. "Ye ready for this?"

"Is anyone?"

"They think they are, but no," Euan said as he went to another table and prepared himself. After he lay down, he looked over at the other two. "As soon as ye close yer eyes, Drew, ye will go."

Drew nodded, then took a deep breath to still his racing heart and closed his eyes. The shift he expected didn't come, and instead there were the sounds of other men talking and movement beneath him. Opening his eyes, he found himself outdoors and on horseback, waiting with a party of men in Cameron tartan with Mal and Euan beside him. They were dressed in clothing Drew recognized, especially Euan, because it was the same thing he'd worn at the gathering.

"Where are we?" he asked.

"Welcome to 1744, my friend," Euan said. "This is the last half of the final day of a journey to Castle Dounie."

Drew looked around himself and then laughed a bit. "This is incredible! And they cannae see us or hear us?"

"No, they cannae. Ye also will nae feel any sort of discomfort because ye are only viewing, though it seems as though ye are nae."

"Euan!"

Drew watched as both the current Euan and the younger version of him turned around at their name being called. It astounded him to see them side by side this way, looking so similar and yet not. There was a confidence in the bearing of the present Euan that didn't exist in his younger counterpart, and it created a rather striking difference between them.

"Aye, Lochiel."

"Are ye and the men ready? The horses rested enough?"

"Aye, Lochiel."

"Good. We should make it before sundown then," Lochiel said as he mounted his horse and the Cameron officers fell into formation alongside him.

"That one looks like ye, Mal," Drew said, pointing at Malcolm.

"Aye, that is my forebear."

"Malcolm Cameron, one of my oldest and best friends,"

Euan explained as the men rode out and they followed.

"Seeing this clothing as it was is so cool."

"Have ye looked at yerself?" Euan asked.

"What?" Only then did Drew look down, gasping to find himself in a similar uniform but wearing Fraser tartan. "Christ! Look!" he got out before he laughed. "Ach, to take this with me!"

"If ye ask nicely, my mam can likely make ye one if ye get the tartan."

"I may take ye up on that. This is surprisingly comfortable."

"Had to be. It was what ye wore all the time, and ye needed to be able to move in it."

"I can see that."

"For now, look around ye and enjoy the ride. Ye cannae get there this way now, and many of the things ye will see along the way are long gone."

Drew nodded, falling silent to absorb as much of this moment as he could. It was an early autumn day, he could tell that much, just past the end of summer. Everything was green, there were still sunny days to be had, and it wasn't yet cold enough to make anything uncomfortable. Beside him, the men of Clan Cameron talked amongst themselves, sometimes breaking into song with things they made up to familiar tunes, and then laughed about because they were making fun of people they knew. Near him, the present Euan laughed, too, because these were *his* memories, and he remembered the people they were singing about. Drew couldn't help the smile it brought to his face. People didn't change; they were always the same in the most basic of ways, in how they interacted with each other and entertained themselves. It wasn't long before the three of them fell into their own conversations and their own songs about people they currently knew, adding them to the ones the past men were singing. Drew was thankful for this, to connect with these two men on such a fundamental level. It was an experience that would be hard to replicate in their modern lives, and more than that, it rooted him even more deeply in his own history.

By the time they reached their destination, Drew had become so comfortable in this new place that he forgot he wasn't actually there, though he gasped in awe as Castle Dounie came into view. It wasn't the one that stood in his own time, as that one had come long after the men gathered here had died, but it was still impressive in its own right. This was the home of his ancestors, the lands where they'd lived, where he'd grown up and where his grandmother lived even now. Although it looked vastly different in the present time than it did here, these were still the same fields, moors, and woods he'd wandered and played in as a child.

"Welcome home to ye, lad," Euan said from beside him.

"Thank ye," he whispered. "I cannae . . ."

"I know," Euan replied, patting his shoulder. "But ye feel it, dinnae ye? Deep in yer bones?"

"Aye, more than I thought possible."

Euan smiled and dismounted right next to his predecessor, and Mal laughed as Euan did so in just the same way he used to. "Cannae take it out of him," Mal said to Drew as they both dismounted.

"Nae sure ye would want to."

"Certainly nae."

"Euan, Malcolm, with me. The rest of ye, see to the horses," Lochiel ordered.

Euan and Malcolm fell in as ordered alongside Lochiel and followed him inside, while the modern men followed behind them. When they stepped inside the castle itself, Drew stopped walking to look around. It wasn't as he'd imagined it would be, but that wasn't a bad thing either. It was larger, laid out differently, but still as grand as anyone would expect.

"Lochiel, good to see ye."

The voice of an older man caught Drew's attention, and he turned his head to find a very familiar man standing there. Simon Fraser of Lovat was instantly recognizable to him from the portraits he'd seen all his life.

"Holy Mother of God . . ." Drew whispered.

"Aye, and ye, Lovat," Lochiel said as the two men shook hands.

"Come in, come in. Take yer ease," Lovat said before he looked at Malcolm and Euan. *"Christ, Euan Cameron, whatever the fae have given ye to make ye the size ye are, stop taking it."*

Younger Euan smiled but remained silent while the current one laughed. "I had forgotten about that," he said as Mal and Drew laughed along with him.

"If ye wish it, Malcolm and Euan can take up residence in the hall with my men while we discuss business."

Lochiel nodded to the two men, who saluted him and went to the hall as Lochiel and Lovat walked away. That was a conversation they couldn't see because Euan hadn't been there, so they followed the men into the hall. The great hall of Dounie still had tables out from dinner, with many of the Fraser officers sitting in conversation with mugs of ale. They all looked up when Malcolm and Euan entered, and a small cheer erupted before they stood up to meet their friends halfway, with hugs and handshakes being exchanged.

"It cannae be just the two of ye," one of them said.

"No, the other lads are seeing to the horses and will be along shortly," Malcolm said.

"Thought so. Come in, sit ye down and have an ale. Nae as though ye will have anywhere to go any time soon anyway."

"Aye, that is the truth," Euan replied.

"Nae for a couple of days at least," Malcolm said as they both sat down and were handed mugs. *"But, aye, probably longer than that."*

"Ye lot always at least stay two nights."

"Ye keep yer hands off our women while ye are here, Euan," another said, pointing at him.

"I cannae help it if they find me," he replied with a devilish smile.

"Oh, and ye do naught to entice them, eh?"

"I dinnae."

"Ye smug, lying bastard."

All the men at the table, including Euan, laughed, as the teasing was clearly of the friendly sort.

"How is yer daughter, Duncan?" Euan asked the man who'd just been teasing him. *"She is, what, 20 now?"*

"Ach, dinnae ye dare!"

Euan laughed and shook his head. *"I will nae, I swear."*

Drew was laughing so hard he found he had to sit down on an empty bench.

"Ye are such an arsehole," Mal said to the present Euan even though he was laughing.

"I was also lying."

"No!"

"Oh, aye. I did nae have to dare because I already had."

"Christ, Euan!" Mal said, though he was now laughing even harder.

Euan shrugged and smiled. "She actually sought me out the last time we were here, so I was nae lying when I said I did nae do anything to entice them. Though, I did nae do it *this* time, so I guess technically I was nae lying."

"Euan!"

They all turned as a younger man's voice called out across the hall, and all the men at the table immediately stood as the young man came toward them, grinning. *"Sit down all of ye,"* he said as he arrived, shaking Euan's hand. *"Good to see ye, friend. Father told me ye were coming."*

"Good to see ye, Simon," Euan replied with a matching grin.

"Can we get ye some ale, Master Simon?"

"That would be grand, Duncan. Thank ye."

"Wait, is that —" Drew began.

"Simon Fraser, Master of Lovat, soon enough to be chief of the Frasers of Lovat," Euan replied.

"Wow. He does nae look as I'd expect."

"No?"

"He was always written about as being a bit indecisive and anxious, but I dinnae see that at all."

"Aye, well, I suppose he could be, just as we all can be at times. When his father is around, ye see it a bit more, just a young lad stuck in the shadow of a father who is larger than life and knowing that someday he will have to step into that role while hoping he can fill the space. I know he never really agreed with his father's penchant for playing both sides."

"I can understand why. It's a risky business."

"Aye, it is."

"Are ye all right, Euan?" Mal asked.

"Aye? Why?"

"Just wanting to check in with ye is all. I dinnae want ye to have to do anything that pains ye."

"These memories are bittersweet, to be sure, but at the same time, I am glad I can visit them whenever I wish, and nae only that, but also share them with others. I am sitting here, looking at myself, only 23, and with no idea of what life has in store in such a short time. I thought it would always be this way, as did the men sitting here with me, the routines and the hum of life that had nae changed for centuries. How wrong I was. . .how wrong we all were. Had any of us known what was coming, had we known that this way of life would soon be wiped from existence, would we have acted differently? Appreciated it more? Held on to these moments a wee bit tighter? It is hard to say, but it is nice to be reminded that there were good times, laughter, and life before it all went dark."

Drew returned his gaze to the men at the tables laughing, joking, and catching up with no idea that in just two years all of this would be gone. The lifestyle that was the only thing they'd ever known and the only thing several generations before them had known, the people here who would never return, even this very castle wiped away in what was the blink of an eye. He had the benefit of hindsight, the ability to know that he should take in all the details he could, even down to the smallest things, because other than Euan and Mal, he'd be the only one who remembered them or even knew they'd existed, and the thought was humbling.

"I will wait here for ye while the two of ye explore the castle if that is yer wish. I know Mal would like to."

"Damned right I would. Ye up for it, Drew?"

"Aye," Drew said as he stood up.

The two of them left the hall, wandering every hallway, stairwell, room, and doorway they could find. It was fascinating to see, fascinating to experience the difference between what was imagined and what actually was. When Drew and Mal returned, Euan was waiting for them as promised.

"Would either of ye like to stay to see a clan supper, or would ye like to move on?"

"It is up to ye, Drew. This is yer trip," Mal offered.

"I think I'm fine. I'm nae sure they're all that much different from the ones we sometimes have now."

"Probably nae. Food is probably different, and the formalities, but otherwise it is as ye would imagine it to be. Let us go then," Euan said. "The mechanism to move is always the same, Drew. Close yer eyes, and we go."

Drew nodded and did so, and the sounds of a hall disappeared and turned into the sounds of footsteps on the ground. When he opened his eyes, he could hardly see a thing, and while Mal stood beside him, Euan was nowhere to be found. The mist was so heavy it obscured everything, even the source of the footsteps they were hearing.

"Where in the hell are we? Where is Euan?"

"I have a feeling I know," Mal said.

Out of the mist came a line of men, walking slowly and quietly, arms at the ready. This was what they were hearing, but anyone ahead of them wouldn't hear a thing until it was too late. In front of the line walked the Euan they knew, sword drawn, and he gestured to them to join him. As Drew took up a spot beside Euan, he looked to his left and there stood young

Euan the officer, his plaid discarded and ready for a fight.

"Welcome to Prestonpans," Euan said.

"I cannae see a thing!"

"Aye, and that was the point," Euan said.

The line of men stopped moving, the mist clearing on the ground near them for a few moments before swirling back in like a blanket, and that moment allowed Drew and Mal to see the regiments on the other side of them and the ones behind them. Present Euan stood next to his former self, whose face was serious and focused.

"Jesus, look at us," Mal said to Euan.

"Ye have nae seen anything yet," Euan replied.

"Ach, there is the prince," Mal said.

Drew turned his head, his eyes going wide at the sight of the young Stuart royal.

"I suggest ye start running when we do," Euan said.

"What?" Drew asked, pulling his eyes from the prince to look at Euan in confusion.

Before anything else could be said, the sound of pipes suddenly filled the air, followed by the screams of clan war cries all around him.

"GO!" Euan shouted to the two of them.

They turned and started running, the small head start keeping them in line with the front of the Cameron regiment. On either side of them, screaming men charged forward, weapons drawn, and as they reached Cope's front lines and the artillery, the sound of bodies and steel colliding surrounded them. Beside them, the former Euan cut men down in a fury, appearing nothing like the man they knew, and although he looked terrifying, they followed him. As bodies fell, the injuries grotesque, Drew fought his instinct to stop and help them, reminding himself that he wasn't really here and even if he was, he couldn't have helped them anyway.

Drew and Mal stopped running when they got past the artillery and saw the battle raging before Cope's men turned and fled, surrendering the field to the Jacobites. Beside them, the younger Euan stood covered in the blood of other men and smiled, bringing a gasp from both men at the sight of him this way. There was no fear, no remorse, no horror at what he'd done; instead, he was happy about it. The smile quickly faded, and he put his hand to his side, grimacing. The mist cleared away, revealing a field covered in bodies, and Euan surveyed it before turning and stumbling back the way he'd come. They could only follow him and found the current one standing where they'd previously been lined up, watching his former self stagger past, and the two of them looked at him in shock and a bit of terror.

"Aye," Euan said. "That is what it was like. That is who I had to be, what was expected of me."

"But ye were nae —" Drew said.

"Sorry? No, I was nae. I did nae feel badly about it at all and still dinnae. They were my enemies, just as I was theirs. If I did nae kill them, they would kill me, and they would feel no remorse. That is war. I *am* sorry if ye see me differently now."

"No, nae really, because I understand what ye are saying. If I see ye differently, it's because I can see the cracks it caused. I can see the reason ye see a Specialist to process all of it safely. I can also see how dangerous ye actually were."

"And still are," Mal added.

"Aye, I am and will be if I must."

"Did ye sustain an injury during the fight? I saw ye hold yer side," Drew said.

"I was injured the previous day. Cope fired on us with cannons when he saw us in a nearby churchyard. I got hit with some bits of stone wall that exploded when the ball hit it."

"And ye could still do this?" Drew asked, incredulous.

"Aye, well, I did nae have much choice. I think I had small fractures in my ribs, which was lucky enough. Then I did this, which made it worse. When I returned to camp and got cleaned off, our doctor scrubbed out the cuts made by the stone from the wall."

Drew grimaced. "Ugh, I'm sorry."

"Had to be done."

"Aye, but still does nae make it pleasant."

"No, that is certain," Euan said with a small chuckle. "I still have scars from that."

"Ye would do."

"I will move us now. This is what Mal wanted ye to see. Ye need nae close yer eyes, as we are in the same place, just a different time of day."

Drew watched in shock as the scene morphed around him. Young Euan moved toward his horse, and Drew could instantly tell he was in a great deal of pain. It was in his posture, the way he guarded himself. He looked pale, his eyes glassy, and Drew raised an eyebrow as Euan took the reins of his horse. "No. . .no, dinnae tell me ye —" But his words were cut off by Euan's scream as he mounted the horse. "Christ almighty! Are ye mad? What are ye doing?!"

"Annnd that was the reaction I was expecting," Mal said. "Though seeing it instead of ye just telling me about it as ye have before is another thing entirely."

"I had to get back," Euan said.

"Nae on a horse!"

"Lochiel would nae allow otherwise because he was angry with me, and this was my punishment. Come on, we'll move forward."

When they did, Drew found himself on the grounds of Holyrood Palace. He knew this place well due to many school trips as a child before he'd moved to Edinburgh for university and medical school. His residence in the city had made him even further acquainted with the palace and its park grounds. "I had no idea a camp was set up here like this."

"Aye, hard to tell now," Euan replied.

The sound of the men approaching reached them, and Drew looked at Euan. "How far was that ride?"

"About 10 miles."

"Ye must have been in agony."

"Aye, I was."

Even if Euan hadn't told him, it was plain enough when he arrived on the scene. Drew could tell the young man was fighting to remain conscious, on the verge of passing out or being sick from the pain, most likely both. They watched the salute, and then saw Euan force himself down, screaming the moment his feet touched the ground. Drew winced and walked forward without thinking as Iain and Malcolm helped him up. Following them as they got him to his tent, he remained when the two men walked out.

As Archibald stripped Euan to the waist, the young man muttered in delirium. "Mam. . .Mam, help me, it hurts. . .it hurts so much. . .Mam, please! Da. . .Da, come and take me. . .make it stop . . ."

Euan's unconscious pleading for his mother and father broke Drew's heart. He'd heard cries just like it countless times, but to hear it from the normally strong Euan only emphasized how much pain he was surely in. Getting closer, he was shocked by what he saw on Euan's body. While there were the cuts Euan had spoken of, there were also deep, ugly bruises that spoke to serious internal injury. In his head, Drew ran over what he'd do if Euan came into Raigmore like this as a patient and realized none of it could be done here.

A movement seen out of the corner of his eye brought Drew's gaze back to Archibald just as he reached forward to press on Euan's ribs. Horrified, Drew tried to grab him and stop him, but his hands passed right through Archibald just before Euan screamed in excruciating pain from the touch. His back arched from the cot he was on, his head tilted back, his face reddening as he screamed, tears streaming down his cheeks.

"Jesus, why did ye do that!" he shouted at a man who was long dead and couldn't hear him now.

While Euan lay sobbing in agony, Archibald pulled laudanum out, administering it to the broken young man who quickly went still and silent. That, at least, was a treatment option Drew could get behind in this particular case.

Leaving the tent, he saw Mal and Euan waiting for him a short distance away, though Mal's face was pale from having heard the same scream Drew had. "Ye are lucky ye survived that," he said quietly.

Euan frowned. "Why do ye say that?"

"Ye had blunt force trauma to the torso, for one. Had the debris ye mentioned hit ye in the right place, it would've killed ye either instantly or painfully over the next several days as ye bled to death internally. Fortunately for ye, it did nae do that. Then, ye ran into battle after sustaining that injury. If ye had been hit, it could've broken yer already fractured ribs and sent them into yer internal organs, puncturing a lung or worse. That would've killed ye, too, as ye had no way at this time to repair that. Ye mounted and rode a horse for 10 miles, both of which could've caused the same thing if ye had jostled yerself just right, though I am sure ye caused a full break mounting the horse. After that, ye landed on the ground here, and ye were damned lucky ye did nae puncture anything there. That scream ye just heard? That was the doctor pressing on yer ribs, which could've fatally injured ye in the same way, and I'm fairly certain he made it much worse by causing a full break in whatever still remained fractured." Drew shook his head. "Ye already had a fever and were delirious."

"Jesus," Mal muttered.

Euan looked at him in shock. "I did nae realize it was as bad as that."

"Well, ye would nae, would ye? Ye were so out of it due to the pain ye probably didn't notice much of anything. At the same time, they wouldn't have known either at this point in history." Drew sighed. "Ye were asking for yer father to come and take ye away and begging for yer mother to make the pain stop."

"No one ever mentioned any of that to me. I suppose Archibald was right; the Lord *was* on my side."

"Must've been," Drew said. "But what a sadistic son of a

bitch Lochiel was to put ye through that sort of agony in the first place."

"Will nae argue it," Euan said, his voice soft.

"We should go," Mal said.

"Aye," Euan replied, seeming to shake off his momentary sadness. "Drew, this will be yer chance to fight alongside yer kin."

Drew closed his eyes, and when he opened them, he was standing amidst a mass of lines of men, all of them in Fraser colors. Looking around and recognizing no one, he threaded his way forward to the front of the group and found himself facing a Hanoverian line as it massed for battle. To each side of him were other clans; to his right, beside the Frasers, were the Camerons, the sight making him smile for a moment before he saw Mal step out from the Cameron lines next to the young officer leading his clan: Euan. It was only then that Drew realized he had weapons in his hands and a sword at his side as he would've had if he'd really been there on this day. He stared down at the pistol and dirk in shock, just as the skies opened up and a torrential downpour began.

"Men at the ready!"

Drew heard the call out from Euan, his familiar voice ringing out with a commanding tone he'd never heard before. It was then passed down the lines to the Fraser regiment, who lifted their muskets to fire at the Hanoverians once the order was given. The weather caused more than a few misfires on both sides, and there were men near him that fell to musket fire, even as he squinted through the rain, to see Dragoons massing.

"Camerons! Pistols! Dirks at the ready for the post volley!"

The order from Euan once again came down the line, the Fraser men around him lifting loaded pistols, and he followed the order along with them. Glancing over at Euan and the Camerons, who were all aiming their pistols forward, including Mal, he knew he'd made the right choice. He had no idea, however, if the weapons they held would fire or if they were just a prop to give them the feel of them in their hands. As the horses came forward, he focused on them as he listened for the orders.

"Aim! Hold!"

"Hold!" he heard Euan call out, waiting for them to get closer. *"Fire!"*

Drew pulled the trigger, surprised by the kick of the pistol in his hand as it went off. In front of him, Hanoverian cavalry dropped from their horses as the lead balls from the pistols they hadn't seen found their marks. Many of the horses spooked and ran in the other direction, but the ones already committed couldn't stop.

"Pistols down, dirks up!"

At the command, the Frasers dropped their pistols, and Drew followed their lead, clutching the dirk tight in his hand as he crouched with the rest. Those horses and riders that charged into the lines were now set upon with dirks, none of them surviving the onslaught. Drew acted without thinking about it, though he came away with no blood on his hands and knew he'd done no actual damage. Hearing a shout, he looked over to see one of the other clans break ranks and charge.

Euan looked annoyed by the lack of discipline as he called another musket volley before standing up. *"Camerons! Charge!"*

"Frasers!" Drew heard called out by the officers before all the men around him pulled their swords in anticipation of the order they knew was coming, and Drew followed their lead. *"Charge!"*

The surrounding men screamed and ran forward, and he charged with them without a second thought. The rush of this moment, the adrenaline, was incredible and all consuming, leaving little room for anything like doubt or fear. Though he knew he couldn't do real harm, it didn't stop him from swinging as if he could while letting the heat of battle take him where it would. He was fighting alongside his clansmen, his ancestors, and it was an indescribable feeling. An anger he'd never felt before emerged as they collided with their foes. He understood now what Euan had said at Prestonpans: It was you or them, and you'd be hard pressed to be sorry for surviving.

When no one was left to fight in front of him, he looked over to find Euan near him, just as he screamed in pain. Drew saw his shirt immediately redden with blood and realized he'd been cut badly. Euan's scream of pain became a scream of rage and the men he cut down found a brutality they likely hadn't expected. The scene immediately changed, the weapons gone, and Drew looked around in confusion, only to find Mal staring at him just as confused. Someone was dragged past them into a tent, and both realized it was Euan. He was swiftly placed on a cot, whisky dumped on the cut as others held him down, and Drew winced, backing away as they immediately began stitching him up. Turning, he strode from the tent, followed by Mal.

"What's wrong?" Mal asked.

"Just. . .do ye have any idea how much that would hurt?"

"A great deal, I'd imagine."

"They are stitching him closed with no anesthetic, Mal. Nothing to numb the area. They dinnae even have time to get him drunk." Drew pointed to the tent as Euan cried out in pain through clenched teeth. "I could nae be that still or make so little sound as that were it being done to me."

"If it was all ye knew —"

"No, even then I would be screaming and so would ye. He is lucky that was a glancing blow and nae deeper, or he'd be dead out there, and luckier that it did nae get infected. I will tell ye this, that man is tougher than we know."

Mal nodded. "Aye, ye are right there. But it was. . .charging beside them was . . ."

"Incredible," Drew finished. "I've never felt anything like it and dinnae know if I will again. That I could do it at all is a miracle, but doing it without fear of injury or death or causing those? That was something else."

"Are ye ready to go on?" Euan asked as he came up near them.

"Aye. Thank ye for this, Euan, for this moment," Drew said. "To know what it felt like to do this."

"There is naught like it, really. I could nae come with ye here as there was something I did nae wish to witness again, so I left it to the both of ye. Ye did well, though. I saw that much. Both of ye acted without freezing up, but we need to work on that sword technique," Euan said, laughing.

Both Mal and Drew laughed with him. "Cannae deny that," Drew said. "I think that's the first time I've even held one."

"We will change that. Now, however, it is time to leave our own history behind us. When ye are ready, Drew."

When Drew closed and opened his eyes, they were no longer outdoors, no longer in uniform, and no longer in the 18th century. They were now in a dingy modern flat somewhere, and Grace stood facing someone, with Euan behind her and a young man between them.

"This was the mission before our last one," Euan explained. "Ye wanted to see the thing about our mission bodies, and this is yer chance. Stand over there," he said, pointing to a spot where they could stand to the side between Grace and the man who was speaking to her.

When the man produced a knife, Grace made a face. *"I think I have some friends who might get you to say otherwise."*

"Ach, here we go," they heard the mission Euan mutter.

"You have friends?" Grace replied, her words dripping with sarcasm.

"Grace, ye legend," Drew said, laughing, just as Mal was.

"I could just kill you."

"You could try."

"I would do more than try," he said before shoving the blade into Grace's chest.

"Jesus Christ!" Mal and Drew shouted in unison.

"Jesus, what are you doing, Ed? Are you insane?"

Grace made what sounded like a pained cry and doubled over, but it became clear that the cry was fake when it faded into laughter as Grace stood up. The other man's face went slack, and all three men watched in shock as the wound to Grace's chest healed and left no trace of anything having happened, with Drew stepping closer to look and be sure.

"What the hell?"

"Oops," Grace said, a wicked smile on her face that Drew had not only never seen before, but also never imagined she could possess.

"Uh oh," Drew whispered to himself.

He stepped back as she swiftly grabbed the arm of her assailant and pulled it out straight, twisting his arm just the slightest bit before she brought her elbow down onto the back of his. The move sent his elbow the wrong way, breaking his arm, and he shrieked in pain. While still holding that arm, Grace yanked him forward and slammed her elbow into his nose before turning and driving a fist down into the side of his face. Both Mal and Drew jumped back with a shout, staring open mouthed at the man on the floor before slowly looking up at Grace. The mission group all stepped over the body and hustled out, leaving the three men alone.

Euan grinned. "God, I love that."

"I mean, ye told me about that, but seeing it was something else," Mal said.

"Aye. Grand, is it nae?"

"Terrifying, more like."

"They should have her come work security at the hospital and take on the drunks," Drew said.

Euan laughed. "That would be interesting, would it nae? They would hit her, and nothing would happen."

"Might terrify them enough to sit down. But that healing? My God."

"It is a grand thing, to be sure. Right, last stop is the mission we just finished."

Euan didn't let them linger long in the most recent one, just long enough to show them the queen, Walsingham, Burghley, Leicester, Mary, and the duke.

All of it left Mal and Drew in a sort of giddy shock when they returned to Observation, and Drew sat up, shaking his head while grinning. "*That* was the coolest thing I think I've ever experienced."

"Aye, I feel that every time I do it," Mal said.

Euan laughed and unhooked himself. "Glad ye enjoyed it. Dinnae tell the lasses I let ye run out into battle, will ye?"

"Promise," both men said at the same time.

"Good. Let us go home, then."

Chapter 22

Later that night, Drew approached the study where he knew Euan and Grace would likely be since they weren't working, finding them both relaxing on the settee with books in their hands, Grace's head resting on Euan's thigh like it was a pillow. Euan looked up from his book as Drew entered, and Grace turned her head toward the door with a curious expression.

"Euan, would ye mind terribly if I spoke to Grace alone for a bit?"

"No, I suppose nae," he replied, his brow furrowed. "It is up to her, though."

"Nothing bad, I promise ye."

Grace nodded and sat up. "Okay."

Euan stood up, kissed Grace on the top of the head, and left, shutting the door behind him as Drew sat down in a chair across from her. "Thanks."

"No problem. So, what's wrong?"

"Why do ye think something's wrong?"

Grace raised an eyebrow, and he laughed.

"All right, fine."

"Did something happen today during Observation?"

"No! No, nae at all. That was actually a really amazing experience, and I feel like an entirely different person."

"You are."

"In a way."

"More than that. You now know more than most of the world does. You've gotten to go back and stand amongst your ancestors, to see them, listen to them, spend time with them even if they didn't know you were there. You aren't the same, and you couldn't be."

"That is definitely true. I feel almost closer to it now, as if they are right there in the next room. I feel like I know who I am when I didn't before."

"You ran into battle beside them, so how could you *not* feel any of that?" Grace said with a sly smile.

"How did ye know?"

Grace laughed and shook her head. "I figured he would let you do that. I know Mal has been dying to, so I'm not surprised in the slightest. When he told you he was willing to take you anywhere, even those places, I knew what he'd do. He's not as sneaky as he sometimes thinks he is, at least not to me, and I can read him like a book. There's one he'll never go to, of course. Was he there with you when you did it?"

"No, he was nae," Drew admitted. "He stayed behind with the other lines at Prestonpans while we went with the past version of him, and he was nae present at all for Falkirk."

"Not surprised. Falkirk isn't a particularly pleasant memory for him."

"He did say there was something he didn't want to see again."

"Yes. He was forced to kill someone he knew well, and it still bothers him. Always will, I expect."

"Christ," Drew muttered. "No wonder."

"It was a great moment for him, too, leading his clan to a huge victory, but it's clouded by that."

"I can imagine so. It's a strange feeling, though, to have done such a thing. I feel as though ever since I have come near ye, I am closer to my history, to my kin. I feel it in me in ways I never did before, and it let me stand up to my mother finally."

"I'm glad. It has always been there; you just hear it now when you didn't before. Being near Euan tends to do that. He's a bit of a bridge."

"I can see that."

"What was it you *really* wanted to ask me?"

Drew fidgeted, not knowing how to begin. "I . . ."

"Yes?"

"When I met ye back at Council Chambers yesterday, I. . .something happened."

"Oh?"

"I saw it."

"Saw what?"

"What happened to ye."

Grace looked taken aback. "You saw —"

"Aye, I saw it. I heard it. I cannae explain it except that I knew it was real."

"I don't know how."

"I assumed it was from ye, somehow."

"The only time that's ever happened was with Euan."

"We'll have to ask The Council, I guess. Even before that, though, I knew how awful it must've been. They showed me the images in Medical."

"Why?" she asked, her voice falling to almost a whisper.

"Did ye think they had only told me? No, they showed me. Because I'm a doctor, they knew I'd find it interesting, and I did, but I knew by looking at them how much pain ye must've been in."

Grace looked up at him, and he could tell she wasn't sure how to feel about what he was saying. All of those here had seen it, but none of them before Drew could understand the reality of it. "It was. . .I can't even really describe it."

"Ye don't have to; I know. I saw what those balls did to ye, what the bayonet did. I saw the damage inside, and I dinnae know how in the world ye got up and kept moving. I know they said there was still some of yer mission body left, but that seems extraordinary."

"I didn't want him to die."

"He was already dead."

"I didn't know that then, and I just wanted to get him

away from there. I thought if I could get him into the trees, he'd be safe and could run when he woke up. It didn't matter what happened to me."

"Why didn't it?"

"I don't know. It's just what I felt at the time. It wasn't that the mission was in jeopardy — even though it was — but I loved him and didn't want him to die. Even if *I* died, he'd be alive, and that's what mattered to me."

"Do ye still love him that much?"

"More. I don't regret my choice, and I never will. I would do it again in an instant."

Drew smiled. "I was thinking it's what gave ye that strength. I mean, obviously the rest, too, but I'm certain that was a big part."

"Probably. That's what creates the energy that allows transport without a Guardian and what creates the bond between a Watcher and their Companion. That decision and the energy mass expended when the Watcher dies is the key."

"But there is more to it than that, isn't there? More to the two of ye."

Grace regarded him with an interested but suspicious expression. "There is. Did he tell you that?"

"No, he did nae, but it's easy to see if ye are paying attention. It's beyond that ye love each other, and my *God* do ye. It's something no one else has, but we sometimes wish we did."

"What do *you* think it is?"

"I wish I could say. I just know I can see it in yer faces. Ye know what the other is feeling because ye feel it, too. Ye can be in another room and know if something is wrong and ye are needed. It's an uncanny thing to watch happen because ye are never sure if that's what ye are seeing."

"No, you're right. That's pretty much how it is."

"Does that extend to physical feeling?"

"No," Grace said with a small laugh. "I can't even imagine how we'd handle that if it did. It's strange enough to feel an emotion you know isn't yours, so I can't picture feeling physical things that aren't. Euan feeling period cramps or child-birth? He'd be *so* angry."

Drew laughed as Grace grimaced. "Christ, I dinnae think he'd *ever* want ye to have a child if that were the case."

"Exactly, and we need to."

"Do ye?"

Grace nodded. "It's kind of a requirement because that's how the family lines continue. We'll have a daughter, at least one, and she'll be the one to take my place if something happens to me when she's young enough, or she'll be the mother to my replacement. That's what happened with my mother, anyway. From what I understand, however, my granddaughter will replace me."

"Wow. So, it cannae be a daughter born from a son, it *must* be a female of yer blood."

"Right. Euan was told that we're the start of a different sort of Watcher, that the Cameron Watcher will, from now on, have very specific traits they are born with that other Watchers and even the other children in their family won't. They even keep the name, regardless of whether they marry or not. They are always a Cameron."

"It has to be strange knowing that."

"It is. Meeting them is also strange."

"Ye have met them?" Drew asked, his tone one of incredulity.

Grace nodded. "Councilwoman Rochford is her period's Cameron Watcher. Rochford is her Council name, but she's the Cameron Watcher."

"Oh, that's right! That makes so much sense now," he said. "I thought there was something about her that was familiar."

"Oh, there is. She's so much like Euan in some ways it's scary."

Drew laughed. "Aye, I can see that."

"Euan has met one of the others, one of the Cameron Watchers beyond the time of The Council we work with."

"Seriously?"

"Yep. Weird, huh? He liked her though, said it was like talking to me."

"It's so odd how all of this is so interconnected."

"I agree, and I feel like there are connections we haven't even figured out yet. Mal is connected to Euan by his ancestor, who was Euan's best friend in his former time. They had an instant bond because there is something in Mal from that former man. The question for me is: Who are *you*?"

"What?"

"Who in your past had a tie to Euan that brings you back into his orbit? There must be someone. You said being around him made you feel things in ways you never had before, closer. You feel it in you. Only Euan can really know."

Drew sat dumbstruck for a moment. He'd never considered it or questioned why he'd felt those things; he just knew he did. Something struck him then, and he gasped.

"What is it, Drew?"

"It's how I know," he whispered. "How I saw it. Whoever it was, he was there. He saw it. I didn't get it from *you*; I got it from *him*."

"That makes a great deal of sense. Hard to say who he was, though, because a great many Frasers were there that day."

"Would Euan even know?"

"Probably not, at least not from that little bit of information. I doubt he was looking to see who surrounded him while he was trying not to get himself killed. Honestly, it might be hard to know at all because he was connected to so many Frasers. The only difference is if you remind him of someone specific, but he hasn't said that to me. It doesn't mean you don't, though, just that he doesn't always tell me everything, especially when he's working through something in his head first," she said with a soft shrug.

"A mystery still, is he?"

"Always. He only allows you to know what he feels you need to, and while I may know a lot, or even most, I don't know everything and never will. I'm okay with that because I'm the same way with him. We understand each other."

"But how is this only happening now? How was it nae something I always felt?"

"You're now in constant contact with a person whose energy connects with what's inside of you and he drew it out, or maybe you did know but you buried it because it didn't make sense to you. Think about it for a while and maybe you'll find instances where things didn't add up but now they do. Euan is the key to all of it when it comes to you and Mal. He's your connection to the past and all that was."

"I'd hoped talking to ye would clear this up, but —"

"But it hasn't."

"No, there are more layers, more questions."

"Welcome to timelines," Grace said, chuckling. "I could tell you some seriously messed up stories."

"I'm sure ye could and will."

"Eventually. Don't want to scare you off since you haven't married Van yet."

Drew laughed. "Maybe nae, but they've already claimed me so it's too late now."

"Ooo, that's true. Maybe another time, though. You'd never sleep tonight otherwise."

"Aye, I dinnae need help with that, I assure ye."

"I imagine not. Emergency medicine is rough."

"Aye, it is, but it is worth it. I love my job."

"I know, and it shows," Grace said, smiling at him.

"Speaking of my job, I should get to bed. I'm on days this week."

"Sleep well, Drew. Don't let Van keep you up, unless it's to have some fun, and in that case, keep it down because we're right next door when we're in here."

He laughed and shook his head as he stood up. "Aye, fine. I'll send Euan back in, then?"

"Please. I know he's nowhere near ready for bed."

"Of course. Goodnight, Grace," Drew said as he left.

Grace sat back against the settee with a small sigh, mulling over everything Drew had just told her. There was something strange about him and his connection to all of this, and she wondered if they'd ever know what it was. There was a discomfort in knowing he'd seen that moment without her sharing it with him even though it wasn't his fault.

"Everything fine?" Euan asked as he returned to the study.

"Yes," Grace replied, tucking all of it away behind a serene smile. "Everything is just as it should be."

ABOUT THE AUTHOR

A California native, Eilidh Miller, FSAScot, has a BA in English and studied history as an undeclared minor to better inform her literature studies. A recent winner of the Robert Burns Literary Award and a Fellow with the Society of Antiquaries of Scotland, Eilidh is very active within Southern California's Scottish community, spending a great deal of time volunteering with the charitable organization St. Andrew's Society of Los Angeles.

A long-time historical reenactor, Eilidh loves research and educating the general public about historical events, as well as entertaining them with tidbits no one would believe if they weren't documented. She extends this same energy to her work, extensively researching the historical periods she includes in her writing to ensure that the information she presents is correct, even going so far as to travel internationally to access archives and scout locations.

She resides in Southern California with her husband, daughter, and her feisty Shiba Inu sidekick.

You can keep up with Eilidh on TikTok – @authoreilidh – or her website www.eilidhmiller.com. You can also join her Facebook page to keep up to date on the next release, special content, and information on appearances.

Before any of them could ask another question, the door opened, and a woman walked in. Everything about her looked severe, from her hair, to her dress, to the very expression she wore. "Whose car is that in my dri —" But she stopped when she set eyes on the group at the table, fixing Anne with an icy glare. "What are *you* doing here?"

"They came to visit Nathan's grave," Dan explained.

"Why? It isn't like he was anything to *you*," she spat at Anne.

"He was my husband, Irene," Anne replied, "and I finally found out where you took him."

"I don't *care* what you think; I don't recognize you as that."

"The State of California says otherwise."

"Mom, look, Grace is here," Eric said.

"Who?"

"Nate's daughter?"

"He didn't have a daughter. This tramp tried to pass off some other man's kid. Hers looked nothing like him; I told you that."

"You might want to look again, Mother," Barbara said.

Irene followed Barbara's nod and examined Grace with a look that could kill. Grace didn't flinch beneath her stare, looking back at the woman with a calm, impassive stare that could — and often did — drive targets and enemies alike crazy. Irene tried to hold it, tried to overpower her, but failed and looked away, dealing with an adult Grace catching her off guard.

"Hello," Grace said.

"Look, she has eyes just like Nathan's, Mother. She could only get those from him," Barbara continued. "She's a lot like him in other ways, too."

Irene said nothing for a moment, then shook her head. "Contacts. I'm telling you that this girl, whoever she is, isn't Nathan's."

Her three children blanched and looked at Grace regretfully, almost as if to say, "See, we told you."

"I don't wear contacts. Come check if you want to. He *is* my father, whether you want to believe it or not, but honestly, I really don't care either way."

The Grant siblings looked at Grace from behind Irene's back, their faces shocked, but Irene smirked. "Then why are you here if you don't care, hm?"

"I'm only here for my mother because I helped her find him. This is for *her*, not for me. She had a right to know where the man she loved was buried."

"She was a liar then and is a liar now. She conned him into marrying her."

"No, I didn't!" Anne cried out, the hurt clear in her voice.

"For what reason?" Grace interjected before Anne could say more.

"What?"

"Do you need me to speak more slowly due to your advanced age? This really is an easy question: What reason did she use to con him into marrying her? A marriage you said you don't recognize, I might add."

"I don't recognize it because it was based on a lie. She told him she was pregnant so he'd marry her."

"No, that's impossible. The timeline doesn't match what you're saying."

"How do you know?"

Grace pulled an envelope out of her pocket, removing her parents' marriage certificate. "See this? The ceremony date was a year and a half before I was born. She wasn't pregnant with me when they got married and couldn't have been. Care to try again? Maybe try a little harder this time."

Irene's face showed a moment of doubt before she cleared it away, sneering at Grace. "Well, you're just an uppity little thing, aren't you?"

"Only when I know I'm right. These three told me he was your favorite; how do you think he felt when he watched you reject his child? I can see why he left, why he didn't tell you about anything, even about getting married. Why would he want to? If I were him, I'd want to stay as far away from you as possible."

Grace's demeanor was calm, as was her voice, and this was a Grace Euan knew well because it was the one he often saw when they were working. It never meant *anything* good for the person opposite her when this side appeared. Barbara gasped at Grace's daring to speak that way to a woman she clearly feared, while Eric and Dan stared at her.

"Who do you think you are, girl, to come into my house and speak to me that way, like you're better than me? Nathan would never speak to me that way."

"He didn't have to, did he? His actions said more than his words ever could."

Grace stood up and took the certificate back, putting it into the envelope before sliding it back into her pocket.

"As for who I think I am? I *know* who I am. Whether you want to admit it or not, I'm Nathan Grant's daughter, and nothing you can do or say changes that. More than that? I'm a Cameron. I've faced worse things than you can even imagine. I've run directly into artillery fire to save a life. I've lived war, pestilence, horror, and death. Hell, I've even *caused* every single one of those things at some point in my career. You don't scare me like you scare everyone else, and your attempts to do so are honestly pathetic."

Irene seemed not to know how to react when someone wasn't properly deferential to her, looking momentarily confused. Grace's last words caused jaws to drop on everyone but

Anne and Euan. They both knew better than anyone that every word she'd just said was true.

"Do you really think that makes you special? Better somehow?" Irene spat, attempting to recover.

A small, cold, smile appeared on Grace's lips. "Oh, it does, you just don't know why, and you never will. You'll never know anything about me. I *am* better than you because I'd *never* do to anyone what you did to my mother, to your own son, and to me. I treat people with kindness and compassion, unless, of course, they've proven they don't deserve it, as you have."

Grace walked around the table, and Euan stood up, as did Anne. As Grace walked past Irene, the woman grabbed her arm, causing Grace to spin around to face her while yanking her arm from her grip. The movement caused Irene to stumble into a chair, and Grace glared at her as she backed away.

"Don't you *dare* touch me," Grace hissed.

"I know what your game is!" Irene shouted, pointing a finger at Anne. "You think you're going to come here and claim Nathan's share of the mill, do you? Broke and too old to get some man to pay for you, so you're going to try to claim his inheritance? Is that it? Or is it *you*?" She sneered at Grace. "Thinking you're going to fake your way into it?"

Grace moved faster than Euan could catch her, and in the next moment she buried the knife Dan used to cut the bread deep into the wood of the table near Irene. Barbara screamed, and all three children scrambled away.

"Did I ask you for anything?" Grace seethed as she leaned over a terrified-looking Irene, her hand still on the blade's handle. "Did I *ever* ask you for one damned thing? Has she? You aren't that hard to find, and if either of us had wanted a penny, you would've heard about it already. I don't want *anything* from you; I don't need it. Between the three people standing here, there's more money than you could hope to spend. But I do hope those land deeds and coins keep you warm at night, because you can't take them with you, and I know your children are going to throw a hell of a party when you finally breathe your last toxic breath. You can only use fear and the threat of money to control people for so long. The Romans found that out the hard way and so will you. Paper and coins burn in hell, just like you will."

Grace turned to look at Barbara, Eric, and Dan. "As for you? Don't bother trying to look for me when she finally dies and sets you free because you won't find me. I have *no* interest in people who do nothing to put a stop to what they know is wrong. You did *nothing* for me. You gave me nothing, and nothing is what you'll now get in return. You'll get to sit there and wonder what happened to your niece, the only bit of your brother left, just like you always have. Except now? Now you know *just* how like him I am. My suggestion to you is that you consider me as dead as he is, because to you? I *am*."